Readers of *Rainbow Baby* will be moved by the story of Samantha and Phil, who struggle with the effects of pregnancy loss on their marriage and family life. Wanner is an accomplished writer who explores a serious and rarely discussed subject with subtlety and grace.

—Glenda MacFarlane, writer and editor

Rainbow Baby

Unravelled by Loss

Tamara J. Wanner

Legacy Reimaged Series: Book 1

RAINBOW BABY
Copyright © 2024 by Tamara J. Wanner

All Scripture quotations marked (MSG) are taken from The Message, copyright © 1993, 2002, 2018 by Eugene H. Peterson. Used by permission of NavPress. All rights reserved. Represented by Tyndale House Publishers. Scripture quotations marked (NIV) are taken from the Holy Bible, New International Version®, NIV®. Copyright © 1973, 1978, 1984, 2011 by Biblica, Inc.™ Used by permission of Zondervan. All rights reserved worldwide. www.zondervan.com The "NIV" and "New International Version" are trademarks registered in the United States Patent and Trademark Office by Biblica, Inc.™

This is a work of fiction. Names, characters, places and incidents either are the product of the author's imagination or are used fictitiously, and any resemblance to actual persons, living or dead, businesses, companies, events, or locales is entirely coincidental.

ISBN: 978-1-4866-2496-6
eBook ISBN: 978-1-4866-2497-3

Word Alive Press
119 De Baets Street Winnipeg, MB R2J 3R9
www.wordalivepress.ca

WORD ALIVE
—P R E S S—

Cataloguing in Publication information can be obtained from Library and Archives Canada.

To my friends who look forward to meeting their
children for the first time by the crystal sea.

Gerald and Janet, Doug and Judith, Kelly and Lani,
Neil and Ronda, Tony and Brenda, Jeremy and Sarah, Cam and Ashton,
Glen and Cathy, Dan and Kathy, Greg and Michelle, Garrett and Jessika, Dirk
and Linda, Derek and Nicole, Justin and Becky...

Contents

Acknowledgments

Gratitude abounds as I marvel at how this story came to be. It began as a response to a writing prompt from a book my sister Sonya gave me. She wanted to encourage a gift she saw in me.

Those first few pages drew some encouragement from the Revisionists, a small writing community in the hamlet of Beechy. In 2022, Glenda MacFarlane, one of the original Revisionists, gave my manuscript a free evaluation when she found out I had written a novel.

2019 saw me take a road trip with my sister and sister-in-law to Houston, Texas for a writer's conference with Margaret Feinberg and Jonathan Merritt. A special workshop led by Beth Moore showed how the pain points I'd written about in my journal could be the very things readers of my book needed to discover hope. I signed up for their Write Brilliant course, which I completed during COVID.

The two-week pause from teaching during 2020 birthed new fruitfulness in my life. My husband retired and we began a new chapter in a different community. My sister-in-law Lani found some great writing workshops through Flourish Writers and I listened to a few of them at her house, intrigued.

Due to pandemic limitations, I joined the Flourish Writers Academy online to reignite my writing passion. I thought I'd write a devotional, but the Creator had different ideas. I am so grateful for the encouragement given by Mindy Kiker and Jenny Kochert during coaching calls and interactions in the private

Flourish community. They introduced me to Ginny Yttrup, who became my developmental editor, as well as my mentor in the Fiction Crafter's Cohort.

My conversations with Janelle Kapeller, EAL instructor at Reflections Equine Wellness, were essential to writing this book. She explained how horses reflect human emotions and demonstrated various therapy exercises for individuals, couples, and families. Nor could I have predicted the impact of the three personal sessions on me.

I'm indebted to my friends who shared their stories of pregnancy loss over the years and the actions that helped or hindered their journey to wholeness. The year my pastor's daughter and his daughter-in-law became pregnant and ended in stillbirth became a catalyst for this story. The events rocked our small church and our pastor. I wondered how someone recovers from that kind of pain. Then I met Kathy and saw how her loss opened doors of hope for others.

I'm grateful for my parents' encouragement to read and to engage with the Word of God as sustenance for daily living.

Bill, thanks for letting me disappear into the office for hours at a time while I wrote. You checked in to see how everything was going with the book even though reading is not your thing. Thanks for making food too.

Serenity, thanks for being my cheerleader with the smallest accomplishment.

Thank you, Cody, for reminding me that healing is complex and takes time.

Lani and Sonya, without your weekly encouragement the first draft would never have been written.

Kathy and Laura, thanks for your prayers, conversations, and encouragement not to lose heart during the editing process.

I'd like to thank the team at Word Alive Press for all their expertise to bring a manuscript to the public in a way that makes it stand out through the editing, formatting, and design process. Evan Braun, thank you so much for streamlining my story. You made it sing in new ways. Ariana, thanks for coordinating all the moving parts of this project. You made sure I felt satisfied with the end result every step of the way.

One

How Did I Get Here?

Samantha stared at her manacled hands in disbelief. The orange jumpsuit, a strange wardrobe for a former elementary school teacher. How had she gotten to this point? Potential manslaughter charges? Assault and battery charges? Her wrists itched underneath the thick dressing still in place from her hospital stay.

"All rise for the Right Honourable Judge Masterson."

Samantha jumped at the bailiff's booming voice. She fixed her eyes on the floor to steady herself and discovered a pair of slingbacks on the floor next to her no-name running shoes. Her lawyer had good taste. When her cellmate had found out who was representing Samantha, she'd said that Phil had found her an excellent lawyer.

Why had Phil gone to the trouble of seeking the best lawyer he could find in Saskatoon? Hadn't he known he'd be better off without her in his life?

"Reply, not guilty," the lawyer hissed.

"Uh, not guilty, Your Honour."

Samantha frowned. How could they think she had meant to hurt Glenda? Surely Phil had told them about the type of relationship she'd had with her. Glenda was Gran come back to life. How had everything gotten so complicated?

If Glenda dies, Cami's doomed to repeat my life, she thought. *Where did things go so wrong?*

"Your Honour, I'd like to read this letter in defence of my client's intent. The police collected it from her home the night of the incident."

"Go ahead."

> Dear Phil,
> Sunlight has disappeared. I can only see a dark miasma of clouds. No matter where I walk, loss jumps me every time. I'll be gone when you get home. Leave the darkness. Start fresh with Cami and find a new love. You won't be stuck with a ball and chain. I know those words were Bob's description of me, but I just hold you back in business and in life. Your abandonment of us shows that work is your mistress. When you disappeared after Micah died...

Samantha felt her throat swell and tighten like an overtuned guitar string. One strum and she threatened to snap. Her own words pierced the unbelief at her surroundings.

The buzz of lawyer and judge swirled into a maelstrom of new terms—and then it was over. Time to return to the holding cell before her transfer back to Grand River Hospital.

She stood up at the bailiff's prompt and turned to follow him out of the courtroom.

As they left, she caught movement from the corner of her eye. Phil's friend Noah Baer, dressed in his full police uniform, approached Phil. Noah looked more like his dad than she remembered.

Hadn't he just gotten a promotion to deputy chief? Had Phil mentioned that once after coming home from the charity golf tournament?

What if Noah's dad hadn't been there that fateful day? Funny how people's stories intertwined with one another. If it hadn't been for the blanket, she might never have connected Noah to her past. She would never have met Gran if Chief Baer hadn't stepped in twenty years earlier...

———◆◦◆———

"Come on out, we made it." The saccharine sweet voice of the social worker didn't calm Samantha's trembling fingers as she undid the seatbelt. The warmth of the booster seat clung to her skin and protested her departure. She tugged down her shorts to soothe it.

Her social worker pulled the small gym bag out of the backseat from beside her. It held the few clothes that the police plucked from her room when her mother had been revived from yet another overdose.

Samantha scanned her new surroundings. Blush pink peonies bobbed their heavy heads in welcome along the narrow sidewalk. Trails of Virginia creeper entwined the railing on both sides of the veranda. Muffled voices trailed out over an open upstairs window from the house next door. A purple banana seat bike promised friendship from the same yard.

A porch swing on the right invited her up the steps when the screen door sprang open. Samantha clutched her middle to stop the butterflies from doing somersaults.

She lifted her head to meet the woman she'd yet to call her grandmother. Samantha's eyes moved from the woman's bright pink flip-flops to the loud floral culottes and handkerchief-styled top. Her gaze lingered on the heart-shaped locket nestled between the woman's collarbones.

"Well, hello there, poppet. You look the spitting image of your mum at your age. Would you like to have a look?"

Her gran opened the locket and she saw a little blond girl perched between her parents, her arms around their necks as she pulled their heads close to hers. Samantha looked into her gran's dancing blue eyes, highlighted by laugh lines, and allowed herself to be drawn into a hug.

Gran drew her into the house. She followed, wide-eyed at the gleaming countertops, the copper range hood, and the large plate of cinnamon buns in the middle of the island.

"Don't be letting those eyes pop out of your head, luv," Gran said. "We'll get to those in a minute. Let's get you tucked into your room first before we nip down for a spot of tea."

Her gran motioned to the social worker to take a seat at the kitchen table.

Samantha followed her up to a small room on the second floor. In a corner sat a small dresser and twin bed with a pink teddy bear atop a simple white duvet. Gran started unzipping Samantha's gym bag to store away her clothes.

Samantha looked at herself in the mirror above the dresser and pinched herself. It was all real. She fingered the soft fluff of the teddy bear. When her mom had left her alone for days at a time, Samantha had become a princess, imagining all kinds of yummy foods brought by servants. Now she stood in her own room with a plate of cinnamon buns downstairs.

Could Chief Baer have been right? Could the Creator love her this much? The gift of the rainbow blanket, the beginning of good things?

When Gran placed the gym bag in the closet, Samantha realized that she hadn't seen her special afghan. Had she left it in the car? She raced downstairs and turned to her social worker, perched on a kitchen chair.

"Um, my blanket? Where'd it go?"

"Good thinking, darling. I forgot that bag. It's in the trunk." When the lady popped the trunk, Samantha drew it out of the garbage bag and hugged it to herself.

Maybe the story about it really is true, she thought. *Do I have a hope and a future, like Chief Baer promised?*

The clang of the cell gate slammed the door on Samantha's future. She had tried to take her life into her own hands, and only Phil's arrival had prevented her. The failure to end her own life had since been paraded through the courts, and all because she had pushed away someone who'd tried to help. Not only that, but she'd hurt the one person who could help her daughter endure their coming long separation.

Shame coated her throat with unshed tears. How could she have hurt the woman who had coaxed her heart back to life?

Samantha sniffed the scents wafting up the stairs as she brought up another load from the dryer. Tonight's menu promised Yorkshire pudding and roast beef.

The white door of the nursery beckoned and she set the laundry basket down in the hallway. When she went in, a flash of colour caught her eye.

"Samantha?"

Samantha turned from the door of the nursery, holding her daughter Cami's greeting card in her hand.

"Samantha, what is..."

She knew Glenda had seen this card before. Glenda's swift look and flush revealed Phil's efforts to lessen her sadness.

"You found the wee lass's handiwork, did you now?" Glenda asked.

"When did she make it?"

Glenda looked thoughtful for a moment. "The first day I arrived, three weeks ago."

"I guess Phil thought it would be safe in here. This is the first time I've gone into the nursery since we lost Micah, you know."

"Well now, aren't you the brave one today, facing these fears?"

"I guess. Time to let go. Join me?"

Glenda stepped into the nursery. "Oh my, that teddy bear wallpaper border is adorable. The blue and white striped feature wall is a stunner. You've got a real eye for decoratin'." She placed her hand on the simple white change table and faced Samantha. "But we're not in here just to admire your handiwork, are we?"

Samantha froze. Could she answer that question? The rhythms and routines of Mrs. Glenda Henderson had created an ambiance of safety and predictability that soothed her. This past week she'd taken Cami to the Fun Factory and crawled through the tunnels with her, thanks to Glenda's encouragement. She'd even managed a little art project for St. Patrick's Day.

"Last week, I felt like a good mom again," Samantha said. "I thought, maybe I'm ready to go into Micah's room. Then I found her card on the dresser and…"

The warmth of Glenda's hand on her arm opened the floodgate of tears.

"Did you ever stop to consider that you are a good mum, whether you go to activities or if you don't go?" Glenda asked. "How many crafts you do with Cami doesn't determine your worth as a mother. Look at that card again, Samantha. Where is she in that picture?"

"Um, she's in between Phil and me."

"What expression did she draw on her face?"

"A smile."

Samantha felt Glenda's hand lift under her chin, causing their eyes to meet. "Samantha, dearie. Cami is secure, safe, and happy. You're a good mum even when you're sad. This card calls to mind what you have: a husband, a daughter here, and a son in heaven. You are *not* a failure, luv."

Samantha couldn't hold Glenda's gaze. Her eyes fell on her afghan, draped over the arm of the rocking chair. A mixture of anger and shame wound about her spirit and choked the hope inspired by Glenda's words.

Some hope and a future. I can't even accept the truth coloured on my daughter's card.

"But you don't know what I've done before this," Samantha cried. "I deserved to lose Micah! It's my fault. That picture doesn't tell the entire story."

She ran into her bedroom and locked the door, then collapsed against the door with the weight of her guilt and shame, sobbing.

Would she ever be free? Her secret taunted her.

Two

Good News?

Samantha's afternoon appointment with the obstetrician dominated her thoughts. It couldn't come soon enough.

She rearranged the calendar on her husband's home office desk, then straightened his pile of reference books. Like nature's rebirth, coloured with swollen yellow and purple buds, she suspected that she too burgeoned with new life. The thought had solidified two days ago when she'd gagged at the smell of frying onions. And yesterday she'd shaken like an aspen leaf while walking to the garage and dropped the keys trying to unlock the door. That had prevented her from driving to the drugstore for a pregnancy test. So she'd gotten a doctor's appointment for today. Unusual for Saskatoon, but the obstetrician's receptionist had just received word of a cancelled appointment. At least this one practiced at Royal University Hospital.

She fanned herself. It seemed hotter in the family office. Why did it seem so hard to breathe?

She rubbed her throat and coughed. Whoa! Why did the room spin like a kaleidoscope? What was going on? Her pregnancy with Cami and Micah hadn't included these symptoms.

She sat down in the office chair, gasping for more oxygen. Leaning back, she closed her eyes and tried to stop the world from spinning. She reached out her hands and clutched the smooth surface of the desk to ground herself.

Oh, that's better. She pulled in a deeper breath. *There!* Then another. The room righted itself. *Steady now!*

She could hear the central vac upstairs.

Good, Glenda's nearby if I need her.

Then she laid her head on the shiny veneer of the desk. It felt so nice against her hot cheeks. Her breathing slowed and it no longer felt as if her heart wanted to jump out of her chest.

Could she stand now? She tested her theory and wobbled her way out of the office and went into her bedroom. Maybe a nap would do her some good.

"Samantha, what's wrong, dearie?" Glenda appeared with the duster.

"I look that bad, do I? I felt a little woozy in the office. I'm just gonna lie down until lunch."

"Did Dr. Ferrier change medications or dosage levels last week?"

"No, she thought she'd leave them alone since I'd had such a good couple of weeks."

"You look a mite peaked, dearie. Do you think you're coming down with something? Your colour's been off the last couple of days."

Samantha twisted her hair around her fingers. "I've got a doctor's appointment later this afternoon. Um, just wondering, do you think you could drive me?"

⟨◦⟩

"All right, dearie, let's get you home. What did the doctor say about why your colour's off?"

Samantha turned to face Glenda in the car. "We're pregnant."

The flatness of her own tone surprised her. She'd been over the moon with the news about Cami and Micah. Why not this one?

"A rainbow baby."

"A what?"

"After you've lost a wee one, the next one is called a rainbow baby. The hardest part is getting past the fear, luv. The fear of losing another one."

"But why is it named a rainbow baby?"

"Maybe it's the joy of hope shining through the vale of tears shed by mums who've grieved a little one. Or maybe it's the way the good Lord put a rainbow in the sky to remind us that He brings colour back into our lives after incredible loss. A reminder of His faithfulness to us, no matter what." Glenda reached over and clasped Samantha's hand. "I told your husband I'd take this job because I knew the pain of losing a little one. I've got a rainbow baby. Her name's Ellen. I'll walk with you through this pregnancy."

Samantha reached over and placed her hand over Glenda's.

"I'm so glad Phil didn't listen to my protests when he hired you." Samantha leaned back in the seat. "I think I'll close my eyes for a bit on the drive home."

"You do that, dearie. Do you want me to pick up Cami on the way home and save Phil a trip?"

"Sure... the car seat's in the back." Samantha turned the vent towards herself. Maybe extra air would help quell the nausea as her mind focused on the doctor's announcement.

"Statistics play in your favour," he had said. *"Everything looks wonderful so far."*

Samantha closed her eyes. So far? Her hands covered her abdomen.

———◦•◦———

Phil Camden paused for a moment to admire his home. Even more than the charming veranda with its wicker porch swing, he adored the view across the river. The stately stone university buildings rose above the treed banks of the South Saskatchewan River. Bright green leaves unfurled the prairie spring. The tight red buds of tulips trumpeted a new beginning.

He knew that hiring Glenda Henderson was the right move for Samantha. Easter had felt like a celebration compared to Christmas, but these last two weeks? Maybe today's news would make a difference.

He burst through the door of his two-story home and tossed his suit jacket on the coatrack.

"Sam, Sam I Am, where are you, honey? We did it. We're in the show." Phil took two stairs at a time to get to their bedroom.

"Daddeeeeeeeeeee!" With hair bows undone and her ballet tutu hitched around her chest, Cami careened out of her room to leap into Phil's waiting arms.

"Guess what, sugar plum? Your dear old dad is going to be on TV!" Phil waltzed his five-year-old ballerina around the landing, waiting for his wife to appear.

"You are, Daddy? Can I come too?"

"We'll see. It might be when you're at preschool. Sam?" Was she in the washroom? He sat on the tufted armchair with Cami still in his arms. With one hand, he loosened his tie. Time to relax!

"Daddy's gonna be on TV. Daddy's gonna be on TV," Cami chanted as she bounced on his lap.

Puzzled by his wife's failure to join them with all the fanfare, he picked Cami up and headed into their bedroom, then paused. Samantha sprawled face-down on the wrinkled navy bedspread. Sleeping? A prescription bottle sat on the nightstand. Had she taken a sleeping pill? Or more? God forbid!

He breathed a little easier as he watched the rise and fall of her chest. Hadn't she thought of all the trouble Cami could get into? A five-year-old left alone in the house?

Phil took a deep breath to settle himself, then tossed Cami on the space of the bed unoccupied by his wife and bent down to kiss her awake. He winked at Cami as he motioned for her to give her mom a kiss, too.

As Cami leaned in to kiss her cheek, Samantha rolled over, stretched, and Cami's kiss landed on her nose.

"Oh, you're home," Samantha said. "What time is it?"

He watched her wince, Cami's bony knees stabbing at her hip as the girl leapfrogged into his arms.

"Daddy's gonna be on TV and we get ta watch 'im. Right, Daddy?"

"Right!" Phil watched as his wife struggled to come fully awake. He reached for her palm, kissed it, and placed it against his face while keeping Cami from falling headfirst into her.

As she focused her dull blue eyes on his, Phil concentrated on keeping Cami in his grasp. Had Samantha grimaced? Smiled? She pulled herself up on one elbow and tugged down a ratty T-shirt she wore, one of his. Her scent wafted his way. How long had it been since she'd showered? He'd always appreciated her modesty, but now he wished she'd wear something that attracted his attention and appreciation.

He plastered a smile on his face. "Wow, honey, I don't know how you could've slept through this commotion, but yes, I have news."

"'Daddy is gonna be on TV'?" Samantha put up a hand to cover a yawn. "Is that the news?"

"Do you remember when I went to the Saskatoon Inn for my initial tryout?" Samantha nodded.

"Well, I got a phone call late this afternoon. July taping in Toronto! They want Tailor-Made Manufacturing to make a pitch on national television!"

Phil scanned his wife's face, seeking affirmation. When her eyes reached his, he saw only lingering sadness. Windows of her soul? More like shuttered barriers!

As her hand withdrew from his face, it felt like she'd dumped a bucket of ice on his excitement.

He forced himself to go on. "Isn't that great news? If we land this deal, we can increase the variety of materials available to our clients."

"That's really wonderful, Phil. I'm happy for you... happy for us, I mean."

Phil had to turn his face away to hide his hurt. How she'd distanced herself from the project they'd built together. How she'd removed herself from a space they'd once shared. She'd accused him many times of not understanding her grief, but he'd never let her see the depth of his. He feared it'd be too much, so only once had he let himself descend into the depths of his own emotions.

It had been eight months since they'd lost Micah. He'd seen glimpses of the old Samantha again just before Easter, but now all that progress seemed to have disappeared. The old Samantha, the flamboyant creature he'd met in university, had always decorated his world like no other woman had. She'd marked the tiniest occasions as a reason to celebrate life.

He had dared to hope today's news would spark that old vibrancy inside her. This TV showcase would put 3D printing in the limelight, and land Tailor-Made Manufacturing on the podium. Designers would flock to his company now!

"Um... maybe we could go out to celebrate," he said. "Get a babysitter and listen to some jazz at The Basement tonight?" He got down on one knee, threw his head back, and worked to entice her using his best theatrical voice: "Your carriage awaits, me lady. Just say the word! Oh, and guess who booked a sleepover for Miss Cami?"

"With Kristina?" cried Cami. "Oh, Daddy, I can't wait! Mommy, wear the blue dress, the one that makes you look like you're going to a fancy party! It's a twirling dress! You gots to have a twirling dress to dance with Daddy, right?"

Phil narrowed his eyes as he watched Samantha. How would she respond? Once he would have been able to predict it, but now?

Samantha leaned forward. "Sweetie, can you get Mommy a glass of water from the kitchen? Remember to use the plastic one you can reach, okay?"

"Okay, Mommy." Cami slipped out of Phil's arms, out of reach of the refusal that Phil suspected would come.

As Samantha waited for Cami to disappear down the stairs, she untwisted her long legs from the bedspread and sat up. "I feel awful. Zero energy. Food holds no appeal. I want to take you up on your offer—"

"—but you can't," he finished. "When will you rejoin the living? You can't even muster enough energy to celebrate one of the biggest moments our young company's ever had? Really?" Phil pushed himself off of his knee to a full standing position. "Haven't you had enough sleep? You were sleeping so deeply that anything could have happened to Cami! Is our dead son so demanding that you can't look after your living child? Do you care at all about what's happening to you? To us?"

Even as the furnace blast left his lips, Phil knew it trumped all he'd done to help Samantha get through the darkness.

The dresser mirror told him that his face no longer appeared red, but his words had lit an inextinguishable flame. He didn't think Samantha's face could turn any whiter until he turned to see Cami's hand trembling with the yellow plastic cup full of water. In her other hand, she held a new drawing she'd made. The tears balanced on her lashes tore at him.

Phil retreated to the doorway, where he knelt to take the cup from Cami's shaking hands. Without another word, he handed the cup to his wife and headed downstairs. He straightened his tie and rolled down his sleeves. Time to find a haven.

———◗ ◦ ◖———

Run away, Phil, back to the safety of your office, Samantha thought once Phil had gone. *It's what you do best when my response doesn't please you. Or your own emotions overwhelm you.*

Well, was she surprised by his anger? The company was his baby! She had just rejected his desire to celebrate its success.

Samantha pushed herself up off the bed to see how Cami was coping with Phil's outburst.

"Hey sweetie, thanks for the water." Samantha sat down on her bed and looked at what Cami had drawn. The highchair that turned into a desk and chair had turned out to be a great investment for their little artist.

Her breath caught as her eyes gazed at the kaleidoscope of colours surrounding the three stick figures. She'd never told Cami the story behind her favourite lap blanket. Was this a message she could trust? Could the story told by Chief Baer be true? "That's a beautiful drawing."

"It's our family. That's you, me, and Daddy. Oh, I forgotted Micah!" Cami took her black marker and drew a tiny stick figure in the sky above the family grouping, still encompassed by the rainbow.

Samantha felt her throat tighten and tears well up. Would these overwhelming groundswells of grief ever stop?

She stood up to wrap Cami's shoulders in a hug and dropped a kiss on her blond hair. "Sweetheart, you're a wonderful artist. I love our..."

Her words choked off, the river of tears overtaking her vocal cords so much that she feared frightening Cami further. She dashed away her tears with her T-shirt and took a shaky breath while Cami added another stick figure in the sky.

"That's okay, Mommy. Our babies are still part of our family."

What? How could she know? Who had told her? Samantha shivered despite the sun's warmth penetrating the window.

Hours later, Phil slid open the bedroom door and edged his way into their ensuite. He breathed a sigh of relief when Samantha's voice didn't pierce the darkness to greet him.

After brushing his teeth, he crept along the wall, but his toe collided with the corner of his nightstand. Biting back a curse word, he pulled back the covers and crawled into bed.

Samantha rolled towards him and he stretched out his arm to enfold her.

"I'm sorry." Phil's words hung in the darkness.

"This afternoon... when you found me in the bedroom... after putting a movie on for Cami, I fell asleep. I had some news to tell you... good news, I hoped. I fell asleep before you came home."

"What news?"

"We're pregnant." Samantha's words waited in the air, daring him to embrace their reality.

Phil forced himself to keep holding Samantha as chills spiralled down his arms. Fear dribbled down his back in tiny rivulets. "You're sure? Have you been to a doctor yet?"

"She figured I'm seven weeks along. The blood work looked good. When I said I didn't feel up to going out... it's because I can't keep food down. I'm scared, Phil. I can't go through another loss. Micah's on my mind. We were at thirty-nine weeks when we lost him."

Unwanted scenes from that day bombarded Phil. He knew what she meant. Work had been a sanctuary, insulating him from the thousand pricks of heartache.

Phil hugged his wife tightly, feeling regret for his outburst. A dark cloud seemed to steal the joy from the day. As her tears wet his sleep shirt, he just stroked her hair. It galled him to feel this powerless, unable to guarantee what tomorrow would bring.

Three

Unexpected News

Samantha's hand splayed over her abdomen as she watched Glenda tell Cami the special news. The scent of iris blooms still lingered about the back deck and Cami's garden plot gleamed green. Robins clustered around the apple tree. Were they waiting for their eggs to hatch?

Cami's squeal interrupted Samantha's musings.

"Wait, I gets to come to your house and Grandpa Tom's for a whole week?!" Cami shrieked and ran to give Samantha a hug. Then she boomeranged back to Glenda to give her a hug before zipping out to the back yard to play.

"Wait, honey, the sprinklers are..." Samantha headed into the house to find a towel for Cami.

"Well, luv, I guess you don't have to wonder if she'll be okay with coming back to our house for a longer visit than just a weekend," Glenda remarked.

How Phil had found this woman, she'd never know, but she had become as big a part of their family as Gran. At first the decision had made her so angry, but now she couldn't imagine life without her.

She sat down on the back deck to supervise Cami, marvelling about that very first day when Glenda Henderson had arrived in their home.

———◦◦———

March maintained its mercurial disposition. This year, no snowbanks lingered, but the air remained cool and frost decorated the muted browns of the grass almost every morning. It mimicked the state of Samantha's soul.

Today felt no different, but could it change with this woman Phil had plucked from the Yellow Pages?

Samantha pulled back the blue embroidered curtain from the office window and watched the older woman park her tan sedan just off the driveway. The salt and pepper cluster of curls emerged from the driver's side, followed by a stylish short pea coat, a muted pink sweater peeking beneath its collar and dark blue jeans.

The woman shut the car door and gazed at her surroundings, taking its measure. Would she find it wanting?

When she glanced up towards the office window, Samantha dropped her hand and retreated into her bedroom. A pang swept through her as she gazed at the closed door in the hall. The white door spoke to Samantha of all she'd lost. Once she'd gladly opened it to bring tea to Gran as she recovered from a fall, but that fall had revealed a greater enemy from which she had never recovered.

Gran had never known about Micah. She'd passed away when Cami turned two. She'd stayed with them for a month before going into the hospice at St. Joe's hospital.

Yes, that white door had opened a pandora's box.

Upon returning home after losing Micah, Samantha had folded up her rainbow afghan and placed it in Micah's room. With a firm slam, she'd shut the door to all hope of a future, and she hadn't gone in since. The whiteness of the door mocked and berated her for all her shortcomings.

Phil couldn't see a hope or a future in her either, so he had hired this woman, a housekeeper. Samantha looked around and saw piles of clothing heaped on every surface.

She stepped into the bathroom to check her hair. The garbage can overflowed with tissues and used pads. Scum around the taps shouted her failure. The snow-white spots mocked her cleanliness record.

"Can't even see through the shower panes anymore!" Phil's voice echoed in the hall of her mind. His patience had worn thin after several months of trying to do everything at work and home.

She pulled the brush through her hair and caught a whiff of her own body odour. Perhaps she should shower at some point today. Maybe Phil's plan felt right. She could use a little help around the house.

His words of love and support shamed her. Ever since they'd lost Micah, he'd done everything he could to aid her in getting back to health. Now he'd given her everything to regain her mental health.

But if he knew the real reason for her grief, he'd leave her for good. She blamed herself for losing Micah. In the mirror, she watched her tears trickle down her face. They dripped into the sink.

She grabbed a tissue and blew her nose. Then she found a clean T-shirt and pulled it over her head. A small thing to show her appreciation of Phil's effort. Time to meet the new housekeeper.

Samantha trailed her hand along the banister and stopped on the second step. Phil's voice floated in from the kitchen.

"Glenda, I'm so glad you're here. Cami's in daycare on Mondays, Wednesdays, and Fridays. She'll be around on Tuesdays and Thursdays. If it's too much work to have her around, I can make other arrangements."

"Don't you worry, Phil. It'll be as if one of my grandchildren were underfoot. I'm sure everything will be just fine."

"Glenda..."

"Yes?"

"My wife isn't exactly excited to have you here."

"Now don't you worry about a thing, dearie. We'll get along just fine. I took this job because I grieved a little one long ago. I know how it feels to have lost dreams and heartache over the death of a wee babe."

Samantha's throat tightened with emotion. Could this woman be an ally instead of a foe? Her voice sounded kind and reminded her of Gran. She'd give anything to drive over to Gran's house and have tea with her again.

She dashed away a tear that had slipped out and went down the remaining steps into the kitchen.

"Hello, I'm Samantha. You must be Mrs. Henderson."

The hand that clasped hers felt warm and soft.

"Hello, I'm happy to meet you, dearie. Phil told me you've been through a bit of a rough spot. Please accept my sympathies for your loss."

"Thanks, as you can see, I'm not... coping well." Samantha gestured towards the sink, piled high with dirty dishes. The counters were covered with papers, stray cutlery, and spices.

"Pish posh. Nothing to be ashamed of. I've been in your shoes, luv, and someone came over, cleaned my bathroom, and did the laundry until I got back on my feet. Now it's my turn to help you find your way back. Oh, and call me Glenda, dearie."

Samantha's heart thawed a little at the flame of hope lit by Glenda's words. Could she find her way back out of this icy white world that had immobilized her?

Glenda turned to Phil. "Well now, why don't you go along to work? Samantha and I'll figure out the cleaning schedule and sort out meals for this week's menu."

Samantha melted into Phil's arms as he reached out to her.

"Thanks for being such a good sport about this," he whispered. "I'll see you later."

She gave him a reassuring squeeze, even if she couldn't quite manage a genuine smile. She so wanted to love him the way he loved her, the way Cami adored him. Perhaps...

A solitary voice in her head goaded her. *Fat chance, you hypocrite. Two-faced liar! You were a liar when you married him. You're a liar now. If he knew the truth about you, he'd never have proposed.*

Exhausted from the constant barrage in her head, she turned to face Glenda.

"I guess I should start with a shower. Would you mind starting with the kitchen and living room? The cleaning supplies are on the top shelf in the pantry. Please put them back after you're done. The mop and vacuum are in this closet. Can we tackle the menu after I shower? I hope I can think better afterwards."

"No problem, dearie. You go right ahead. I'll think on it while I redd up this kitchen and see what kind of grocery items you have in the pantry."

Glenda bustled off to the pantry while Samantha dragged herself up the stairs, determined to do what she'd just said. The covers on her bed called her name, but she ignored the sirens. Glenda sounded too much like Gran for her to succumb.

———◦◦——

"Mommy! Come see, there's a rainbow in the sprinkler!" Cami tugged Samantha out of the deck chair. "You can see it if you turn your head this way!"

"Ooh, that's beautiful. Thanks for showing me, honey." Samantha noted her daughter's joy, and also her blue lips. "Sweetheart, let's go sit on the back porch for a bit. I think you need to warm up and dry off before supper."

"Aw, do I have to?"

"Yes, you do, but maybe you'd like a story while you're warming up?"

"Well, can I hear one about when you were a little girl?"

That startled her. Her childhood didn't really make for happy stories. Had she ever told Cami how the rainbow afghan had brought her to Gran's house? She'd have to skip some parts, but the story fit the current moment.

"It was a long time ago when I walked to Hands-On with my mother. I was wearing my favourite purple jacket. It was cold outside. I was hungry, so we stopped there for a snack 'cause it was free. That day, they handed out free blankets to families. I got a rainbow one, 'cause the lady said it matched my jacket."

"The one in Micah's room?"

She stared at Cami. "How did you know?"

"Daddy got mad when I played house in there one day."

Samantha stiffened. "Oh?"

"He said it was your special blanket. I said I was sorry, and I didn't take it for my dolls."

"That's okay, kiddo. Daddy was probably just worried I'd want it back some-time. He knows I've had it since I was a kid just like you."

Samantha rubbed her hands up and down Cami's back and arms with the towel to warm her, since Cami had started shivering.

"I was hiding in the closet 'cause I was scared something bad had hap-pened to my mama," Samantha continued. "She was sick a lot, and she was just lying on the floor. Somebody must have noticed and called 911 'cause the police showed up. Mama told me that police officers were scary and would take me away. I hid in the closet until Chief Baer walked into my bedroom. He saw the blanket and told me this story."

"I was scared when you went to the hospital and Daddy didn't come to see me for two days."

"Oh, baby girl, I'm sorry you felt scared." Samantha squeezed her arms a little tighter around this child who never ceased to amaze her with her honesty. "Thanks for telling me how you felt. Do you want to tell me more, or should I start the story?"

"The story, Mommy!"

"First, Chief Baer told me he had a little boy called Noah who had a blanket just like mine."

"Really? Someone has the same blanket as you?"

"Yup. He said his mom made it for Noah and it came with a story. He asked me if I wanted to hear it."

"You said, 'Duh, of course I wanna hear it.' Right, Mommy?"

"Actually, I was too scared, so I just nodded my head. And then he told me about some guy who liked to cheat and made his brother super mad, so he had to leave and live somewhere else. He fell in love with a girl, but her dad made him work for seven years before getting married. Then, just like he tricked his brother, the dad tricked him by giving him the sister of the girl he loved."

"That's not fair!"

"Nope. So the dad told him he had to work another seven years to get the girl he loved."

"How'd he get tricked?"

"When those people got married, the lady wore a veil, kind of like the burka some ladies wear at the mall, so he didn't notice until later. Anyhow, the girl he loved finally had a baby boy after waiting a very long time. The man loved this little boy very much. Then the little boy's mom died, which made his dad very sad."

"Mommy, I don't know if I like this story. Are there any more good parts?"

"I think the dad must have noticed how sad the little boy was, so he made his little boy a very special coat with all the colours of the rainbow. Then he told him about a promise the Creator had made to his own dad and grandfather. 'One day, our family will be a great blessing to every nation on earth. When you wear this coat, I want you to remember my love for you and that our family has a future, and a hope promised to us by the Creator.'"

"Is that why it's your special blanket? So you don't forget love and stuff like that?"

"Sort of." Yikes, this girl liked to get to all the hard stuff inside. Had Samantha forgotten about the love she'd been shown?

"Did your mommy die?"

"No, she didn't, but she was sick for a long time. I got sent to live with Gran and Pops until she got better."

"Is that the lady in your locket?"

"That's right, sweetheart. She lived with us for a while when you were two, but you're probably too little to remember her. She stayed in Micah's room."

"I'm warmed up now. Can I go back and play in the sprinkler?"

"You bet, snow jet!" Samantha stood up and hung the towel on the railing. She then leaned against the pillar, watching Cami duck and weave under the arc of the sprinkler. Her shrieks of joy filled Samantha with hope. But with her track record, how long would it be until loss punctured it?

Four

Difficult News

The view of the alley behind Phil's office did nothing to enhance his mood. He watched rain bounce off the dumpster. He'd just called his acting business partner into the office to discuss their latest supplier issue. Bob Harrington's resume had impressed him back when he'd needed to hire an operations manager, but as acting partner he didn't seem to be as invested as he should be. Instead he was just sitting there, licking the chocolate off his hands from a donut.

"It's about time you got here." Phil slammed his agenda shut and pushed away from the desk. "Another supplier has politely declined to work with us..."

Frustration was getting the better of him. Should he let Bob know that Samantha was pregnant again? It seemed odd to talk about his wife. The relationship between the two had been rocky. Samantha had bristled every time Bob called her the "little woman" or Phil's "ball and chain."

"What's got you all riled up today?" Bob asked as he stood, stretched, and strolled over to Phil's office window.

"I just wish I could figure out what's spooked our suppliers."

"Erin's sent out the cheques on time, correct?"

"Yes, everything looks like it did a couple of months ago. I don't know where the bad press is coming from."

"Well, you'll knock 'em dead in Toronto," Bob said. "Samantha's going with you, right?"

"Yeah, we'll do a few fun things after the television shoot." He hesitated for a moment. "But Samantha's pregnant again, due early January. I'm worried about it. Everything's fine. She's fine. The baby's fine. The nausea's quit, so it'll be our last little adventure before the baby comes." He hesitated again, even longer this time. "I sure hope the presentation goes well. It's nice to have Sam back in the loop. She sees things I don't. I've been practicing my pitch with her after Cami's gone to bed."

"Don't forget the hard work I've been doing to keep things afloat while you've been home taking care of stuff there over the last couple of months. I still think I deserve a promotion to partner, rather than just acting partner. The hours I've put in and the extra responsibilities in the office I've taken on deserve something."

"Yeah, I know. I appreciate it, but I can't swing it right now. Maybe we can amend your contract later on to reflect that or change your title."

"Your ball and chain keeps you on a pretty tight leash. Glad I'm not in your shoes."

Phil gripped the desk to keep from throwing his mug at Bob. He counted to ten. Were these the same sorts of remarks Bob had made to Samantha? Is that why she had been so averse to Bob becoming a partner?

He looked at Bob and held his gaze. If he didn't depend on Bob so much to keep the warehouse humming, he'd rethink hiring him in the first place.

As Bob closed the door and left, Phil slumped down in his office chair and spun around to gaze out the window. Samantha had told him that she felt uncomfortable around Bob. Was his attitude towards women always so derogatory? He would have to check with Erin and see how Bob treated her.

During the drive home from work and daycare later that day, Phil listened to Cami's chatter with half an ear. He kept thinking about Bob's proposal to make him a full partner. Was it a sound plan? He hoped Samantha would have the energy to serve as a sounding board tonight.

There were a lot of problems at work. He couldn't figure out why the company's cashflow seemed to ebb more than flow. The numbers didn't add up. Even though business kept increasing, the suppliers seemed reluctant. What was he missing?

Phil couldn't shake the feeling that there was more to the problem than what lay on the surface. Was he just jittery and seeing doom everywhere simply because Samantha was pregnant?

On days like these, Phil wished he could pick up the phone to call his dad and sort out his thoughts.

He drove into the driveway and shifted into park. As he turned off the vehicle, he reflected on how much he needed his wife. He then got out of the car and walked around to the rear passenger door. He made a silly face at Cami as he pulled it open.

"Got your card for Mommy?" he asked.

"Yup, I drew the pony at Grandpa Tom's house for her."

"Hey, that's the best pony I've seen you draw yet!"

"Thanks Daddy!" Cami raced into the house ahead.

At least this card wouldn't stir up any hidden fears, unlike the one he'd hidden from Samantha a few months ago right after Glenda arrived.

"Got your card for Mommy?" Phil asked his daughter as they arrived home. The raw March wind felt warm compared to the icy shiver that zipped down his neck.

"Yes, Daddy!"

Phil glanced down at the drawing on the homemade card. He loved the three stick figures holding hands with big smiles on their faces. Then he noticed the tiny horizontal stick figure in the middle of a rainbow, next to the proverbial sun every child seemed to instinctively draw at the corner of the page.

His heart skipped a beat. What would Samantha do or say when she saw that?

Cami had already undone the car seat and raced past him.

As Phil entered the house, he picked up Cami's winter coat and hung it on the hook. He also moved her boots onto the mat. After throwing his gloves into the basket and tugging off his coat, he loosened his tie and rolled up his sleeves.

He moved into the kitchen. The counters gleamed and three place settings adorned the table. Intoxicating scents filled the air.

Where had Cami disappeared to? He listened and followed the sound of voices up the stairs into Cami's room, where he found Glenda sitting on the bed with his daughter.

"Daddy, this is Mrs. Henderson."

"Yes, honey, I know. I met her last week."

"Did you know she has a pony, Daddy?"

Phil shook his head. "Didn't take you long, pumpkin!"

"Oh, it's all right, Mr. Phil," Glenda said. "She's doing what every four-year-old does. It takes thousands of questions to figure out this world and its happenings."

The housekeeper got up from the bed and stepped into the hallway. Positive that the girl's toys would keep her occupied, she motioned for Phil to join her. Phil followed, mystified by the secrecy.

"Your wife took a shower and helped me figure out a menu for the week. We tackled your bathroom upstairs. She fell asleep about an hour before you got home. I didn't let Cami wake her. I saw the card... it's precious, but I think it'll be hard on Samantha."

Glenda handed him the card.

"You're right," he said. "Thanks again for your time. The house looks great."

"You're welcome, dearie. I'd best be off. Tom will be eager to hear how my first day went, and I can't wait to tuck into his famous meatloaf and mashed potatoes."

"Sounds good. See you tomorrow."

Once she'd gone, Phil opened the white door and gazed at the empty crib for a moment. He placed the card against the lamp on the chest of drawers, then touched the rainbow afghan.

Would the vibrancy come back into their marriage? Their family? His colourless wife had disappeared into the family fabric rather than standing out like the woman he'd married.

He turned and walked into their bedroom to wake Samantha for a fantastic meal, judging by the smells. Maybe those would coax her into joining them.

Glenda's call shook him to the core.

"I'll be there in fifteen minutes." Phil excused himself from the video conference, citing a family emergency. He slammed his fist on his desk and raised it to the heavens. "Why? Haven't I lost enough already?"

He pushed away from the desk, tipping over his office chair in his rush to get to his vehicle.

"I'm gone for the rest of the day. Cancel everything." He glimpsed Erin's look of concern but didn't stop to explain. The office manager could roll with anything that came her way. In fact, Erin was invaluable.

He left the building in her capable hands, knowing that he needed to get to St. Joe's.

A wave of nausea hit him when he got in his car. This couldn't be happening again.

Phil rolled down the window as he got onto the street. No amount of air rushing past his face could quell the roiling of his stomach.

"Where is she?" Phil asked as he burst past the admitting desk and stormed into the hospital's emergency ward.

"Sir, wait." The harried receptionist chased him down. "Please register over here."

"I'm looking for my wife, Samantha Camden. She's having a miscarriage." She typed the information into the system and waited. Phil's foot vibrated up and down, tapping out his distress. "They've taken her up to the obstetrics ward."

Phil shook his head. Didn't these people get it? No one losing a baby wanted to be in the same place where others were celebrating the arrival of their hopes and dreams.

He stomped to the bank of elevators and punched the button. He wished he could restart this day somewhere else.

As he pushed open the curtain, he saw the standard blue and white blanket wrapped around Samantha.

Glenda released Samantha's hand. "I'll be in the hallway if you need me."

Phil's anger and adrenaline melted as he looked into Samantha's eyes. Her anguish fettered the spark that had once lit his world with fireworks.

He let the railing down and crawled in beside her. "I'm here, I'm here."

Phil's fingers felt like lead as he typed, changing the name on the upcoming flight to Toronto. Instead of going with Samantha, he would have to bring Bob. It wouldn't be the romantic getaway he'd imagined. Not the send-off he'd hoped for as he kissed Cami goodbye at Grandpa Tom's house.

Samantha had stayed behind in their darkened bedroom, her lips seeming cold and unmoving as he kissed her. Was she mad at him for leaving? For continuing with his plans for Toronto? The business was at a crisis point and he had to make this work.

He really didn't want to be travelling with Bob, but what choice did he have?

"That man is not quality material," Samantha had said to him the previous night. "What were you thinking when you offered him an acting partnership in March?"

"What could I do? You hid in our room, ignoring the world. I needed someone to meet clients."

"He's one of those guys who never grows up. He always makes jokes in public that paint you in a terrible light."

This Samantha had sounded more like the woman he married.

Get your mind on the game, Phil, he thought to himself. *You're going on national television. You can't think about Samantha now. She's going to be fine. All she needs is a little bed rest. She'll bounce back.*

The image of his wife huddled under the covers, pale and unmoving, replayed in his mind. He couldn't focus on that right now.

━━━━●○●━━━━

Three... two... one...

The producer motioned for Phil to begin his journey down the stairs. Time to pitch Tailor-Made Manufacturing to five venture capitalists. He needed to nail this presentation. The company was losing money and he didn't know why. The potential cash injection from any of these five people could buy him enough time to sort everything out.

Samantha should have been with him, not Bob, but it was too late now.

Be present. Stay in the game. You've got a job to do.

He shook his head, forcing himself to reset his mind.

Glenda had claimed Cami for the week. Phil wished he could see the look on Cami's face when Grandpa Tom announced to her his plan to add a cart to his pony rides...

He arrived on the landing, but the spotlight blinded him just as he made the turn. Misjudging the distance, he overstepped and had to grab the railing to keep from falling. Shoot! His stride faltered.

When she sees this, Sam I Am will smirk about it for days.

With that thought, his mind focused. Lifting his head, he smiled straight into the camera for his girls. He straightened his shoulders and launched into his pitch.

"Good afternoon. My name is Phil Camden and my company is Tailor-Made Manufacturing. Our goal: support local entrepreneurs who want to decrease their overhead in the 3D printing business. We supply the raw materials and technical expertise to bring their visions to life..."

Upon his return from Toronto, Phil trudged up the stairs, exhausted and disappointed in himself for not having scored the big deal. His only hope was a phone call he'd received afterward while waiting to board the plane home.

He'd pick up Cami tomorrow from the Glenda's. Right now he just wanted to feel Samantha's arms around him and process the event with her. Or rather, he hoped she'd be up to processing it with him.

Bob had guzzled enough alcohol on the plane to need a cab ride home, so he had no chance to debrief with his acting partner.

When he climbed the stairs at home, he noticed that the nursery door was ajar.

"What are you doing?" he said.

Samantha rocked back and forth on the glider. Her fingers pulled at woollen strands, unravelling the rainbow afghan that hadn't left her room until Micah's death. The pile of yarn grew on the floor, and with it Phil felt his hope unravel too.

"It's a lie," she murmured. "There's no hope and a future for me. I don't deserve to have this wrapped around me. I'm such a fool to believe in fairytales."

Samantha's bleak words made Phil shudder. He didn't know what to do as the pile of yarn grew deeper around her feet. He knelt by the rocker and slipped the afghan out of her hands, then tugged her out of the chair and stepped behind her. They cried together once he had pulled her into his lap. How could he fix this?

Five

Plans Change

Phil got out of his car, grateful that for once he would be able to keep his promise to Cami to get home early. The air felt heavy, as if foretelling a coming storm. He unfastened the buttons on his suit jacket as he gazed towards the river. There were no clouds on the eastern horizon, just a faint haze that dimmed the bright blue summer sky.

It was odd to find Glenda's car parked along the curb. Hadn't he arranged for her to stay from one-thirty to four-thirty on Thursdays? Maybe something had gone wrong with her vehicle.

Phil hurried up the steps of the veranda and opened the front door. He took off his jacket and hung it in the hall closet.

"Samantha? Cami?"

He stood for a moment, expecting to hear Cami rush to greet him, followed by her joy-filled "Daddy!" as she launched herself into his arms.

Instead he was met by silence.

"Glenda?" If Samantha had taken Cami out, at least their housekeeper should still be here. "Mrs. Henderson?"

Samantha usually texted him if she left the house. He checked his phone again. No missed calls or texts.

He loosened the knot of his tie as he walked into the kitchen, his steps coming to an abrupt halt.

"What the... Glenda!" His heart hammered as he took the last few steps to where the older woman lay inert on the floor near the island. He bent down on one knee and tapped her shoulder. "Glenda, can you hear me?"

Eyes closed, face pale, she didn't stir.

With trembling hands, he fumbled for the cell phone in his pants pocket and punched 911 into the keyboard. He hit the speaker icon, then set the phone on the floor next to him.

"C'mon, answer!"

He lifted Glenda's wrist to feel for a pulse. *God, let her be alive. Let her —*

"Where's your emergency?" The dispatcher's voice came through the phone's speaker.

"146 Baileywick Place, Saskatoon," he shouted in the phone's direction. Leaning his face next to Glenda, he felt relieved to feel her faint breath against his cheek. "Yes, the front door's unlocked."

"What's your emergency?"

As Phil relayed information to the dispatcher, his first aid training came back to the forefront. He scanned the room for clues about what had happened.

"I don't know what happened." Phil glimpsed blood on the floor, but he couldn't tell its origin. Panic arose as he traced the blood to a trail leading upstairs.

Oh God, no. Not my girls.

"There's a trail of blood going up the stairs. My wife and daughter..."

Phil snatched his cell phone off the floor and headed up the stairs two at a time. Rounding the landing at breakneck speed, he followed the blood into the bathroom.

"Oh, no, no, no..."

Samantha's tousled blond hair lay below the taps, her white alabaster skin matching the porcelain. She lay in a pool of blood. Was he too late?

He dropped to his knees beside the tub, slipped his arms underneath her featherlight frame, and moved her onto the floor. When had she lost so much weight? His baggy T-shirts must have disguised how much she'd lost in the last few weeks.

Her right arm flopped onto his knees. The jagged cuts looked raw and puffy. They oozed blood in three different places. On her other arm, geyser after geyser of blood shot out with each faint heartbeat.

Oh, God, help.

"My wife, she's bleeding from her wrists. Jagged cuts from..." Hand shaking, Phil reached for a kitchen knife lying on the floor.

"Sir? Sir, you need to stop the bleeding."

He left Samantha on the floor and scrambled to the vanity, where he searched for clean towels to press against her wrists. Discovering none, he ripped open two sanitary pads and held them against her cuts to slow the bleeding. He put pressure on both arms.

"I don't know... where my daughter is." He couldn't seem to pull any oxygen into his lungs. Had Cami seen anything? Had Samantha hurt their daughter before trying to take her own life?

His wife's face swam before his eyes as he struggled to maintain pressure.

"Yes, I hear the sirens." The sounds of the front door opening reached Phil. "I'm up here!" he yelled.

When the paramedics reached his wife, Phil turned his attention to searching for Cami. He scanned the back yard from the master bedroom window. Nothing. He checked her bedroom and closet, in case she was hiding. No sign of her.

Skirting the second set of paramedics working on Glenda, Phil opened the door to the basement and pounded down the stairs, flying through the rec room and checking the spare bedroom. Nothing there either.

He zoomed back up the stairs, past the paramedics steadying Glenda's transfer to the stretcher, then headed for the front door. He froze on the front porch. His neighbour, Mary Ann, stood on her veranda, taking in the scene.

Suddenly, Mary Ann's screen door popped open and Cami came out. The girl started down the steps towards the gate in the neighbour's front yard.

His knees buckled in relief, but he caught himself before tumbling off the steps.

"Mary Ann, Mary Ann!" He waved his arms frantically. He couldn't let Cami come across the street.

"Cami." Mary Ann caught the girl and scooped her up in her arms. She carried her back into the house.

Phil moved out of the way as the paramedics took Glenda into the ambulance.

"Her pulse is weak and thready," one of them was saying. "Looks like a head trauma..."

He leaned against the pillar of the veranda. How could this be happening?

He waved the second ambulance onto the driveway as the sirens of the first ambulance cranked up. It was headed, Phil assumed, to St. Joseph's hospital.

The second set of paramedics came out of the house with Samantha. Moving closer to the stretcher, Phil drank in her colourless face underneath the oxygen mask. He stroked her forehead, then leaned in to kiss her.

"Please fight to stay with us. Cami needs you. I need..." He choked back tears and stepped away as they lifted the gurney into the ambulance.

"We're headed to St. Joe's. You can meet us at the emergency admittance bay." The paramedic's stark, cursory instructions gave Phil hope. "Are you okay with driving there? You in shock?"

"I just need to..." Phil made himself hold his breath for ten seconds before blowing it out. "I need to organize my daughter's care."

Phil's gaze followed the ambulance until it turned off their street. He then dropped his eyes and discovered that his shoes were speckled with blood. His knees were stained red. He'd need to change before seeing to Cami.

He dragged himself back inside and upstairs to the primary bathroom. What a whirlwind! He washed his hands and watched the red liquid swirl down the drain, wishing the lingering effects of this trauma would disappear as easily.

After stripping off his bloodstained clothing, he dressed, found a large suitcase, and dumped his daughter's dresser drawers into it. He swept her favourite stuffies, blanket, and pillow off her bed. He unplugged her tablet and charger and tossed them in as well.

When he returned to their bedroom, he grabbed his electric shaver and antiperspirant from his gym bag and then added some clothes for himself. He crammed it all into an overnight bag. He could camp at the hospital for a few days if needed.

His blood pressure rising, he punched his mother's number into his phone.

"Mom... I need you... C–c–can you drive in to the city right away? I've got a situation. Samantha's on her way to the hospital. I don't... know if she'll make it."

Hearing his mom's empathetic murmurs made it hard for him to swallow the giant lump in his throat. But he went on to tell the story of his afternoon.

"Phil, leave Cami's suitcase at Mary Ann's for me," his mom said. "Take the booster seat out of your car and leave it there, too."

As he headed down the stairs, he paused as his mom's words registered. "I'd have forgotten about that. Thanks, Mom."

Outside, Phil wrestled the booster seat out of his car and started over to Mary Ann's place. Before he'd crossed the street, the door opened and the neighbour's high-pitched voice broke through the flotsam of his mind. Her questions came like rapid fire.

"What happened to everyone? Was it a break-in? How bad are the injuries? I didn't notice anyone lurking around. But I've been busy with the girls. We were in the basement—they were making cards while I was scrapbooking."

"I'm not sure what happened to Glenda," Phil confessed. "She wouldn't wake up. But my Samantha, she... she slit her wrists."

Using the booster seat for support as the gravity of what had just happened sank in, Phil forced the next steps into words.

"My mom's coming into the city to get Cami. I don't know what will happen next. I need to get to St. Joe's. Glenda's husband Tom needs to be contacted. I..."

As Mary Ann took the suitcase and booster seat from him, Phil felt bereft of those supports. He fought to take in what Mary Ann said next.

"Talk to Cami before you go. She has some questions and is a little worried."

Her gentle tone penetrated his adrenaline saturated brain. "Can you get her, please?"

While waiting for Mary Ann to extract Cami from her play with the neighbour's own daughter, Kristina, Phil sank down to the steps on the porch.

Next step: text Tom. He pulled out his phone.

There's been an emergency, he typed. *Call me when you get this. I'd rather tell you on the phone.*

Cami's arms circled his shoulders and he reached around to slide her onto his lap.

"Sweetheart, Grandma is coming to pick you up after supper." He took a deep breath. "You get to have a mini-holiday out on the farm."

Cami's blue eyes gazed up at him. Her soft hands on his cheeks forced him to maintain eye contact, challenging him to be honest.

"Do you have another trip, Daddy? How come there was an ambu... ambulance at our house?"

"Mommy got sicker. And she needed one to take her to the hospital."

"But why can't I go to Mrs. Henderson's house like your other trips?"

"Mrs. Henderson isn't feeling well."

"Is that why she rode on a bed?"

Phil swallowed hard. "Yes, honey." She'd seen more than he had thought. He hugged her tightly. "I need to go see Mommy in the hospital, Cami. I'll come get you as soon as I can. Okay, sweetheart? I'll call you tonight and read you a story just like I do when I'm on my other trips."

The tears filling Cami's eyes undid his emotions, threatening to swallow him whole.

The sound of the door opening brought salvation. As Mary Ann sat down beside them, he mouthed "Help." Her silent solidarity bolstered his feeble attempts to comfort Cami. Mary Ann's soft murmurings of God's love for her mommy resurrected long-forgotten Sunday school lessons.

Soon Cami relinquished her death grip on Phil, moving to Mary Ann's arms for comfort.

Phil leaned over and kissed Cami. "I'll talk to you tonight, sweetie-tweetie. Give Grandma a kiss and a hug from me."

Mary Ann ruffled Cami's hair. "Let's get you washed up for supper. Can you go inside and tell Kristina it's time to wash up?"

After the screen door banged shut, Phil and Mary Ann got up. Mary Ann grabbed the booster seat and suitcase she'd left on the porch.

"My mom should be here by seven-thirty." Phil stopped and turned back. "Do you think she should wear her pyjamas? Mom needs about an hour and a half to get here. Cami's bedtime is eight o'clock. It'll make it easier if Cami's already wearing her pyjamas."

"I'll make sure she has them on," said Mary Ann. "Poor kiddo."

"You have an extra housekey, right?"

Mary Ann nodded.

"I think I grabbed everything," Phil said. "If Mom thinks of something I forgot, she can use your key to get into the house."

"I have the key. Don't worry about anything. Call us for anything. We'll be there. The hospital's a hard place to be when you're alone. This situation is tough. Randy'll be home soon if you need him."

"Uh, thanks. I'll call if things spiral downhill. But for now, I better get going."

Phil drove away after punching in the address of St. Joe's into his GPS. He didn't want to take any wrong turns.

As he headed towards the hospital, the questions he'd held at bay swarmed. What if Samantha didn't make it? What then?

Mouth dry, he swallowed. Losing Micah had left him hollow. But losing Samantha, too? He massaged his neck to relieve the tension.

Six

Emergent Care

Waiting to merge onto Twenty-Fifth Street, his phone rang. Before answering, he pulled into a side street and answered the call.

"Hi Tom." Phil paused. How did one tell a guy his wife was on the way to the hospital? "Your wife went by ambulance about twenty minutes ago to St. Joseph's." Phil cringed at Tom's gasp. "When I arrived home, I found her unconscious by the kitchen island. She wouldn't respond. I kept... I kept calling her name, Tom. She didn't move and I couldn't hear or see my girls anywhere..."

As Phil relived the scene, his grip on the steering wheel tightened.

"Phil, are you there? You're not driving, are you?" The deep concern in Tom's voice pulled Phil back to the present.

"No, I pulled over. Tom, I saw a blood trail and followed it to find Samantha... my Sam, bleeding. She... she tried to take her own life." Phil shook his head, still stunned to hear himself say the words out loud. "I don't have any updates. No details. I'm so sorry."

Tom's voice pierced the darkness. "What about Cami? Is she... she, okay?"

"Yes, she's fine. Mary Ann had her... she saw the ambulance... she saw your wife. Tom, I wish I knew what happened."

"You and me both, Phil. I better get going. I'll see you there."

The rest of the drive to the hospital passed in a blur. Upon arrival Phil parked his car and rested his head against the wheel, gathering strength for the next challenge.

After a couple of deep breaths and wish-filled thoughts, he opened the car door and strode towards the emergency entrance. He followed the signs to the waiting room and stood in line for the information desk clerk.

Before his turn, a wave of nausea hit him. He plugged his nose and breathed through his mouth. Cold rivulets of sweat trickled down his back as other ER memories rose like the bile he'd just swallowed.

The receptionist's voice interrupted the images racing through his mind. "Who do you want to see?"

"Samantha Camden. I'm Phil Camden, her husband." He fumbled with his ID.

"Have a seat. A nurse will come get you when they're ready."

That sounded ominous. Was it still touch and go? Had he not arrived home soon enough? His chest tightened.

A few minutes later, a nurse came by and told him to follow her into his wife's exam room. The buzz around his wife's bed increased his worry.

"Mr. Camden, do you know if she's on any medication?" the doctor asked in a brisk tone.

"Um... she's on antidepressants, or at least she was..."

The activity in the room swirled at a feverish pace as the doctor called for additional equipment. Phil had to turn his head as they threaded a black tube down Samantha's throat. The pungent smell of the contents of her stomach had him plugging his nose so he wouldn't lose his lunch. Only the doctor's pronouncement that there weren't any pill fragments caused him to finally exhale.

Like sentries hovering over his Samantha's head, the IV poles held life-giving bags of saline and blood. His glance followed the tubes cradled around his wife's arms to the thick gauze dressings packed around her wound. Phil's face warmed at the thought. How could anger and pity dwell together?

He gazed at his wife's matted blond hair, her tiny freckles vivid against her pale face. Oxygen prongs had replaced the mask, assuring her of receiving enough life-giving oxygen while her body recovered.

Oh sweetheart, where are you? Come back to me fully.

As if aware of his longing, her eyes fluttered open. She turned her head away from him. Would she never stop pulling away?

Phil ignored her signal and leaned over the rail to kiss her forehead. While reaching for her hand, he realized that restraints were pinning her arms to the side of the bed. Had she continued to fight the doctors and nurses? Or was it something worse?

He collapsed into the corner chair, overwhelmed. The thoughts came like incoming missiles. It seemed hopeless.

All the publicity about your wife's depression will send business down the tubes, he worried. *You'll never attract an investor. Cami will act out at school and...*

Propelled by the thought that any of this could harm Cami, he got up, leaned over the railing, and waited until his presence forced Samantha to make eye contact with him. He needed answers. She had them.

"Glenda's been hospitalized." He took a deep breath as he worked to keep his tone even. "What the... what happened, Samantha?"

He held her gaze and waited.

"I didn't want din... wan... her to stop me. I din wan her ta call the para... paramedics..."

"She wouldn't wake up when I shook her, Sam. How did she get hurt? Exactly how did she get knocked out?" His tone punctured the hiss of the oxygen in this sterile, inhospitable environment.

Samantha's gaze fell. The silence sizzled like a hot iron poker. With no answer, the fight in Phil stilled.

Just then, the doctor motioned to Phil from the hallway. He sighed and walked away from the woman he no longer felt he knew.

"Hello, Mr. Camden," the doctor said. "I'm Dr. Whitmore. Your wife is stable. She had close to twenty-five stitches in each arm."

Dr. Whitmore's eyes held his. Why did he feel on trial for what his wife had done?

"She's had considerable blood loss, which is why we're transfusing her. She became combative once conscious, so we had to restrain her. I looked at her chart and saw she had a recent stay here." The doctor flipped the page on the chart. "I'm so sorry for your loss. Is she getting some help?"

"Dr. Nancy Ferrier at Southside Counselling Centre."

Like that had done a lot of good. Samantha had begun counselling with Dr. Ferrier after her grandmother passed away. He had thought it would help keep the dark clouds at bay, but now?

Dr. Whitmore made a note on the clipboard he held. "Was she on any anti-depressants?"

Phil nodded. "She had been improving before Easter, so her dosage decreased. Then she stopped taking the meds when she became pregnant."

He raked his hand through his hair. "After she miscarried... I don't know if she went back on them or not."

Why was he just now wondering whether she'd taken her medication again? Had he stopped caring?

"Should I have insisted she get back on them?" Phil asked. "After the loss, isn't it normal to be sad for a while?"

"Antidepressants provided the missing chemicals Samantha needed. It's based on bloodwork, not just standard procedure for those struggling with depression. Miscarriage or not, her psychiatrist should have seen her or ordered new bloodwork. But hindsight won't change the present. I'm so sorry for your loss, Mr. Camden. I am going to recommend her admittance into Grand River Hospital."

Phil didn't know how he felt about Grand River Hospital. It meant traveling an hour and a half away from Saskatoon. But a plan always made him feel better. His shoulders relaxed a bit. Maybe this would be the fresh start they all needed. A timeout, so to speak. He'd have to sort out the implications of this move later.

He plunged into his next line of questioning. "Dr. Whitmore, what's the prognosis of the other woman? The one who came in with my wife? She's our housekeeper, Mrs. Glenda Henderson."

"I'm sorry. I can't give you that information." Dr. Whitmore turned to go, then looked back at Phil. "Oh. Isn't that her husband at the nurses' station?"

"You're right, that's him. Thanks, Dr. Whitmore."

The doctor went into the next patient's exam room.

Phil headed to the nurses' station. "Tom... wait! Do you have a minute? How's Glenda?"

Tom turned and glanced at Phil. "It's not looking good. She has a compressed fracture at the base of her skull. Internal bleeding in her brain is putting pressure on her brain stem. She's headed into surgery right now. She had a bloody handprint on her chest, Phil. The paramedics contacted the police. They believe your wife pushed her."

Phil stared at Tom in disbelief, and then he remembered his wife's response to his question about what had happened. God, how could this be happening? Would they incarcerate Samantha? Would she end up in prison? Was her past coming full circle?

Only Cami didn't have a grandmother nearby to help care for her.

His manufacturing business had soared since his televised pitch in August. It remained all he could do to stay ahead of it all. Bob kept asking him to find additional sources for materials so they could expand. That alone made his head spin. But would the business crater when the bad press got out? Would they topple under the weight of lawyer fees?

He leaned against the ledge of the nurses' station to keep himself upright.

"Excuse me, Phil, I think the less time we spend together right now, the better," Tom said. "I need to call our daughter."

How could Samantha have stooped to hurting their beloved housekeeper, especially after losing her own sons?

He felt torn between providing for his family and grieving yet another loss. He wanted to crawl in a hole with his wife, but how could he? Cami deserved normality.

A soft touch on his arm interrupted his thoughts. It was the nurse. "You can go back into your wife's room now."

Without Glenda's presence and support, he didn't know how he would cope with work and also take care of Cami and Samantha. The image of her in the bathtub taunted and jeered at him. Home no longer felt welcoming.

Phil returned to his wife's exam room and watched as the nurse and aide attached the IV poles. They unplugged the oxygen cannula and turned off the heart and oxygen monitors.

"Um, where's she going?" he asked.

"We're admitting her to the mental health ward for seventy-two hours."

"Oh. Can she have visitors there?"

"After the seventy-two-hour hold." The nurse halted her preparations as two police officers entered the exam room.

One officer cleared his throat. "Would you mind waiting on the transfer until we've discussed some things with Mrs. Camden?"

The nurse raised her eyebrow, then stepped out. The aide followed.

"Ma'am... Mrs. Camden, we need to ask you some questions about what happened this afternoon."

Samantha opened her eyes and attempted to focus on the men beside her bed. Her dull expression didn't leave Phil with any confidence that she even cared about the reason for the police's visit. Was she even aware enough to answer their questions? Unlikely.

He moved closer to hear her responses.

"Sir," said one of the officers. "I realize you'd like to hear your wife's answers, but we really need you to step aside."

Step aside?

Just like that, Phil travelled backwards in time to a series of memories he'd blocked. *Step aside.* Words spoken by paramedics. *Step aside...* The doctor. The surgeon. The pastor. The neighbours.

Step aside.

Sixteen-year-old Phil had been pacing in the surgical waiting room while his mother begged him to sit.

"Why didn't he say something after he hit the fence?" Phil asked his mother.

"You know your father. He always plays down his injuries."

"What if he doesn't make it?"

"Don't worry. The surgeons are fantastic at RUH."

"Didn't you hear the paramedics say they got to him too late? If he'd gone by ambulance earlier, he wouldn't have lost so much blood internally."

"Son, it's not your fault."

"It is. I didn't secure the feed bag, and it startled the three-year-old that dad was working with."

"Your dad's been working with horses from the age of four. Sometimes things are out of our control. It's not your fault he got tossed onto the corral rail. That one was temperamental from the get-go."

"But I should have told you right away to come down to the corrals to look at Dad."

"He told you to do what you always do after a training session, and you did it. Taking good care of our animals is important to our business and our reputation, no matter if they hurt us or cause trouble."

The image of his father slumped over in the tack room burrowed into Phil's brain. But the next slide pushed it out as he watched his mother crumple into the chair at the surgeon's words: "We did everything we could."

A cone of silence descended on events to follow. Like a string of dominoes, the lack of insurance led to the horse auction and then drought compounded the loss.

Phil got a job the first month after his dad died. He balanced school and farm work. Every extra penny went into keeping the section of pasture so one day his mother's dream of boarding horses could come true. He sold his horse rather than ask his mom for a loan for his first semester's tuition. And he honoured his father's last request.

But he'd never been able to bring himself to go riding again.

At least, not until his mom had pushed him into holding Cami on a horse for the family photos. It had felt like a betrayal of his old horse, Buck.

What would he have to give up this time?

The officers requested that Phil move to a chair in the hallway.

"I want answers, too," he had protested as the door closed, shutting him out.

Seven

Storytime

The vibration stirred Phil into action. It was a text from his mom: *Can you call Cami right now? I just finished tucking her in and she's ready for bed.*

He rubbed his eyes and texted a quick *Yes*. He looked for a quiet space away from the hubbub of the ER and settled on the stairwell. Hopeful for decent reception, he dredged up a smile for his daughter.

"Hi, sweetheart," he said as the video chat started. "Grandma braided your hair. So pretty! Did you have a fun trip with Grandma?"

"Yes, Daddy. Is Mommy okay?"

"Yup. She's still sick, though, honey. She needs to stay at the hospital for a while."

"Is she gonna die like baby Micah?"

Phil's heart sank a little lower. "No, the doctors gave her the medicine she needed and fixed her all up."

"What about Mrs. Henderson?"

"The doctors are helping her too. Now, what kind of story do you want tonight?"

"A story about Cami!"

"Hm, a story about Cami. Can you help me if I get stuck?"

"Okay, Daddy."

"Once there was a little princess named Cami, and she loved the colour..."

"Purple!"

"She loved the colour purple so much that she decorated her entire room with it. She had purple lilacs in a purple vase. A purple pillow for her cat. She had violet curtains..."

"Daddy, just purple, not violet."

"Violet's another name for purple, Cami."

"Oh, that's a pretty name."

"She had different shades of purple pillows in her reading corner, but her favourite part of the room was..."

"The purple rocking chair."

"Princess Cami loved the purple rocking chair. Every time she sat in the purple rocking chair, something magical happened."

Phil paused and waited for Cami to chime in. When she didn't, he thought she might have drifted off to sleep.

"What happened to Princess Cami, honey?"

"She gotted to travel to her mommy and daddy."

His heart winced at that addition to the story. "That's right, honey. The purple rocking chair would always take her to where her parents were so they could tickle her and kiss her good night."

His mom caught those last words and smothered kisses all over Cami, gently tickling her.

"It's time to say good night to Daddy, Princess Cami," she said. "Blow him a kiss, sweetie."

Phil captured the kiss with his hands and brought them to his cheek, then watched as the screen went dark. He stuck the phone in his pocket and headed back to the exam room.

At the sound of his footsteps, one of the exiting police officers glanced backwards and recognized him. He touched the other officer's arm and they both stopped to wait.

"Mr. Camden, do you have a few minutes?" asked the dark-haired officer. He looked weary. "They took your wife to her new room."

"I'm not sure if I have anything to add. I arrived after the event."

"That's all right. We're just establishing a timeline for what may have happened."

The two police officers looked at one another and the second one pulled out his notebook.

"Could we have this conversation after I check on my wife's status? I haven't had supper. I don't feel very coherent right now."

"Meet at the cafeteria in thirty minutes?"

"Sure."

Phil eased down the hallway towards the admitting area. After finding the elevator, he punched the eighth floor button and leaned against the railing. His adrenaline rush had disappeared. Would this day ever end?

His legs felt encased in cement as he lurched out of the elevator. Each clomp of his foot grew heavier until he arrived at the double doors of the unit.

He tried the handle. Locked.

He buzzed the door of the psychiatric wing. A few minutes later, a man in dark blue scrubs opened the door.

"May I help you?" the man asked.

"My wife, Samantha Camden. I hoped to see her before the seventy-two-hour hold."

"Come with me. There are some additional forms to fill out."

Phil wondered if all nurses were so terse. Maybe they were just conserving energy?

After filling out his wife's insurance card information at the nurses' station, the man in the dark blue scrubs came by again. Hadn't he just had to go through these same forms? Ugh, bureaucracy!

"Follow me. You have fifteen minutes."

Fifteen minutes? That's all? Phil was too tired to argue. He raked his hand through his hair and rubbed his eyes.

"She also has to agree to see you," the man added.

What? What if she didn't want him? What would that mean? His stomach clenched and his eyes tracked the nurse as he disappeared into room 812.

A moment later, he appeared.

"She'll see you," the nurse said briskly. "Fifteen minutes only."

How should he make use of the short time? He didn't know what to expect. Medication and counselling had supported her during her depression, so this felt brand new.

After pulling open the door, he threaded his way through the curtains to find Samantha tucked under the austere white blankets with the blue stripe. A metal stand with a bag of plasma and saline solution hung next to her, its life-sustaining tubes connected to the woman he had promised to love in sickness and in health.

A pang of guilt assailed him over his anger earlier. How had he let his business reputation take priority over his wife? What kind of husband was he anyway? He'd been busy with work and too exhausted to connect.

Nope, his dad would have called them excuses.

The paralysis of Samantha's grief terrified him. Work gave him a buffer.

Spying a chair near the back, Phil pulled it closer to the bed before his legs gave out. Work seemed so far away now. Could his words make a difference?

"Samantha, I love you," he said, his voice breaking. "You'll get through this. You'll get help. We..."

"Phil, I can't," she whispered. "I want it to stop because it hurts so much. I keep failing. My body keeps failing."

Leaning his head on the railing of his wife's bed, Phil reached for her hand and held it. The waning and waxing buzzes of hospital machinery wove in and out of his consciousness. Without looking up, he deciphered the blood pressure machine from the constant blip of the heart monitor. Like Rorschach inkblots, the teardrops on his pantlegs pronounced the state of his emotions. He didn't know what to say.

Phil lifted his head at Samantha's sniff and noticed that her sinuses appeared blocked by tears. The black restraints anchored her arms to the railing and kept her from wiping her tears or blowing her nose. He grabbed several tissues and gently wiped her face.

"Thank you." Her voice sounded hoarse.

He felt comforted knowing he'd done one thing to help. A start.

When the charge nurse arrived to check Samantha's stats, Phil squeezed her hand and left.

Seeing those restraints pushed long forgotten memories to the surface of Phil's consciousness. He remembered the ridealong with his friend, Noah, the one that had ended with a young man screaming profanities in the emergency room as personnel worked to restrain him.

Really? His mind needed to bring that up? Stay focused on the now, Phil!

When the charge nurse left, Phil ducked back in to say his goodbyes.

"I love you, Samantha. I promise to be here for you. Mom picked up Cami from Mary Ann's house. She's safe and looked after, so I can focus on you." Phil caressed her hand and kissed her forehead. "I'll see you Sunday."

Samantha's brow wrinkled. "Sunday?"

"It's the ward's policy. No visitors for seventy-two hours."

"Oh." Samantha's eyes closed again.

The charge nurse poked his head in. "Time's up."

"Can I bring you something from home on Sunday?" Phil waited, but Samantha didn't answer. He'd need a list of what to bring before her transfer to Grand River on Sunday. Who would be the best source of information? The nurses station?

He dragged himself to the basement where he located the cafeteria. He picked up the day's special of lasagna and Caesar salad and found a spot to sit away from everybody else. Real cutlery helped dispel some of the day's surreal qualities.

Phil made quick work of the simple meal. The coffee seemed to melt the frozen spot where his feelings were all balled up in a tight knot.

He swallowed the last of the coffee as he saw the officers come his way.

"This spot work for you, Mr. Camden?" one of them asked.

Phil wiped his mouth with a paper napkin, then crumpled it in his fist. "Sure."

"I'm Detective Flynn and this is Sergeant McKnight."

"Phil Camden of Tailor-Made Manufacturing."

"About what time did you arrive home this afternoon?"

"Five o'clock"

"What did you do after you got there?"

Phil quickly summarized the events for the officers.

"I left for the hospital by six-thirty, I think."

"Thank you, Mr. Camden. In order to further our investigation, we'll also need your cooperation to go through the evidence in your home. Afterwards we can release your home back to you."

"Uh, what do you mean?"

"Well, the testimony so far suggests that your wife pushed Mrs. Henderson. Mr. Henderson wants to press charges for assault and battery. A team of forensic specialists needs to collect evidence. Who can we talk to in order to confirm your departure time from the office?"

"Uh, Erin, my office manager."

"Do you have a business card so we can contact him or her?"

Phil dug around in his wallet for a business card. "It's her..."

Stunned, he tried to draw a breath. It felt as though someone had punched him in the gut. He put his head between his knees and slowly counted to ten before blowing out slowly. He took a few more slow breaths, then raised his head and nodded.

Detective Flynn stared at him for a moment. "You okay?"

"Yeah, I think so." Phil finally found a business card to slide towards the detective.

The detective patted him on the shoulder and murmured something that escaped Phil's understanding.

As the officers exited the cafeteria, Phil slumped, head in his hands. *Can I say something to Tom? What if Glenda dies? How will I cope as a single parent? Would Samantha survive inside an institution? Could she survive prison? Will people know me as the husband of a convicted murderer? Will venture capitalists still be interested in franchising our operation? Will negative publicity destroy our brand?*

He sat up and sighed. How could I be so selfish?

He could let Tom know that he'd given his statement to the police. Guessing that Tom hadn't eaten, he got up to grab sandwiches, a muffin, and a hot cup of coffee before heading to the second floor.

He found Tom in the waiting room, idly flipping through the pages of a magazine. Phil set the food down on the coffee table beside him.

"Didn't know if you'd had supper yet," Phil said. "It's yours if you want it. Any updates?"

Tom's granite stare collided with Phil's solicitous tone. "Phil, I met with the police. I'm pressing charges against your wife."

"I know. I just gave my statement and my permission for them to investigate the scene at my house."

Phil tried to infuse as much compassion and care into his voice as he could, knowing that Tom was holding it together the same way he was. After all, the Hendersons were like grandparents to Cami.

"Thanks for the sandwiches." Tom cleared his throat. "I couldn't bring myself to leave. I'm not hungry, but I should probably try to eat something. The nurses promised a bed or cot for me to crash in tonight."

"I need to find accommodations, too. And an extra toothbrush. I think the gift shop is still open. Do you want a toothbrush?"

Tom stared at Phil.

Eight

Dazed and Confused

Her arms were bandaged and the black restraints snaked around the railing of the hospital bed. It made Samantha long to escape. A sense of horror invaded her thoughts as she confronted the reality of her situation.

The doctor entered the room and picked up her chart. "Hello, Samantha, my name is Dr. Mochar. How can I help? Any questions?"

"I... the officers asked me if I pushed her. I don't remember..."

"Pushed who, Samantha?"

"Glenda. Mrs. Henderson." Samantha's throat tightened and squeaked out the next words. "She's our housekeeper."

"I can't give you any specifics of another patient's care. I know she needed surgery. That's all I can tell you at the moment."

Surgery? Surgery means something bad. The weight on her chest increased, making it hard to breathe.

"She's still alive, isn't she? I didn't mean for her to get hurt." Straining to sit up, Samantha cried out, her voice hoarse. "I just wanted the pain to stop. She begged me not to hurt myself. I just tried to get away from her."

"Speaking of surgery, you're going to need some, too. You injured your tendon."

What? Energy coursed through her; twisting and turning, she tried to get away from the images replaying in her mind. When the dam broke, she couldn't stop herself. She started coughing and choking.

The nurse finally loosened the restraints and handed her some tissues.

"I... can't... breathe... help... me."

Between gasps, she watched the nurse inject something into her IV line. Dr. Mochar wrote something on the chart, and then the nurse laid her cool hand on Samantha's head.

Ahhhh, thought Samantha. *That feels like my grandmother's hand when I was little and got sick.*

She felt her body shudder and twitch with each outcry.

"There, there, Samantha. You're safe. Let's try to take a deeper breath. Through your nose."

Samantha absorbed the calm strength conveyed by the nurse. Her breathing slowed and her tears ebbed. However, it did nothing to stop the tornadic motion of her thoughts.

If only Phil had come home just a few minutes later, I'd be dead. Dead, just like my boys. I would be with my boys and Gran. No more worries for Phil. He could simply dismiss my death as a symptom of depression...

But she saw a glimmer of the pain her death would bring Cami. The same pain she'd experienced.

A verse memorized long ago wandered into Samantha's mind before she drifted into sleep.

"Or didn't you realize that your body is a sacred place, the place of the Holy Spirit? Don't you see that you can't live however you please, squandering what God paid such a high price for?"[1]

How could her body be sacred if it couldn't bear life?

The scrape of metal rings and the rush of light forced Samantha to acknowledge she was alive. She willed her eyelids to open. They felt glued to her face, like the stubborn bit of yolk that wouldn't give way to a scrub brush.

She rubbed her temples in circles, trying to silence the drummers in her head. They competed with her own memories for attention. The metallic taste in her mouth begged to be erased. The smooth round straw pulsed with each sip of water she drew, but it couldn't combat the fire in her throat.

She'd tried to tell them she'd taken no pills, but the tubing threaded down her throat holding the charcoal slurry, preventing her protests. The frantic flurry replayed in her mind.

---

[1] 1 Corinthians 6:19–20 (MSG).

———⊸∘⊶———

"Do you know if she's taken any pills, Mr. Camden?"

Phil sounded tired. "She's taken an antidepressant, but I can't remember the name right now. I... I don't know. I–is she going to make it?"

His voice held an uncertain tone Samantha had never heard before. Fear? The clatter of the ER didn't drown out the brief gasps of air she heard beside the stretcher. Was Phil terrified?

"We've gotten the bleeding stopped, so she should stabilize soon. Trying to head off any breathing issues if we need to take her into surgery for tendon repair. We'll pump her stomach just to be sure."

Samantha felt Phil's presence move away from her head. She wanted to say something, but the words wouldn't come together in a sentence. The world spun as the nurses tilted her head and the taste of plastic filled her mouth. She struggled and tried to twist away, but two hands cupped her head and held her in place.

"There, there, Samantha, almost over."

Thank goodness!

"No pill fragments, Doctor."

"One less thing to worry about. Highly unusual for this type of attempt, though. Results of her blood alcohol limit?"

"Nonexistent."

"Hmm. Does she have a child?"

"I could ask the husband."

"Do that."

Samantha wondered what was so unusual about her suicide attempt. Lots of people slashed their wrists.

The rings on the curtains shivered as the nurse returned.

"They have a five-year-old girl."

"That explains the deep slashes on her left arm. She probably used a topical numbing cream they kept around for their little girl's cuts and scrapes. These on her right are much more tentative."

How had he figured that out?

———⊸∘⊶———

Even though the restraints had come off the night before, she felt so woozy that she pressed the call button. Once the aide arrived, she assisted Samantha to the toilet and then closed the door.

The mascara under her eyes looked like she hadn't slept in days, but the remnants of the activated charcoal made her look ghoulish.

While trying to rinse out the grey facecloth, she caught the sink with her left hand and almost fainted from the pain. She crouched beside the sink, head lowered between her knees, and panted until the blackness and nausea passed.

The aide tapped on the door. "Everything okay in there?"

"No."

The aide carefully opened the door and assisted Samantha to her feet. With help, she shuffled towards the bed, nearly stumbling as she reached for the bed railing. The aide had straightened the covers and pulled them back in order to make it easier.

"Could I have a heated blanket?"

"Sure."

The warmth of the blanket soothed Samantha's jittery stomach. She felt her muscles relax. It reminded her of Gran, the way she'd tucked the blankets around Samantha each night, covering her fears with love and softness. If only she hadn't destroyed the one thing that reminded her of Gran. A reminder of a hope and a future.

The sound of the dinner trolley penetrated Samantha's consciousness. A tray scraped across her portable table and the aroma caused Samantha to open her eyes, but the view was anything but appetizing. A scoop of potatoes covered in a brown gelatinous glaze, overcooked green beans, and slices of roast beef beckoned her reluctant appetite.

Desperate to get the taste of last night out of her mouth, she forced herself to swallow a bite of the instant mashed potatoes. The potatoes soothed her raw throat. She took the plastic lid off the pale green mug of coffee and blew on it before trying a sip. Ugh! Tasted like bleach water. Maybe the apple juice? The small sip burned like fire down her sore throat. Pudding for the win! At least it was her favourite: tapioca.

Shortly after, the nurse came in, took her vitals, and handed her some pills.

"Is there any ice water?" Samantha asked. "My throat's raw."

The nurse disappeared, came back with the water pitcher, and poured her a full glass. Liquid cooled the ache and washed away the acrid taste of the pills.

She took a bigger sip to capture the ice cube, letting the icy cube numb her aching throat.

"You're awake." Dr. Mochar entered the room. The doctor's voice vibrated and took the tympanic beating in her head to a whole new level. "Do you have any pain?"

He scanned her chart for the latest update, she supposed.

"My head's pounding right now."

"Typical for those with acute blood loss. Anything else hurting you?"

"My throat's sore, thanks to the charcoal slushy tube. And my left hurts more than my right arm. Why is it so hard to move?"

"It's going to take your left arm a little longer to recover since you nicked two tendons with the knife. We had to restrain you longer than most. The surgeon didn't want you moving that arm after he repaired the tendons."

"What day is it?" Samantha asked.

"Saturday."

"It's Saturday? Not Friday?"

"No. Between the transfusion and surgery late Thursday night, we sedated you for twenty-four hours in order to give your body time to recover."

"Oh. I guess that answers my questions. Um, so what happens next?"

"A transfer to the Grand River Hospital in North Battleford on Sunday afternoon. You'll be there until your preliminary hearing. Forest Acres Wellness Centre might be an option for you after your preliminary hearing. They'll begin physiotherapy and occupational therapy. We don't want you to atrophy."

"A preliminary hearing? For a suicide attempt?"

"Your housekeeper, Mrs. Henderson, got hurt that day. Do you remember anything about that?"

What had she forgotten? She'd waited until Glenda had taken Cami over to Mary Ann's for a playdate. Then she'd crept down the stairs to the kitchen after daubing the topical cream over the area she intended to cut. She'd just finished sharpening the knife and made a decisive slash when the front door opened. The stream of blood had mesmerized her, pouring into the sink...

Glenda's voice startled her. "Oh no, dearie, no, no, no. Your life is precious."

"I'm not precious." Her reply echoed in her mind. "You won't stop me, Glenda. Let go of me! *Let me go!*"

By this time, she'd dragged herself and Glenda to the foot of the stairs. She pushed the housekeeper away and ran to the bathroom to finish what she'd started.

Had Glenda fallen? Had she gotten hurt?

"Whatever happened, Samantha, it was bad enough for someone to press charges against you for assault and battery. If she doesn't make it, the charges move to the next level. Like manslaughter."

The pronouncement resonated through her whole body. Her pulse raced. If Glenda died, she could be convicted of murder...

Oh, dear God, what did I do?

Samantha vaguely remembered answering some questions after she was brought in, but everything felt fuzzy.

She tried to take a breath. "Help, I can't... uhh, b−b−breathe?" She clawed at the gown around her neck. "This gown is too tight... it's cutting off my air."

Her clumsy clawing did nothing to relieve the weight of the doctor's words.

"No, I need to finish what I started. My life's a burden. I shouldn't be alive! I just want to die!" She tried to fight off Dr. Mochar even as the nurse came in to Velcro her arms to the railings. "Stop... don't! Get these off me. Not another needle. I hate need−"

When she awoke, terrifying thoughts pummelled her. Would Glenda live or die? Would they incarcerate her for what she'd done? Would Phil divorce her? Would Cami learn to live without her? They refused to be caught, like a piece of litter skittering across a parking lot.

There was a knock on her door. Since when did nurses knock?

Oh, this guy looks familiar.

"Hello, Samantha, it's been a while. How's your little girl doing?"

As soon as the man spoke, Samantha remembered him. When was the last time they'd gone to church?

"Hi, Pastor... Brad?"

He was the one who'd done Gran's funeral. His goatee was no longer black but a salt-and-pepper grey.

"That's right," he said.

"What are you doing here?"

"It's my weekend to act as chaplain. I come to the waiting room around the ICU on Saturdays. Sometimes I'm on the mental health unit. Anything I can do for you?" Pastor Brad looked at her empty water glass. "Fill up your water?"

Samantha nodded.

After he set her glass back on her tray, he looked at her. "Could I pray with you?"

Memories of her nighttime routine with Gran filled her mind. She could almost feel the wrinkled hand wrap around hers.

"Poppet, say yes. Never refuse someone who wants to pray with you."

When was the last time she had prayed? Not since, not since...

"Um, sure," she said reluctantly.

The pastor closed his eyes. "God, You see Samantha. You saw her from the moment she existed in her mother's womb. Her heart's broken. Remind her in practical ways that You are near to the brokenhearted. Amen."

From the moment I existed? she asked herself. *In my mother's womb? Then why'd I have to go through so much as a child?*

She realized that Pastor Brad had quit praying.

"Well, at least you don't go on and on like Gran did. Most nights, I'd pretend to fall asleep before she finished. Now I just wish..."

Tears filled Samantha's eyes as she turned her face away.

"Let me guess. Now you wish you could hear her prayers for you over and over you again."

"I don't think they took. I mean, look what I did. Look where I am!"

"I'm pretty sure they took, Samantha."

Quit being cryptic, Pastor Brad!

She turned to look him in the eye. "They took?"

"You're alive. You're here in a place where they stitched you up and gave you protection when you couldn't protect yourself from harm. Doesn't that sound like the answer to a grandmother's prayers for her grandchild?"

Pastor Brad's gentle response slipped past her barricade and pushed open a door Samantha thought she'd done her best to nail shut.

She rolled over to hide her sudden interest. *What are you doing talking to a chaplain anyhow? There's no way he'd even give you a second chance to set foot in his church if he knew what you've done.*

"Samantha, your husband's here. Interested in seeing him?"

As Samantha tightened her hand around the rail, she gasped in pain. Phil was here?

"Um, why now?"

"Don't you want to see him?" asked the nurse. "Say goodbye before you leave for treatment? Maybe talk a little."

She twisted the sheet between her fingers. "No."

"You're sure?"

"Yes."

She could hear Phil's protests at the nurses' station. Then silence.

Dr. Mochar came into the room, rolling her suitcase with the purple stripes behind him. "Your husband brought your things. I'm starting rounds, so you're the first stop."

Samantha wanted to disappear under the covers. What must Phil think of her refusal? The suitcase! Why hadn't she realized she would need clothes for her stay in North Battleford? Ugh! So embarrassing!

Suddenly she noticed her afghan draped over Dr. Mochar's arms. Who had fixed it? Phil? Glenda?

"So why the reluctance to meet with your husband, Samantha?"

"It's easier for him."

"In what way?"

Samantha thought the doctor would quit pursuing the issue, but not a chance. "Um, he came here to make himself feel better."

"I thought he came to bring you your things and say goodbye."

Samantha didn't answer.

"So you want to make him feel badly about your situation, your suicide attempt, because you think he doesn't feel bad enough?"

She looked at Dr. Mochar and just shrugged. She couldn't reciprocate her husband's unconditional love. He had called her his best friend, his favourite confidant, as newlyweds. When she'd lost the babies, nothing had comforted her, so he'd distanced himself. She had feared she would lose him for good.

Her inability to love her husband couldn't steel her from the hurt in his eyes when she pulled away from his hugs. How could lying make her look so bad?

Nine

Shattered

At the nurse's words, Phil wanted to hurl the flowers through Samantha's door. Instead he waited for the doctor to exit. He drummed his fingers against the nurses' station. This hospital was pushing him into facing his past.

"Phil?"

He turned and saw a distinguished gentleman stride towards him in dark jeans, T-shirt, and sportscoat. He looked familiar, but Phil couldn't figure out why.

Then it came to him.

"Pastor Brad. Visiting someone?"

"Yes, but I've got a moment if you need one."

Phil set down the vase. "Samantha's here, but the doctor's with her right now."

"Hmm, I've got a few minutes. Step into the empty room over here?"

"Maybe not. I don't know how long the doctor'll be and I don't want to miss Sam before she, uh, goes to…"

Phil studied his feet, unsure of whether to say more.

"Before your wife goes to North Battleford?"

Phil snapped his eyes up and met Pastor Brad's gaze.

"Your wife and I chatted last night for a few minutes," the pastor said.

"Oh." Phil's shoulders relaxed. "Yeah… that."

Pastor Brad glanced at his watch. "I only have a few minutes before my wife comes looking for me. I'm free after the evening service. Why don't you pop by then? Or come to the evening service?"

"I'll think about it. I need to talk to Sam."

Phil crossed his fingers in his pocket and waved as Pastor Brad exited the doors of the psych ward.

Upon hearing the door to Samantha's room open, he turned his face and saw the mountain of sheets created by Samantha's legs, and then nothing as Dr. Mochar stepped through the doorway and closed it behind him.

Dr. Mochar motioned for Phil to follow him into an empty room.

"I couldn't get her to change her mind, Phil. I'm so sorry. This isn't unusual behaviour. Give her some time to get through some treatment sessions. Shame's a powerful emotion. Don't view this as a rejection. It's more like she's protecting herself against facing the real consequences of her actions."

"All right. That helps a little, but it's hard to take."

"Most definitely. Grand River's an excellent facility. Make sure you mention the name of the Forest Acres Treatment Centre to Samantha's lawyer. Given the circumstances around Samantha's attempt on her life, you could bring it up for the judge's consideration. During the preliminary hearing."

Phil's stomach clenched as he thought about what Monday would entail.

He reached up his hand to massage his right shoulder. "Uh, thanks for taking the time to help me understand. Guess I can go now. Could a nurse give the flowers to Samantha later?"

"I'll make sure they travel with her to her room at Grand River."

"Is she going by ambulance?"

"No." Dr. Mochar reached his hand towards Phil's arm. "Police van."

———◖◦◗———

Samantha, clad in an orange jumpsuit and accompanied by an officer, disappeared through the exit in the courtroom.

Phil pushed himself up from the bench behind Samantha's lawyer, extended his hand, and mumbled his thanks. Perfunctory handshakes done, he made his way to the back of the courtroom, thrumming with energy to meet his mom and leave.

He also noticed Noah, in his full dress uniform, standing at the back of the courtroom. Phil reached out and shook his friend's hand.

"Thanks, man," Phil said. "You didn't have to come."

"Course I did. What are best friends for? Lesley sends her love and prayers."

"Mom's waiting, so I can't chat. Thanks again for being here."

"No problem. I'll take your calls anytime at work. Even if it's just so you can have adult conversation. Lesley tells me that's important when you have kids."

Phil clasped Noah's hand with both of his and then kept walking.

Cami, who seemed frantic, ran towards him and wrapped her arms around his legs. She clung tight. "Whoa..."

"Daddy, can I come home now?"

His daughter's anxious face peered up at him and he scanned the surroundings. Where had his mom tucked herself away?

Ah, there she was. He smiled at the contrast between his mom's western gear and the look of the rest of the crowd, dressed in fancy suits and ties, every hair in place. Gotta keep up the image...

His mom rounded the gothic pillar in the foyer, toting the large black suitcase. It bulged with the sum of his daughter's belongings. The suitcase had been packed two weeks ago in a frantic ten minutes.

"Didn't know when court would wrap up for you in there," she said. "I got here as soon as I could. The mare's about to foal and Mr. Graham, the stable manager, is still recovering from that gate accident."

"Thanks, Mom. I really appreciate everything you've done."

Phil leaned over, Cami still wrapped around his leg, and gave her a long hug. He then bent down and disengaged Cami and picked her up.

"Say thank you to Grandma for the visit," he said.

"Thank you, Grandma, and give Dancer a kiss for me. Can you send me pictures of the new baby horsie?"

He set Cami down and took hold of the suitcase in one hand. He then gripped Cami's hand in his other hand.

"You bet, sugar plum. Be good for your daddy."

His mom jetted out of the courthouse so fast that he couldn't keep up both lugging the black appendage and hanging on to Cami.

Suddenly, Cami jerked her hand out of his and ran back towards the courtroom.

"Cami, come back here. Where are you going?" Phil hustled back with the lumbering black suitcase bouncing off his ankle with lightning accuracy. He halted as he saw her tug a cute teddy bear suitcase behind her.

"Sorry, Daddy, I forgotted this by the door. Grandma gived it to me. She said I don't have to give it back."

"I'm glad you remembered it, but next time can you tell Daddy where you're going and what you're doing?"

Phil counted to ten and blew out slowly. It kept his mouth and emotions in order and also prevented him from exhibiting his frustration and fear in this very public place.

"Sorry, Daddy, it gots my favouritest stuffed animal in it and I would be really sad if I forgotted it."

"Well, I'm glad you didn't forget it."

Looking through the window beside the revolving doors, Phil noted the crowd of photographers. The taxi had arrived. Time to run the gauntlet.

His business deserved better publicity than this. Had it been only a month since he'd been on TV? He hadn't made a deal, but he'd certainly gotten noticed. Were it not for that moment of fame, he might have avoided this circus now. That's what being in the limelight cost him.

Flashes of cameras lit up the doorway as Phil pulled his hat lower over his face. He pushed his way through the revolving door, dragging the black behemoth of a suitcase. Cami scurried beside him, trying to keep up with her little teddy bear suitcase bumping along beside her. With his free arm, he picked up his daughter and barrelled his way down the stairs through the mob of photographers.

The cab driver popped open the trunk. Phil set Cami down and then hefted the luggage in the trunk and slammed the lid down. After depositing Cami deep in the cab, he collapsed the handle of her little suitcase and set it on the seat next to her. He got in and wrestled the suitcase aside in order to latch his seatbelt.

"Let's get out of here." Phil slammed the door to halt the questions from reporters. "146 Baileywick Place."

"Daddy, will Mommy be all right?" Cami twisted her blond hair around her finger.

"Yes, she'll be fine, but I don't know... I don't know when she'll come home, sweetheart."

"What do you mean, Daddy?" Her earnest blue eyes challenged him to be truthful.

Phil swallowed the lump in this throat. It grew larger with each question. "Mommy is going to be away. We'll get to see her, but she won't live at home."

Cami's head drooped. "Oh."

He reached for her tiny fingers and enfolded them in his hand. Sometimes words wrecked moments like these.

When the taxi turned down the last stretch before their street, he leaned closer to Cami. "Did you have a good time at Grandma's house?"

"Yes, Daddy. She tooked good care of me. She even let me sleep in her bed. I got to watch TV every morning. I gotted chocolate chip pancakes with smiley faces."

"That's nice, honey. I really missed you these last two weeks."

"I missed you too, Daddy. I missed Mrs. Henderson and Mommy soooo much. I cried sometimes at night."

Phil snuggled Cami close. "I'll let you in on a secret. I cried a little at night, too." His voice wobbled as he smiled down at his daughter's golden strands. "But I'm so glad my big helper girl is coming home with me tonight. I am glad we'll be at home together now."

"Me too. Daddy, do you know how to make breakfast? I'm hungry."

When the taxi stopped in front of their home, Phil paid the taxi driver. Perhaps he'd neglected being at home just as Samantha had accused him of being, that he'd been avoiding dealing with his own grief over the loss of their babies.

He dragged his mom's latest gift to Cami to the back of the taxi and wrested the suitcase out of the trunk. He then realized Cami remained in the taxi.

"Is it stuck, honey?" A lone tear rested on her cheek. "I won't leave you."

Phil undid Cami's seatbelt and walked with her hand in hand towards the house, dragging the reluctant suitcases over the cracked cement of the driveway.

"Would you like cereal or toast, honey?"

"Toast with strawberry jam, please!"

"I think I can manage that." He fumbled through the keys, searching for the one that unlocked the front door.

He prepared the toast and jam for Cami and then made himself a peanut butter and jelly sandwich. He sat near the kitchen island, watching his little girl munch away, and wondered what life would be like now that a psychiatric institution had sequestered Samantha. If it was a matter of treating her depression until stabilization, they'd get through it. But her treatment didn't define her. Her length of stay, and place of stay, would be determined on whether their housekeeper lived or died.

Housekeeping became his job now. Or had it always been his job, and he was only just realizing it?

Cami looked at him. "Daddy, is Mrs. Henderson coming to do laundry today? The man beside the snack machine said it was Thursday. She always comes on Thursday. I know when it's Thursday, because she comes then."

"Not today. Today we're going to do Mrs. Henderson's job. She said you were a good helper on laundry days. What's your job?"

"I gotted the soap for her and turned on the washing machine. And sometimes I used the clean laundry basket for a boat."

"Well, at least I have an experienced helper. Let's get the clothes from the hampers and start the laundry parade."

Cami prattled on about her friends at daycare while they sorted the clothes into piles. He was no stranger to laundry, but he hadn't really handled its details since college. Laundering clothes hadn't changed that much over the years. The machines had just gotten fancier. He balled the lint in his hand and shot it into the garbage can.

Still got it.

"Nice shot, Daddy. What now? Can you play a game with me? Mommy and me play dominoes. Do you know how to play, Daddy?"

"I think I remember how. But if I forget, you can remind me of the rules, okay?"

Dominoes? Card games? Board games? These all used to be a regular occurrence in his world thanks to Samantha. Whose house had they always invaded to play those all-night board games? Right! Bob and Patty's...

———◖•◗———

Phil rubbed his temples and leaned away from the books he'd placed in the library carousel. A pair of feminine hands covered his eyes.

"Sam, quit it. I've got to ace this final. I've got to keep studying till it's solid."

"What do you mean, study? You studied all afternoon." Samantha tugged on Phil's arm. "It's time to take a break!"

"Sam, just because you finished all your finals doesn't mean I have!"

"You already studied for this one. I know your quirky study habits."

"I know, but this is the last one before the internship and it's the one all businesses look at to see if you have what it takes to understand risk and reward and calculate what it takes to fly in the entrepreneurial world."

"All you're doing is reviewing. You had these same textbooks out two weeks ago. Then you wrote out your study notes. You always study for your last final first."

"It's a good thing, too, because I've got this girlfriend who always seems to interrupt me." Phil gathered up his textbooks and notes and shoved them into his backpack. "I cave. Who are we playing against?"

"First we get pizza. It's all you can eat for five dollars. Then we go over to Patty and Bob's place. Capiche?"

"That sounds way better than peanut butter sandwiches again."

———◁•▷———

"Daddy... Daddeeee, it's your turn."

Phil snapped back to the present. He still defaulted to peanut butter sandwiches for an easy meal.

He added his domino to the maze of dots spread across the tabletop. "Okay, honey."

"Daddy, is Mrs. Henderson going to die?"

Just how much does Cami know? he asked himself. *How much did she see?*

Ten

It's a Zoo Day

"I'm in the kitchen, sweetheart. I had waffles for breakfast. Do you want some?"

"Yes, please! Is today the zoo day?"

Phil pulled out his smartphone and navigated to the calendar screen. Friday's date appeared alongside the word zoo in large capital letters.

"What word do you see, Cami?"

"Z–O–O," she spelled. "Oh, we *are* going!" Cami bounced up and down for several minutes, chanting. "We're going to the zoo, we're going to the zoo, hi–ho the derry–o, we're going to the zoo."

He dropped two waffles in the toaster. Her letter recognition was great.

Phil chuckled as she continued her bouncing; it was a good thing they were going to burn off some of her energy. She hadn't even had sugar yet!

He poured a liberal amount of syrup on the waffles and handed Cami the plate and a fork.

After breakfast, they headed out the door with umbrellas in tow, just in case it rained. She wouldn't want to be forced to leave the zoo like the last time, because Samantha and Glenda had forgotten the umbrellas. Phil catered to her wishes.

He checked the seatbelt. Was it in the right place on her booster seat? He shut the door, climbed into the driver's seat, and started the engine.

A local news van passed the car as he headed out of the street. He automatically turned his head in the opposite direction so as not to be recognized. He had purposefully taken taxis to and from the courthouse to avoid contact with the media. Keeping the SUV parked in front of the house and using the garage in the back for his car also seemed to discourage curious onlookers.

He parked close to the zoo entrance, in case he had to make a quick exit. It had been a while since a stranger had come up to him and asked if he'd appeared on TV. The previous day's trial had stirred up renewed interest, with all the new photos and video of their exit from the courthouse.

After he paid for their zoo passes, the vendor craned his neck towards the window as if to get a better look. Phil wondered whether it was due to his recent fame.

Keeping a watchful eye out for a media presence, he and Cami began exploring the zoo. Cami's chatter kept him occupied.

"Why do snow leopards like being cold?" she demanded. "Do you think they were hot in summer? Why do they gots a ball? Do they play catch? Is the fence high enough? Do you think they could jump over and eat me? That tree looks dead. Why is there a dead tree in there?"

"Maybe they use the tree for a scratching post, like Grandma's cats do in the barn. Let's watch the prairie dogs for a while."

Fascinated by the way the prairie dogs darted in and out of their holes, Cami's attention focused on where they would pop up next.

Phil scanned the crowds for camera crews. Maybe he was just paranoid, but he didn't want to be cornered by a reporter with Cami in tow.

"Aren't they the cutest things ever, Daddy?" She tugged on his hand. "Can we go see the pig goats?"

"Pig goats?"

"You know, the tiny goats. I think they're by the big sheep."

Phil pulled out the walking tour map and realized what she meant. He stifled a smile. "Sweetheart, they're called pygmy goats. Pygmy is a fancy word that means small."

After admiring all the different unique ungulates, they headed to the cafe for lunch. Phil felt grateful for the anonymity of being tucked in a back corner booth, but when he paid for the food he noted pitying glances from the cashier.

His unease building, Phil headed over to the children's zoo so Cami could see the reptiles, insects, and Goeldi's monkeys. He worried he would never get Cami away from watching the monkeys swing from rope to rope, so he bribed her with a chance to go to the meerkat house.

His attempt to exit came to a halt.

"Excuse me, are you Phil Camden?"

"Yes, and who might you be?"

"My name is Stephanie Lindbjerg of Global…"

A journalist. "Look, Stephanie, is it? I'm in the middle of enjoying my day at the zoo with my daughter and I'd appreciate it if I could continue enjoying my time."

"I just want to ask you a few questions."

"No comment, Stephanie."

"It wouldn't take any time."

"Daddeeeeeeeee! Look, that monkey is grabbing the fruit and eating it."

Wheeling around, Phil realized that his daughter had run back to the monkey exhibit. He hurried after her and crouched down. She had her face pressed to the window, oblivious to all but the activity in the monkey exhibit.

"You're right, honey. What kind of fruit is it?" Phil glanced over his shoulder. Had he lost the reporter?

"Oranges. Or maybe melons?"

There was Stephanie again. "Phil, what went through your mind? When you saw your housekeeper unconscious on the floor with a trail of blood going up the stairs?"

Where in the world had she gotten that information? He couldn't remember that detail coming out in the courtroom. Had Tom said something?

Phil mashed his lips together and scanned the area to see if there were any park personnel or security guards.

Ah! One guard stood near the information desk. Phil's body, as tense as an offensive linebacker before the snap, moved into position behind Cami.

"Security… security, get this woman out of here!" he shouted. "She's harassing my daughter and me!"

He picked up Cami and exited the children's zoo area. He headed over to the zoo's playground through a cement tunnel at a dead run.

"Ow, Daddy, you're hurting me."

Phil adjusted his grip. "Sorry, honey."

"Daddy, I'm not done. Did you know monkeys can hold on to things with their tails?"

"No, sweetheart, I didn't." Phil slowed his breathing in order to calm down. "There's a fancy word for that, but what is it… um… opposable? No, that refers to their thumbs…"

"Daddy, what's a blood trail?"

Fisting his hands, he silently cursed the woman who hadn't shown the courtesy to recognize a child's presence before opening her big mouth.

He opted for the simplest explanation. "It means drops of blood going in a line."

"Like when I get a nosebleed and Mommy wipes up the drops after she helps me stop it with a tissue?"

"Yes, honey, just like that. You're one smart cookie."

"Daddy, can you help me swing like a monkey?"

"You bet, honey!"

Phil lifted her up to the hanging rings and helped her to swing. While spotting his daughter like a gymnastic coach, he kept a watchful eye out for the reporter. When Cami reached the end of the hanging ring and jumped onto the platform, Phil breathed a sigh of relief.

"Wow," he said. "You couldn't do that when you were four."

Cami clenched her fists and showed off her biceps.

"That's my strong girl. Able to jump over buildings in a single bound!" Phil felt his heart rate slow. Until...

"Daddy, were you scared when you saw the blood?"

"Yes."

Cami threw her arms around him and hugged him. "Daddy, you don't have to be scared anymore."

Phil stared at her in amazement. She zoomed towards the twirly slide and went up and down it several times.

"Honey, it's time to go."

She ran over to the treehouse next. Before she could start climbing the ladder, Phil plucked her off and set her down on the ground. "Honey, I said it's time to go."

"But I don't wanna go home! No! No!"

Cami flung herself on the ground, kicking and screaming. It was reminiscent of the previous evening's night terrors. How she could go from happy to mad in the blink of an eye, he'd never know.

Yeah, kiddo, I don't wanna go home either, he thought. *But like it or not, I have to. I'm the grownup.*

He looked at his watch and wondered whether they could sneak in a train ride before supper. Right now, all he wanted to do was get her to stop screaming.

"Honey, do you want to take a train ride?"

Her screams stopped. She rolled over and sat up. Phil caught himself before he groaned aloud at the grass stains on her jeans.

"Oh, Daddy, that would be the best! I never have time with Mommy or Mrs. Henderson."

She hiccupped and wiped her nose on her sleeve. Phil sighed. Anything to stop the screaming.

Surely the reporter would have been called away by now. There must be some accident, anything more interesting than reporting on his wife.

Maybe the train ride would keep them out of the reporter's way.

"Daddy, I hafta go potty!"

After making a pitstop at the washroom, they headed around the backside of the meerkat exhibit towards the train departure site.

"Gimme a fist bump, kiddo. No waiting for a train. It's leaving in five minutes."

They exchanged a mismatched fist bump. Phil kept his hand out in order to give Cami a high five.

He watched her carefully attach the chain to the side of the train car.

"All set, Daddy."

The train halted and allowed a family of peacocks to cross. While the male unfolded his blue glory and strutted his stuff, the female chased after the young ones.

Have I been strutting my stuff, God, leaving everything on Samantha's shoulders? How could work be more important than my wife and daughter?

They exited their train car and made their way back to the front gate of the zoo. Drat! The news van was still visible in the parking lot.

Phil scanned the area to see if the reporter was nearby. How was he going to get back to the car without that reporter hounding him at the gate with more questions?

"Phil, Phil… is that you?"

He turned around to see his neighbour, Mary Ann, alongside her children Kevin and Kristina. They were coming out of the wolf exhibit.

"Hi, Mary Ann! Are you just starting or just finishing the tour?"

"We're done. Er, I mean *I'm* done."

Phil laughed. "Want to trade children until we get out into the parking lot? I'm trying to avoid a reporter who's probably waiting by the exit for me. Do you remember what colour my car is?"

"It's blue, right? Sure, I'll do that for you. By the way, how's Mrs. Henderson?"

Cami piped up. "She's sleeping a lot. Daddy said it helps her get better."

Bending down, Phil said, "Kevin, would you mind trading ballcaps with me until we get to the parking lot?"

"Sure, Mr. Camden."

Phil gave Mary Ann his keys. She then dug hers out from the recesses of her backpack. Next, Phil handed his cap to Kevin and watched while Kevin turned it slightly until it sat at just the right angle.

"Say, Kevin, am I wearing this cap the right way?"

Kevin reached up and slid the cap on Phil's head slightly to the right and tilted it upwards. "You look good, Mr. Camden."

"Thanks, Kevin. Do you and Kristina want to pretend to argue and act like you don't want to leave? I'll take both your arms and pretend to march you back to your van, only you're going to have to walk me to the correct van, since I don't know where you parked it. Okay?"

Kevin and Kristina both nodded. Kevin gave Kristina a shove.

"You touched me!" Kristina glared at Kevin.

"No, I didn't."

"Better watch out or the grizzly bear will chase you."

"He's in a cage, silly."

"He could dig out from it."

"No, he couldn't."

The ruse was on. Mary Ann and Cami went out the gift store exit and Phil started marching the other children in the other direction. Even though the reporter stood in front of the gift shop, she kept talking to her cameraman and didn't notice them.

After getting through the exit, Kevin and Kristina kept arguing about whether grizzly bears could dig a tunnel under the cage and get out. Kevin tugged Phil to the left towards a light standard, where a tan-coloured van sat.

Phil breathed a sigh of relief as he waited for Kevin and Kristina to buckle their seatbelts.

Getting in the driver's seat, he drove the short distance to the next row of parked vehicles and angled the van so the driver's side aligned to his own car's driver's side. He then handed Kevin's hat back, plopped his own ballcap firmly on his head, and jumped out of the van door. Mary Ann was just tucking the seatbelt around Cami's booster seat.

"Thanks for doing that, Mary Ann."

"You're welcome. Glad to help." She handed Phil his keys. "Do you and Cami have plans for the rest of the weekend?"

"Nothing set in stone. If the doctor gives the go-ahead, tomorrow or Sunday will be our first official family afternoon at the Forest Acres Wellness Facility. Apparently, they have horses and ponies there. I'm not sure what to expect."

After a sympathetic glance, Mary Ann peered through her van window. "I'd better get going. World War III is about to erupt."

Phil chuckled as Mary Ann slid into her van and shut the door on her boisterous children's argument.

He opened his driver's door and noted that Cami's head was already leaning on the side of her booster seat. He quietly started the car and drove away, the reporter none the wiser.

Eleven

Colour Refresh

Samantha studied the grey walls of the office. Tasteful black stitching embroidered the pillow on which she rested her left arm. If only her stitches would stop itching so she could concentrate on Janet's questions.

"I thought we'd spend our first session just laying some ground rules and getting to know one another a little. These sessions are confidential. Let's get you ready to re-enter your world with your husband and daughter."

Samantha shifted on the couch. "What if I don't feel like talking? I talked with Dr. Nancy every other week for the past two years. Other than medication and the side effects, I didn't see much change in my world. How is this going to be any different?"

She folded her arms over the pillow and rubbed her arm against the embroidered nubs.

"Are you allergic to horses?" Janet asked.

"I don't think so."

"Let's walk out to the corral. It's a beautiful day."

Janet led Samantha down the hall to the exit that led to the barn.

"What size are your feet, Samantha? We'll change into some cowboy boots before we go."

"Size seven."

"Just put your shoes in this box. I'll label the cubby as yours. After we're done, you can put your cowboy boots in here for the duration of your stay."

Shielding her eyes, Samantha drank in the warm sunshine on her face and breathed deeply. The unusually warm weather spelled a second summer. The azure sky beamed like a benevolent father as sparrows swooped and flitted amongst the dappled gold leaves of the poplar trees.

Notes of apples and pine trees refreshed her senses as she followed Janet out the barn door and into a fenced area where several horses roamed. Two dun-coloured horses stood loosely tied to one of the fenceposts. Overhead, two hawks rose high above the trees towards the white wisps in the sky. Samantha wished she could join them.

Instead she joined Janet and leaned on the corral fence while Janet explained the next steps.

"Let me introduce you to some new friends. This black and white appaloosa is Daisy. She just foaled in January. Tied up over here is Duke, a retired quarter horse. The one in the corner by herself is Star. The other dun-coloured quarter horse is Jack. He learned to unlatch the gate. It's why he's tied up." Janet took a deep breath. "Today is a walk and talk. You choose which horse you would like to take for a walk."

"Okay."

Samantha looked over the horses. Were any of them safe? Daisy appeared skittish and Jack tossed his head up and down. Nope, not him. A snort followed by his restive pawing on the ground convinced her.

How had they come up with the name Star? She appeared to be completely black. Star turned her head as if sensing Samantha's gaze. Then she paced along the fence as if looking for someone or something. A five-pointed patch on her forehead stood out from her raven black shiny coat.

Star stopped, held Samantha's gaze, and bobbed her neck up and down gently. Samantha felt drawn to Star. Why wasn't this horse with the others?

"Can I try Star?"

"Sure! Any reason you picked her?"

"Um, she looked lonely. Is there a reason she's not with the other horses?"

"Well, she had to come here alone. We didn't have room for the foal and the breeder wanted to keep it."

"Oh." Tears welled in Samantha's eyes. She could relate. She missed feeling Cami's arms around her neck.

"What started your tears, Samantha?"

"I miss my daughter."

"Can you tell me about her?"

"She's a blond, bright-eyed ball of energy. Loves sparkle glue and really wants a puppy. She's incredibly imaginative."

Samantha remembered the time she had caught Cami playing teacher with her stuffies. She'd almost burst out laughing when Cami raised one eyebrow at her "students" and put one of them in timeout. She'd backed away from Cami's door.

Funny. She hadn't thought about Cami taking after her profession for a long time. When was the last time she had spied on Cami's playtime?

"Samantha, where'd you go?"

"Oh, sorry. Got lost in a memory."

"About Cami?"

"Yeah, she's a great little hugger. Her hugs are the best."

"You sound like a very proud mama. Why do you call her hugs the best?"

"She loves fiercely," Samantha said. "Her hugs are the only touch I can take right now."

She missed her daughter's hugs so much. Startled by the intensity of her feelings, she focused on Star's eyes in order to regain her equilibrium.

Janet's voice punctured her emotional tempest and drew her away from a potential abyss. "Here's a lead rope."

"What do I do with it?"

"See Duke's lead rope? And the metal ring on his halter?"

"Yes."

"Pull back the lever on the spring snap and hook the lead onto Star's halter."

"Then what?"

"Hold the extra length of the lead rope in your left hand like a figure-eight. Wrapping it around your hand is dangerous. Sometimes horses get startled and run from sounds, like a plastic bag or a small animal. You don't want to get dragged by a horse because you've got the lead around your hand. Always walk towards Star's head. Avoid walking around the back of any horse unless your hand is on her rump, so she knows you're there."

"Uh, okay."

Samantha took the lead from Janet and started walking towards Star. She clipped the lead rope to the halter.

"Hi Star, I'm Samantha."

She awkwardly touched the horse with her right hand. When the horse shied away, she dropped the lead rope. She bent, gathered up the lead, and tried to get Star to face Janet.

"Remember, hold the lead like a figure-eight in your left hand," Janet said. "Place your right hand just a few inches from the halter under her chin."

The simple task felt complicated.

Next, Janet set up pylons and asked Samantha to lead Star around the small paddock. Plodding along at a comfortable pace calmed Samantha until they drew close to the other horses in the corral. With determined force, Star turned her head against Samantha's shoulder and pushed Samantha to go in a different direction.

When it happened a second time, Janet intervened. "What's going on, Samantha? Are you having trouble with Star?"

"Um, I can't get her to walk past the other horses."

"Remember, you're the one leading her. Don't let her lead you. Try it again."

Star went around partway and then lunged towards some grass by the edge of the paddock fence. Samantha tried getting her head up and away from the grass, but Star turned her whole body away and kept eating.

Samantha looked at Janet and shrugged. "I guess that's it for today, huh?"

"Why so?"

"She appears hungry. I don't want to deny her food."

"How'd you feel when Star turned her body away from you?"

Samantha's heart raced and she clenched the lead rope closer to herself. "Ignored. Unimportant."

"When have you felt unimportant? Tell the horse about all the times you felt that way. Put your hand on her neck, get closer to her ears, and whisper to her."

Samantha leaned into Star's neck and whispered. "Um... I felt unimportant when the young married couple at church didn't include me in the conversation."

The heat of that nine-year-old's embarrassment flooded her cheeks again. She took a deep breath.

"I felt unimportant when Phil stopped sharing his company woes with me and shared them with Bob instead. I felt unimportant when Phil came home and showered kisses on Cami, but only gave me a peck."

She stroked Star's neck, then clenched the lead rope as the next memory came up.

"Phil went back to work the day after we left the hospital. It felt like a slap in the face."

She swiped tears from her cheek, then buried her face in Star's neck.

"When we lost... Micah."

Her silent cries contorted her body as she clung to Star. She continued her broken whispers after she had regained control and could stand without Star's help.

"Being told that the infection from the stillbirth had scarred my fallopian tubes and adoption may be the best route. The nurse's suggestion about using better birth control after I left the clinic."

Star's ears turned towards Samantha. The horse moved close, as though shielding her with her body. Had Star just tried to comfort her?

Just when she thought she'd regained control of her emotions, they flooded her whole being. Tears streamed from Samantha's eyes and she swiped at them with her sleeve. Shaky, she clung to Star's side for support.

"Samantha, you can brush Star's neck," said Janet. "Follow the direction of her hair as if you're soothing her. She needs to be relieved of the burdens you shared with her. I want you to tell her all the ways she's important and thank her for listening to you."

Samantha stroked Star's neck. "Star, you're so good at listening to me. You're doing important work. You've been so patient with me when I don't know what I'm doing."

She rested her head against Star's shoulder and stroked her flank. The earthy warmth and rhythmic breathing of the horse calmed her. Her shoulders dropped as she breathed in sync with Star.

"I'm sorry you can't be with your baby. Thank you for being here with me. You help so many people. You have a place. Thanks for staying with me when I cry. Thanks for not running away to the other side when I dropped the lead rope."

Star snorted and shifted away from Samantha as if released. Was Star laughing at her ineptitude?

"Anything you appreciated about Star that you wished someone close to you would do?" Janet asked.

"I thanked her for staying with me when I cry. My family and Phil always avoid me when I cry." The clarity of that sentence walloped Samantha. The muscles in her throat constricted as she worked to blink back tears. "I wish I could thank her for staying with me when I cry."

"What did it mean to have Star stay near you while you cried?"

Samantha tilted her head and thought about the warmth of Star's coat against her cheek. Its softness reminded her of her afghan of many colours. It felt like having Gran reach out and say, "You're my favourite, Poppet. There's a plan and a future waiting for you. Don't you forget it now, luv."

"She could handle my emotions," Samantha said. "I'm safe with her. My emotions weren't scary to her."

"It's time to say thank you to her in another way. You get to feed her some oats. They're one of her favourite treats. Sit over here in the lawn chair and pick up the bowl behind it. Put some oats in your hands if you like."

Samantha balanced the bowl on her lap and scooped some oats into her hand. Star's velvet lips closed around the oats until they were gone. When Star's head pushed aside her hands for the rest of the grain, Samantha had to stabilize the bowl. The oats disappeared in minutes.

Star's snuffling for more grain startled Samantha. She giggled when Star nudged her hands and chest as if to ask if any had been kept from her.

Gently pushing Star's head away, Samantha stood, unclipped the lead from her halter, and patted her. She looped the lead over a fencepost and then slipped out the gate and closed it.

She closed her eyes and took a deep breath of pine mingled with the dusky scent of horses. Slowly, she blew it out. She gazed at the iridescent blue sky dotted with wispy clouds; she noticed the burgeoning red and yellow of maples and elm trees peeking through the stand of evergreens. She heard the black slash of geese before tracking them above the tree line. When had the world gained colour? Somehow, the black cloud seemed to have drifted further away.

Had she ever experienced this feeling of lightness after a counselling session? Her kinship with Star felt like nothing she'd ever felt before. She felt different, heard.

"Leave your cowboy boots in the cubby," Janet said. "I'll look forward to seeing you tomorrow."

Janet waved goodbye and brought one more horse into a stall at the end of the barn.

Samantha made her way to the storage cubes, where she sat on the rough, worn bench and tugged off her boots. Her socks gave off a faint leathery scent. She pulled the laces out of her shoes, pulled back the tongue on each shoe, then slipped one foot and the other into her running shoes. They felt cool on her damp toes.

Janet poked her head out of the stall. "I'll leave some homework in your cubby tomorrow before your afternoon session."

Samantha nodded and tied her shoes. She headed back to her room, taking time to absorb the fall colours as she walked. Like wine-tasting, she sniffed the fall air and detected faint nuances of straw, mowed grass, newly turned earth, and manure. A distant combine whirred.

A mixture of deep fryer oil and barbecue sauce assailed her as she pushed open the door to the primary facility.

Must be having burgers in the dining hall tonight, she thought. *Wonder what Phil and Cami eat these days? Maybe Glenda is helping them out—*

No! She hadn't thought it through. How could Glenda help them, since Samantha had been the one to put her in the hospital?

Playing with horses won't bring her back, Samantha. You'll never be free of the albatross around your neck.

Twelve

Clouds with Purple Linings

Like an automaton performing its prescribed movements, Phil flipped over cards and continued his role in the memory game. His mind also engaged with the contents of the letter Samantha had written to him. The police had picked it up as evidence when they'd searched his home. Hearing it read in Samantha's defence had benefited her, but not him. Echoes of phrases poked like a forgotten shard of glass that had embedded itself in one's foot.

Phil turned another card over.

"Daddy, can I go visit Mrs. Henderson? I miss her." Cami quickly flipped two cards, got a pair, and then went again.

"Um, I'm not sure."

Phil gamely flipped two more cards and watched as Cami found two more matches before his turn again. In their last conversation, Tom had warned him against making contact.

"Can we send her some flowers?" Cami asked. "Mrs. Henderson helped Mommy send flowers to Grandma when she hurt herself on the fence last year."

"That's a good idea. What kind do you think we should send?"

"She likes pansies. They're happy flowers and she needs a card. I can make a super duper one."

As he shook his head, Cami's eyes pleaded with his and then fell. Watching her shoulders slump sent his heart in a downward slide.

"Well..."

Seeing a chink in her daddy's armour, Cami redoubled her efforts. "Pleee-ase, Daddy, can you text Grandpa Tom right now? I'll get out my special purple paper so it matches the purple pansies."

"Okay, I'll text him. Then Daddy's going to clean up breakfast and figure out our schedule for the week. Maybe you and I can go to the zoo again one day."

"Yeah!"

Cami ran up the stairs to her room. Was it odd that Cami didn't want to make Samantha a card? Should he be worried?

He wished he could find the same energy to tackle the dishes, the laundry, and all the schedules.

Please, God, don't make Samantha face homicide charges, he prayed. *Let Glenda regain consciousness, please! Let the judge hear the cry of Samantha's heart. Please God, help her see another solution. Help her find hope. Don't let the judge sentence her to jail for assault and battery.*

His heart sank as he recalled a phrase from Samantha's letter: "my death solves all my problems." That sentence had crushed him.

When his cell phone rang, he glanced at the display. He figured he should answer it, if only to distract himself from the swirling doubts in his mind.

"Hello, Bob. How's everything going at the warehouse? You been keep-ing up with everything?" He listened as Bob rattled off the latest production numbers and the second quarter sales. "What do you mean, how's the ball and chain? That's my wife you're talking about!"

Phil hung up after Bob's apology.

He shuttled the few dishes into the dishwasher. If only he could clean up his mistakes with Samantha as easily as dishes!

"Do you even stay long enough to notice what I do all day long, Phil?" he imagined her saying to him. *"You couldn't even stay with me in the hospital after we lost Micah."*

She hadn't remembered the first two days after losing Micah. He'd been there continuously—until she finally came to. He'd had to go pick up Cami because she wouldn't stop crying at his mom's place.

Now then, what to have for lunch? He pulled out a container of leftovers and opened it. He started dry-heaving after one whiff. Hadn't he gotten rid of this already?

"Am I that repulsive to you, Phil?"

No. The word repulsive described the containers collecting multicoloured fungus in the fridge. *Never you, Samantha, never you.*

He gulped the last swig of coffee. If only he could wash down some of the revulsion he felt about himself...

The phone rang again. He checked the display and answered.

"Hi, Mom. Thanks again for taking care of Cami these past two weeks. It really helped."

"I hope you picked somebody who knew what they were doing to redo the flooring."

"Mom, gimme a break. I hired a professional. I'm not taking chances."

"Samantha said you had to cut back at the company. I know things haven't been going that well. Just wondered if you could afford it."

"When'd she say that? I didn't think she paid attention to anything I said after the last miscarriage."

"Son, she put her heart and soul into that company when you first launched. I know it's been rough for the two of you lately, but you'll get through this. Don't try to carry things by yourself like when your daddy died."

"Mom, rough doesn't cover it. I had insurance, so we're good. End of story." Phil slammed the refrigerator door. "I gotta go."

"Phil, get a hold of that temper. Cami needs all the TLC she can get."

He rolled his eyes. She'd given him that same admonition throughout all his teen years. Then again, he hadn't felt this much stress since his dad had died.

"Did my grandbaby girl have any night terrors last night?" she asked.

Phil rubbed his forehead. "Yeah, twice."

He opened the fridge again and opened the crisper to discover food edible enough to eat: buns without mould, and even some ham and cheese. Lunch problem solved!

"Did you handle it the way I told ya too?"

He sighed. "Yes, Mom."

"Don't you take that tone with me! Now, how about filling me in on the court happenings? I didn't want to take the time yesterday to ask, especially with Cami around."

"Well, things were kind of..." A flush of the toilet alerted him that Cami had come out of her room. "Mom, we'll talk about it later, like when my little pitcher with big ears is asleep."

"Good idea, son."

"Oh, Mom, what about Dancer's baby? Is it a colt or a filly? Any pics you could send? It'd be a great distraction."

"Email or text?"

"Oh, just text. Thanks."

He hung up just as Cami appeared in the doorway, waving her very sparkly purple card, along with a rainbow arc of sparkles that flew through the air.

"Look, Daddy, it's done. What do you think?"

"It's incredibly sparkly, honey. Almost as sparkly as you!" Phil brushed sparkles off Cami's nose and winked at her.

"Ready for lunch? Let's go wash our hands."

Cami put her hands on her hips and tossed her head. "I wanna go see Mommy."

"We can't."

"But if I can go see Mrs. Henderson and she's in the hospital, why can't I go see Mommy in her hospital?"

Phil stalled by putting some dishes in the dishwasher. How could he answer? *"Because your mom's too sick for visitors. Because she thinks we're better off without her."* His hand clenched a fork and his face flushed with a sudden heat.

"Mommy's hospital is too far away, so we can't see her today. Her doctor will let us know when we can come visit."

"Daddy, are you mad at Mommy?" Cami's question froze Phil in midstep. "'Cause you're using the bad driver voice."

Phil turned. "The bad driver voice?"

"Mommy said not to be scared of it. She said you use it when you're scared someone might hurt us with their bad driving."

He moved back to the dishwasher and closed it, buying time to absorb Cami's question. She stood near the island, the island that had almost destroyed her beloved Mrs. Henderson.

"Sweetheart, I'm mad, but I think I'm sad as well. And sometimes it's hard to tell those feelings apart. Are you ever mad and sad at the same time?"

"Like when my friend Kristina has a friend over and I wanna play, too?"

"Exactly, but maybe you and I can take a break from talking about being mad and sad and see if we can find some of those special flowers you think will cheer Mrs. Henderson up."

"Did Grandpa Tom say it was okay to come visit?"

Phil squirmed. He hadn't texted Tom for fear of getting rejected. Cami's wondering face challenged his first impulse to lie.

"I didn't text him. We'll check at the hospital desk and find out if it's okay to go see Mrs. Henderson. If it is, we'll drop off the flowers and try to see her. If not, we can leave the flowers at the nurses' station and they'll make sure she gets them."

He pulled into St. Joe's parking lot. So many memories!

"Let's go, Daddy, come on!" Cami had unlatched her seatbelt and was already opening the door. Phil hurried around to help her lift the pansies out.

He soon stood at the information desk with Cami. "Good afternoon! Which room is Glenda Henderson's?"

The receptionist typed Glenda's name into her computer, then stared at the screen for a moment. "She's in room 545." The receptionist leaned over the desk. "They don't usually allow"—she motioned to Cami— "on the ward."

Phil appreciated the receptionist's discretion. "Thank you very much."

"Thank you," Cami echoed.

They headed towards the row of elevators, Cami's head hidden behind the mound of pansies.

"Careful, honey, you just about walked into that chair." Phil grabbed for the plant as it bobbled when Cami touched the elevator button to go up.

They stopped at the nurses' station where Cami piped up.

"Excuse me, please," said Cami to the shift nurse. "I gotted these special flowers for Mrs. Henderson. Can I give them to her?"

Phil caught the nurse holding back a smile.

"Oh, honey, those are beautiful," the nurse said. "But Mrs. Henderson can't see anyone right now except her husband and daughter."

Despite the kindness in the woman's voice, Cami's eyes still welled up with tears. "But I wanted to give her a hug and tell her about the baby horsie at Grandma's house."

"Mrs. Henderson is sleeping now, and that sleep is helping her get better, okay?"

Phil bent over and met Cami's gaze. "Want to peek in the window and see her sleeping?" He put his hands together as though praying that Cami would accept it.

"Okay." She looked back at the nurse. "Can I watch you give her the card and flowers?"

The nurse smiled at Phil. "Determined little thing, isn't she?"

As Phil held Cami up to the window of Glenda's room, the nurse placed the flowers near the window ledge and set the card on the movable tray near her bed. Two bags hung on IV poles and their slender tentacles held a grip on Mrs. Henderson's life.

Only two? Phil thought. *Is that good or bad?*

———◦◦———

Phil crawled into bed and relished the scent of clean sheets. He scrunched his pillow into the perfect shape and rolled onto his side to face the empty pillow. At first the sight intensified his loneliness, but then he remembered the first time Samantha had instituted the ten-minute pillow talk rule.

"Well, you're not here, Sam I Am, but I'm gonna follow the rule," he whispered. "I can't remember the last time we had a ten-minute pillow talk. And that's okay. Tonight I'm bringing it back, hoping it helps me remember the good things about us. Here goes.

"The best thing about my day was shopping with Cami. She's hilarious. First, the pansies for Glenda weren't the right shade of purple. If they had any dried leaves, she turned her face away as if she'd seen something horrible. Did you ever take her to a greenhouse? Anyhow, we got it delivered. That was the hardest part of my day, seeing Glenda lying there so still. She sported fewer tubes, but I dunno. I'm scared, Sam."

Phil punched the pillow into a better position.

"What am I thankful for? The good routines you've instilled in Cami. I know you thought you were a horrible mother, but it's amazing what you and Glenda accomplished. I just wanted you to know that I noticed. Is there anything you need or anything I can change so your day goes better tomorrow, Sam? Wish you were here to answer that."

He pulled up the comforter around his shoulders.

"Good night, Sam. Love you."

Phil yawned, then texted his mom to say he was too tired to talk. He just needed to sleep, and talking about the hearing wouldn't be sleep-inducing.

———◦◦———

At 2:00 a.m., Phil woke with a start and sat up in bed. His heart pounded in his chest.

Then the sound came again. Cami! The screams came from her bedroom. He threw back the covers, grabbed his robe, and ran to her room.

"It's okay, Cami. Daddy's here."

The nightlight cast a warm glow across Cami's bed. She sat up, staring blankly, and continued screaming.

He sat next to her and wrapped his arms around her. "Shhh... Daddy's here."

She struggled against him, her screams piercing his ears. He held her tight. "Cami, it's okay."

Finally, Cami quieted in his arms and she slumped against him. He wiped away her tears, and his own, then laid her down and tucked her in.

He dragged himself back to his own bed, only to awake to a repeat performance at four o'clock. At seven, he woke again. This time, Cami was pushing his eyelids open.

After getting up, he'd flipped on some cartoons in his bedroom for Cami to watch as he showered. When he was done, he opened the door to find Cami wrapped in his wife's housecoat, rocking back and forth on the floor, tears on her face. He rushed to her side and wrapped his arms around her.

"Oh, honey, can you tell Daddy what's wrong?" He stroked her back. "Do you miss Mommy?"

"I... I thought you were gone, too... just like Mommy."

A lump rose in his throat and he took a deep breath. "Oh, sweetheart, I didn't mean to scare you."

Cami burst into sobs and wound her arms around Phil's neck and held him tight. Sobs continued to shudder through her little body.

Phil cradled Cami's legs, picked her up, and carried her to the rocker where he sat with her on his lap. He slowly rocked back and forth, stroking her hair and back. Cami stilled and her breathing slowed.

Silent tears streamed down his face. His commitment to stay home in the afternoons suddenly turned into a long-term proposition.

Thirteen

Time to Pivot

As Phil sipped his coffee, he couldn't get the morning's events off his mind. Was working from home a possibility? Could he trust Bob to run the company? Samantha's misgivings about Bob bothered him. He'd dismissed them as the operations side of the business improved with Bob's oversight. However, Samantha was an excellent judge of character.

God, I want my wife back. I need her to help me figure this out. Was her people radar still accurate, God, despite the depression?

Maybe Pastor Brad could help him figure things out. His understanding of corporate life helped. Not that Phil had attended church much since high school. Two funerals and a baby dedication didn't count.

The night Samantha had refused to see him, Phil attended the evening service at Hope Fellowship. Pastor Brad had invited him into the privacy of his office after the service. That conversation had given him hope.

Pastor Brad clapped Phil on the back. "Phil, I'm so glad you came by the church tonight."

"Thanks. How come you were up at the hospital yesterday?"

"A couple of us older pastors take turns being the chaplain on weekends. I visited with your wife on Saturday evening. It's part of the chaplaincy routine to pop by the psychiatric wing. We had a quick prayer. I was up to visit another person today, and that's when you and I ran into each other."

"Thanks for seeing her. Beyond that, I don't know what to say."

"I just wanted to let you know I'm here. Available to listen to anything you want to talk about. I'm sure you have a lot on your plate. Samantha mentioned her upcoming hearing."

"I'm grateful she did say something. My mom has Cami right now, but she can't keep her beyond the hearing. I need to cut back on my hours at work so I can be around for her after school and in the evenings."

"Actually, Phil, I was wondering if you needed to chat about how you're dealing with things at an emotional and spiritual level."

Pastor Brad had a way of digging up things Phil preferred to keep buried.

"You mean counselling?"

"I'll make time in my schedule for you in the next two weeks," the pastor said. "Even if it means meeting after work. I won't push, but I think you need someone to talk to. Suicide attempts are messy, traumatic, and difficult to process. Working through it now will help you support Cami when she returns home from your mom's place. It'll be a big signal of your intentions towards Samantha as well."

Phil knew the dark circles under his eyes and unshaven face shouted his exhaustion.

"I think she feels guilty about the burden she's placed on you," the pastor said.

As long as he kept moving, he could track what Brad was saying, but his hands were getting chapped from pleating his pants so often. "I know I need help but..."

Phil teetered on the edge of the edge of the chair as he shoved his hands under his legs. His grandfather's advice came to him: "Whatever and whomever you invest in with your time and energy will pay big dividends." That saying had applied to all aspects of life.

He hadn't invested in his wife and Cami for a long time, with the exception of hiring Glenda. It was time to make a shift.

He looked at the beige carpet with its tasteful pattern. He raised his head, straightened his shoulders, rolled down his sleeves, and buttoned the cuffs.

Phil looked into Pastor Brad's eyes. "I need to change. I need any help I can get right now."

"I can see you mean business, but how about we save the tough stuff for our first meeting?" Pastor Brad leaned forward. "How's business? I was sad when you didn't get the venture capital investment you were looking for."

"I didn't think pastors relaxed and watched TV!"

Pastor Brad chuckled. "Before going to seminary, I used to live and breathe the corporate life. I love that show. It lets me relive some of that excitement, but it also reminds me why I left. My past life helps me understand the businesspeople in my congregation."

"Something's off and I don't have the brain space to sort it out," said Phil. "I need fresh eyes to figure out why we've lost some clients. Bob's kept things running during my absence. His updates are always positive, but things aren't lining up. We gained a few clients after my TV appearance, but our cashflow doesn't seem to match the uptick in interest."

"This might seem odd to ask, but you might want to check to see whether your incoming payments match outgoing invoices. If they don't, one of your employees may be committing fraud."

Phil sat back in his chair, pant legs forgotten. Could things get any worse?

"What part of your business are you willing to let go of responsibility for?" Pastor Brad asked.

"Before we had Cami, Sam handled the marketing and trained new staff. Then she stayed home. When she got a part-time teaching job at Wilson Park, she loved that the school had a daycare attached to it. Cami was never far away. She didn't go back after we lost Micah. In June, she talked about coming back to do the marketing and make informational teaching videos. But then she had her miscarriage..."

"Marketing's your biggest need?"

"Yeah, but I don't have the cashflow to hire someone new. I need to pay a lawyer, too." Phil shrugged, but the lump in his throat remained.

"Take a minute, Phil. It's been an impactful weekend. Have you been able to sleep yet?"

"In bits and pieces. I keep seeing Thursday's events in my dreams. I haven't been able to sleep in my own bed yet. Police released the scene yesterday, but everything needs to be cleaned up."

"That's not surprising."

"I guess not, but it all costs. Tomorrow I have to find that lawyer. She could accept a public defender, but I want her to feel like I went to bat for her. You know what I mean?"

"Lawyers are expensive, but Samantha's worth it. Cami needs her mom. You need them both."

"I just can't see how I can keep burning the candle at both ends and parent, too."

"My son Ryan brought one of his old friends by the other day. I think his name was Gabe. If I remember the conversation, Gabe talked about looking for work in the Saskatoon area as a marketer. He seemed like a good guy. Do you want to see if I can get a hold of his contact information?"

"I'm not sure about anything these days." Phil slumped against the armchair and rested his head on his right hand. "It's been a long couple of months. I'm cash poor right now, so I don't even know what I might offer this... this, uh, Gabe guy?"

Pastor Brad moved towards Phil and placed his hand on his shoulder. "Mind if I pray an out loud prayer for you right now?"

"I don't mind." Phil bowed his head.

"Father, you see the weight Phil's carrying. Thank You that Your yoke is easy and Your burden is light. Give Phil eyes to see that You're with him. You long for him to cast his cares on You. Ease his path forward and make things clear. Remind him that You're the same faithful God that provided manna in the wilderness. Amen."

Phil pushed himself to his feet and stretched out his hand towards Pastor Brad. "I'm grateful for the time you've given me today. I'll give your words some thought."

But before he turned to leave, he thought of a question.

"What did you mean about manna?"

"It was a food that fell from heaven to feed the Israelites in the wilderness." Pastor Brad smiled. "Sounds like you could use a few people around to support you while you're going through this. The Old Testament is full of stories about God showing up when His people were going through tough times."

"Sam has a rainbow blanket. She used to say it was her hope and promise blanket. She destroyed it after the miscarriage in July. I'd like to know more about that."

"Anytime, Phil. My door is always open, unless it's not. Then it means I'm away. Book your appointments with my secretary after you sort out your Monday. Deal?"

"Deal."

Phil smiled and headed home.

——◦●◦——

Phil yawned. Cami's weight pinned him against the rocker. Early morning night terrors were no picnic. It was only eight in the morning, but it seemed like he had fit an entire day in the middle of the night.

He missed having his regular conversations with Pastor Brad. He'd have to try to get to the Sunday morning service with Cami on the weekends when they didn't head out to North Battleford, or wherever Samantha's treatment took her.

Okay, I need somebody to pound the streets for my company, he thought. *What's the name of that new guy in town? Gabriel? Gabe? That's it.*

He inched his way out of the rocker, deposited his precious bundle onto her bed, and tucked her in. Hopefully she'd get a little more sleep this morning while he sorted out what was happening next in their world.

He slipped into his home office and dialled Pastor Brad's number at the church, and waited. Eight-thirty might be a little early, but Phil hoped that the man started office hours early on Fridays.

"Hello, Pastor Brad," he said when the pastor picked up. "It's Phil Camden here."

"Hello, Phil. How did the first night home with your daughter go?"

"Cami and I are doing okay, although she had a lot of screaming episodes that night and again last night. I think I'm ready to take your advice. Do you think Gabe is still in town?"

"Gabe? I'll ask Ryan. Give me a sec."

Phil decided that a cup of coffee might help clear the muddle in his brain. He picked up his cell and headed downstairs while he waited for Pastor Brad to get back to him.

"Phil, are you still there?"

"Yes."

"Ryan said he's staying at the hotel near the airport. Do you want his contact info? I've got his cell number and email address. I didn't know if you wanted to send more of a query letter, something that outlines the job, before phoning him."

"Boy, I'm lucky to have you in my life, Pastor Brad. I'm so tired I would have missed that step. Good thing you used to live in my kind of world."

Pastor Brad's warm chuckle filled the air. "Ah, don't worry about it. You'd have thought of it once you woke up a little more."

"Thanks again." Something else occurred to him. "Oh, wait. Do you know somebody who might help Cami? Like counselling or something?"

"I'll text you some names and agencies, all right?"

"Okay."

Phil sipped his coffee and headed back up to the home office. He took a quick peek to see if Cami remained asleep. His glimpse reassured him that he had a few more minutes to himself.

He sat down at the computer and saw that Pastor Brad had already sent over the details about Gabe. His full name was Gabe Michaels, marketing consultant, and Phil was pleased to see that he had a master's degree behind his name. He began to compose a letter.

> Dear Gabe,
>
> My name is Phil Camden. I'm the CEO of an innovative 3D printing company. We specialize in a niche market by empowering designers to get their new product to market. Our business allows them to create small product runs here in our warehouse. We provide the infrastructure and materials for them. It's taken off. I'm looking for someone to run our advertising division since my partner had to leave the business because of health reasons. Would you be interested in coming out for a tour this week to see what we do?
>
> Sincerely,
> Phil Camden
> Tailor-Made Manufacturing

He pressed send.

God, I know You and I are practically strangers, but could You make this work somehow? I can't fly solo anymore. Sam is the person I need. I want her here more than anything. But she's not, so could Gabe be a good fit?

Half an hour later, he got a response from Gabe, along with the man's personal dossier and reference letters. As Phil read through it, he noted the extra seminars Gabe had taken to enhance his resume. Some of those would stand him in good stead as an entrepreneurial consultant.

It was nice to know someone in the marketing field understood accounting and accounting law when presenting a pitch. It might be a valuable extra service to provide clients.

But would it be possible to afford this guy? The tightness of their cashflow had him worried.

He sent a reply, suggesting that they meet the following Tuesday morning. He then emailed Erin with all of Gabe's references and asked her to set up a couple of video conferences with them on Monday in preparation for the interview.

His phone chimed. He called Bob back at the warehouse.

"How's everything going, Bob?"

"Everything's hunky-dory around here. Erin forwarded me an email from a potential new client, so that's good."

"Oh, really? That's great, Bob. Did the new shipment come last week?"

"Uh, no. Something about payment not arriving in time."

"That's strange. Did you contact them yet?"

"I figured it could wait till you got back on Monday."

Phil's stomach tightened. He'd established great trust with all his suppliers. Had he forgotten to send out a cheque?

"Maybe I'll check with Erin to see when we sent out the cheques," Phil said. "You know, it might just be an issue with snail mail."

He rubbed his eyes. A faint thrum of pain hinted at the possibility of a headache. He hoped the payment issue was just something to do with the postal service.

"Sure thing, bossman."

"Quit calling me that. You've been practically running the show there for the last few months."

"Yeah. My paperwork has tripled, not to mention all the cheques I have to mail to keep the printers rolling."

"Doesn't Erin mail them on her lunch break?" Phil asked.

"Usually, but I offered to do it while you were gone from the office."

Phil's stomach felt like it was doing gymnastics. Had Bob forgotten to mail the cheques? Was that why the supplier had stopped delivery?

Maybe it was time to act on Pastor Brad's suggestion that someone, maybe Bob, was siphoning money from the company. He just couldn't get his head around it. Yet how did one go about figuring out where the money went? Could an auditor figure it out?

"Nice that you gave Erin a break," Phil said. "See you Monday."

"Sure thing, bossman."

His stomach growled as if on cue. Phil headed downstairs for breakfast and a second cup of coffee. Ten minutes into breakfast, he heard Cami calling him as she galloped down the stairs.

Ready or not, single parenthood. Here I come!

Fourteen

Daily Living Struggles

Samantha struggled to open her eyes, then glanced at the clock. 7:30 a.m. Time to rise and shine.

What did the list tell her to do? Go to the bathroom, wash her hands and face, brush her hair and teeth, get dressed.

Samantha made her way through the list of ADLs, or activities of daily living. Exhausted by the effort spent on these simple tasks, she sat on her bed and waited for the orderly to open her door so she could eat breakfast. After three days at the facility, she was still uncertain of the protocols and unsure of how to get permission to connect with other people.

"Good morning, Samantha," said the orderly. "Today is your lucky day. How do you feel about joining the others for breakfast this morning?"

"I'd rather eat in my room than make small talk with strangers."

"Let's make a start. Go to the dining room, pick up your tray, and then you may eat in your room. Baby steps."

After picking up her tray with fruit, granola, and yogurt, Samantha added a glass of water and cup of coffee. An attendant handed her a spoon. Phew! No eye contact, no weird introductions, no catcalls... just the normal hubbub of a cafeteria.

The orderly walked her back to her room. "See you in half an hour for goals group."

Samantha's appetite fled. She pushed the granola and fruit around her bowl with the spoon. She looked at the whiteboard: *Take one bite of yogurt and two bites of fruit.* She sipped some water, scooped up some yogurt, and swallowed it. Next, she spooned up two chunks of melon. Next, coffee.

Now she could tell the group she had accomplished two ADLs.

As she sat at her designated table, she wondered about the stories of each person sitting there. Yesterday she'd learned their common characteristic: they were all mothers. Each table had a shared factor around which they crafted daily routines. Hygiene and activities like meals and laundry were universal to all. Establishing daily routines helped each client regain the skills they had let go of in their depression.

The counsellor handed out their previous goals list. Samantha stamped the date beside the two goals she had accomplished.

"Today we are going to add one more goal to our list," the counsellor said. "Choose snacks that improve your serotonin level. Here's a list of nuts and seeds that help. Turkey, cheese, eggs, and salmon are also good choices. They provide tryptophan, which your body needs to produce its own serotonin. Bananas, pineapple, kiwi, plums, and tomatoes also contain high levels of tryptophan. Avocados, dates, grapefruit, and cantaloupe have smaller amounts."

Samantha grimaced at the thought of walnuts, so instead she checked peanuts, cashews, and almonds on the list. When she saw that pistachios, her favourite, had lots of tryptophan, she checked it off. She could handle pumpkin seeds in salads. Maybe she could sprinkle flax on her yogurt. She could try having a banana and kiwi fruit for afternoon snack.

She added two more goals to her ADL sheet.

As the counsellor initialled each box beside the new goals, she encouraged each person to share their recent additions.

Samantha looked at the clock. It was almost time for gym activities. She crossed her fingers that it would be time to go before it was her turn to share.

When the person to her right shared, Samantha looked at her feet, refusing to make eye contact with the counsellor.

"Time to go to the gym," he said. "Today we are doing stretches and some cardio."

Sometimes rigid adherence to a schedule had its benefits! The counsellor began rearranging the groupings of chairs and tables for the next session.

Samantha headed back to her room and pinned her updated ADL schedule with a flower magnet to the whiteboard.

After changing, she pressed the buzzer. The door opened and she headed to workout with the same group of women from goals group. She huffed and puffed with everyone else and completed the series of stretches, running, skipping, and dance steps.

She headed to shower instead of using her phone break. Phil and Cami were coming up tomorrow for the first visit, so it didn't seem necessary to make a call. She could hardly face the prospect of looking at her husband, let alone talking to him. Plus, if she showered she could check another box on her ADL list.

It felt good to feel the warm water on her wrists. She slowly towelled off. She found clean clothes and got dressed.

The intercom buzzed.

"Samantha, please answer your intercom."

"Yes?"

"Are you ready to see Dr. Andrews? She's waiting for you in the process group room."

"I'm exhausted. Could I rest before lunch instead?"

"Would you rather meet her outside in the courtyard?"

She sighed. "Okay."

The orderly opened her door and followed her out to the courtyard where Dr. Andrews was waiting. Samantha hung back along the wall beside the door. The doctor moved close enough to hear Samantha but not close enough to spook her or make her feel like shrinking away.

"Rough day, Samantha?"

"You could say that. All day I've just done the next thing to keep from thinking about Phil and Cami's visit tomorrow. Going to group gives me too much time to think while other people are sharing."

"What bothers you about the visit?"

"I keep seeing Phil's face, the one he made while trying to help me. You know, on that... day."

"What did you see?"

"He looked so panicked." She walked along the pathway, fixing her eyes on the paving stone design.

Dr. Andrews joined her. "Why does his fear bother you?"

"Because it means he cares."

"Why does his caring bother you?"

"It means... it means..."

Samantha stopped. She didn't want to think about his fear of losing her. His fear and panic wrapped around her mind like an octopus's tentacles. He still loved her. The stories she told herself weren't true.

Her breaths shortened and she had to fight for air. Her pace slowed, and finally she stopped.

Dr. Andrews waited a few moments before speaking. "Why don't we walk around the courtyard?"

Samantha followed with halting steps and concentrated on breathing. She breathed in on the count of four and out on the count of eight.

"Samantha, great job of using breathing techniques to regain control."

Dr. Andrews's praise pleased her.

As they completed a few more laps around the courtyard, the only sounds breaking the heavy veil of silence was their breathing and the soles of their shoes on the pavement.

"Samantha, are you ready to see your husband and your daughter?"

"I don't think I have a choice. I'm a mother. A mother doesn't avoid her child... but the last time Cami saw me, I was being loaded into an ambulance."

Her response sounded wooden to her own ears, filled with duty and obligation. Was anxiety the only emotion she could feel? Where had yesterday's progress gone, with Star? Had it all disappeared?

"So the answer is yes, for Cami," murmured Dr. Andrews. "And Phil? How would it feel if I was to tell him, 'I'm sorry. Samantha's ready for a visit with Cami, but not with you'?"

Samantha cringed at the blunt words. "It sounds harsh and cold. I don't want to be that person. But I don't want to process my suicide attempt with him. I'm not ready to talk about it. I'm afraid he..."

"Won't come? Won't bring Cami? Won't respect this boundary you've set for yourself?"

"All of the above?"

"Well, despite not going to process group today, you did well at exploring the edge of your relationship with your husband and daughter. It's time for your break. Will you be making a phone call or just taking some time to journal about what you learned in this last hour?"

"I think I'll just journal."

They exited the courtyard and parted ways. An orderly walked Samantha back to her room, where she asked to have her lunch tray delivered.

She picked up her journal and jotted down three things she was thankful for. First, she was thankful for the opportunity to be outside walking while talking to Dr. Andrews. Second, she was grateful that her anxiety attack coping techniques were becoming more automatic.

When the orderly arrived with her lunch tray, she dove in. She finished eating in record time and then picked up her pen again.

Third, she was happy that the lunch of beef stroganoff and blueberry spinach salad tasted good today.

Stretching out on her bed felt glorious. She relaxed until it was time for her next equine therapy session.

While heading out to the barn with the orderly, she spied Star in the corral. She went over and stroked her neck while she waited for Janet. She couldn't wait to introduce Star to Cami, but seeing Cami would also mean seeing Phil. Was she ready for that?

Samantha watched Phil wrest a sobbing Cami into the vehicle. He shut the car door and turned to her.

"I better go," he said. "She's beside herself."

Samantha nodded, not trusting herself to speak. Phil gave her a quick peck on the cheek and left.

She clutched her stomach with her left hand and gave a feeble wave as her family turned out of the parking lot. She collapsed onto the nearby bench and sobbed. The afternoon had been a disaster.

"Samantha, it's time for supper."

She hadn't noticed the orderly arrive. "Not hungry."

"Do you want to speak with someone?"

"Wouldn't help."

"Do you want a light tray sent to your room?"

"Could you people just leave me alone?" Samantha pushed herself away from the bench and took rapid strides back to the facility.

Every illusion of hope disappeared as the reality of what she'd done sank in. Her family was a tangled skein of wool and she was the one who had unravelled it. She'd stripped Cami of security. She'd added chaos to her husband's overloaded life. And she'd removed the one person in their lives who had begun knitting their hearts back together.

"Excuse me, but you need to return to your room if you're that upset."

Samantha drooped. "Fine."

All the rage she felt towards the facility rules dissipated. It turned into a barrage of pointed accusations directed at herself.

She entered her room and sat on the bed.

Her door buzzed.

"What now?"

"It's me, Dr. Andrews."

"Oh, sorry for snapping."

"That's okay. The orderly said your visit ended in tears. I thought you might want to process what happened."

"I wrecked my family. I wrecked any chance of finding a future. End of story."

"Because of your daughter's overtired meltdown?"

"No, because I took away her feeling of safety. Did you know she's having night terrors?"

"I can see how that might distress you. You're a very caring mother."

"Phil would deny that."

"Then why would he make the effort today?"

"It's the long weekend. Cami can sleep in tomorrow. Kind of logical, isn't it? She starts school on Tuesday."

"But it's pretty typical for a five-year-old to have a meltdown after a full afternoon. Few kids that age actually enjoy stopping an activity they love."

Samantha shuddered, the words Cami had flung at her before Phil shut the door still reverberating in her mind.

"Mommy, why can't you come home? Why did you leave me? Why did Mrs. Henderson leave me, too? I don't want to leave you. Don't make me leave you. Why is Mrs. Henderson in the hospital? She didn't move in her bed, Mommy. She didn't look at my flowers. Why, Mommy? Is she gonna die, Mommy? What happens if she dies? What then?"

The sound of those words struck at the core of her being. "I won't come home," she decided. "Cami will resent me for the rest of her life. She had so many questions I couldn't answer."

"Will any of those questions move you towards healing?" the doctor asked. "Or are they a distraction to keep you from doing the hard work of discovering the truth?"

Samantha remained silent. Wallowing in self-pity kept people at bay, including her family. Glenda had been the one to challenge that wall, just like Gran had. Now Dr. Andrews?

Fifteen

Work-Life Balance

"But I don't wanna go to kindergarten, Daddy! I wanna stay home with you!"

Cami's folded arms and wide stance challenged Phil, daring him to step into her arena and fight. Dark half-moons under her eyes warned of overtired dramatics ahead. Maybe a minor distraction would work?

"Cami, look at my phone and see what's on the calendar."

"No!" She turned her back towards Phil, stamped her foot, and kicked her backpack away from the kitchen island. Phil left his phone open on the island and carried on with the morning's tasks.

Cami edged closer to look.

"What picture do you see?" he asked.

"It's a desk."

"That's right. This morning, you and Daddy have to go to work. You work at a school. Daddy works at the office."

"But..."

"Now, Cami, look at the next picture."

Her face lit up when she saw the picture of the fast food restaurant just down the street.

"That's right. After we go to work, we're going to get hamburgers. But you have a playdate. We can't meet your friends from school unless you go to school."

"Oh, okay. I'll get dressed."

"Thank you, Cami. Race you! First one down gets to choose our breakfast food."

Phil raced to the bedroom and pulled out his dress shirt and tie. He smiled as he heard Cami's door slam and the thunder of feet down the stairs.

After slipping on his loafers, he headed downstairs. He gulped down his coffee while Cami spooned cereal out of her favourite bowl.

He looked down at his watch and saw the time. "Let's get going, kiddo. Brush your teeth and meet me at the back door."

The process of dropping his daughter off at the elementary school for Cami's first day wouldn't be quick. Sure enough, he heard a sniff from the back seat as he parked in the school lot.

"I guess we'll have to take turns reading stories after today, right?" Phil teased.

He got out and waited for her to unlatch her seatbelt and punch the red release button on the side of her booster seat.

"Daddy, I am going to..." Tears shimmered on her lashes. "...miss you so much!"

Phil's eyes stung and he blinked to clear his clouding vision.

He cleared his throat. "Remember the book about Chester the Brave?" Seeing the small nod, he continued, "Here's one kiss for one hand and here's another from mom. She sent it last night, remember?"

A glimmer of a smile peaked through Cami's tears. She nodded a little harder.

"All right then. Let's go meet your teacher. Got your backpack?"

"Yup. And thanks for buying the cheese bits."

"Look, Cami, I think I see a rainbow over the door of your classroom down the hall. It's like Mommy says, 'If there's a rainbow, there's a future.'"

"I don't think Mommy remembers what a rainbow means anymore."

Phil tugged Cami close and bent down to see tears once again, clustered on her lower lashes.

"Hey, of course she remembers. That's why she sent you a kiss for today, right?"

Cami nodded.

Phil wasn't sure whether Samantha remembered the significance of the rainbow, but he didn't want to sound as hopeless as his daughter. He needed her to be brave. He needed to be brave, too, and not lose heart.

He guided Cami into the room and helped her locate her locker and find her nametag on the table. With a last hug and two more kisses, he moved out of the congregation of parents back to his car, determined to make it to work by nine.

He pulled into the parking space between the warehouse and the offices. Noticing Bob exiting the warehouse, he paused and waited.

"Morning, Bob. How are you?"

"Can't complain. Nice to have you back today. Ball and chain doing okay? 9:30 meeting, right?"

Phil bobbed his head in affirmation and clenched his teeth to keep from saying anything else.

Together, the men entered. Bob ducked into his office doorway while Phil strode towards the reception desk.

"Good morning, Erin. Have a good long weekend?" He waited for her to nod in acknowledgement. "Could you please give me the most urgent emails, the correspondence I need to deal with in the next thirty minutes? Also, could you set up the conference room with some coffee and a copy of Gabe Michael's dossier? I think I cc'd you that on Friday."

"No problem, Phil."

When he and Bob had hired Erin, their efficiency had increased fivefold. If Gabe Michaels could bring that same level of efficiency to marketing, the company could rise to the next tier.

Phil sat down at his desk and opened the most recent bank statement. He frowned. Something wasn't adding up. He compared the order list to the receivables, then the balance in the raw materials/operations budget category, and the accounts payable...

Bob poked his head into Phil's office.

"Oh. Hi, Bob. Ready to give me an update?"

"Here's where we are, bossman. Currently, we have sixty-five clients using our services for small niche markets, such as costume jewellery and household areas. We may need to change our ventilation system if we expand. Some suggested materials require an upgraded system because of the fumes. Or we get more eco-friendly and capture the education market."

"Bob, what's PLA made from again? Samantha had just started telling me about it before I left for Toronto. She thought I could use it in my pitch, but she didn't have enough time to finish the research. I know it's known as the green plastic."

"From sugarcane or cornstarch. Ideal for elementary and high school uses."

"Send me some specs and potential revenue captures. I'm focusing on marketing and customer relations while I'm here today. Make a list of changes we'd need to make and the associated expenses."

"Got it. Anything else you want on my to-do list?"

"Please doublecheck the invoices, material amounts, and cheques for product produced in the last month." Phil pushed his desk chair back and stood up. "The auditor's coming by this month as part of our year-end checks and balances. I'd like to be prepared."

"Sure. Done by Thursday morning. Anything else?"

"I'm interviewing Gabe Michaels today for the marketing position. I'd like you to meet him."

"I have a truck coming in soon. What time were you thinking?"

"Why don't you join us at 11:15? I'll have interviewed him by then. Great references. I talked to a few on the holiday Monday, and I've got one more to call after the interview. Ask Erin to send a copy of his resume to your inbox. I won't decide until you and I chat."

Phil pushed a piece of paper across the desk containing the job description he had written up.

"This looks about right," Bob said, reading from the paper as he paced. In the process, he almost knocked Samantha's photograph off Phil's desk.

"Hey, watch it. I've got work to do, and so do you."

"Yessiree, Mr. Bossman."

"I told you to quit calling me that. We're practically partners."

"Practically, but not officially."

"I've been too busy to create the official paperwork."

"Well, I'll get out of your hair so you can get back to it," Bob remarked. "I won't miss the extra work now that you're back in the office."

Phil breathed a sigh of relief as he watched Bob head out the door to the warehouse. He then got up to stretch his legs and find the file he'd missed taking home the other day.

Erin poked her head in. "Mr. Michaels is here. I seated him in the conference room." She handed Phil some sheets of paper. "Here's your copy of his resume, as well as your notes on potential salaries."

"Thank you, Erin. Coffee in the room?"

"Yes. All ready, sir."

"You know, you could drop the sir. You're not talking to my dad."

"It's a habit, I guess. I'll try."

Phil strode into the conference room, excited to meet Gabe in person. The younger man's lean physique matched his age. His ash brown hair was cut in the latest fashion, and his skinny blue button-up and khaki pants bespoke confidence.

"Good morning, Gabe." Phil reached out to shake the young man's hand. "Pastor Brad had good things to say about you. Where did you two meet?"

"Through his son Ryan," Gabe said. "We were groomsmen at the same wedding. So when I moved here this spring for a temporary position, I looked up the church. I wanted to stay in town, which is when Pastor Brad mentioned your company. I liked what I saw on your website."

"Well, I'm happy you stayed in touch with Ryan. Do you want some coffee?"

"Thank you. I take it black."

Phil poured Gabe a cup and handed it to him. "What do you think of the mug?"

"It's lightweight and has a comfortable handle."

"Our company designed and printed it right here at our facility. We made it of the most common type of plastic. It's called acrylonitrile butadiene styrene, or ABS. Bob printed all our office tools, tableware, filing cabinets, and tables with this. We're exploring adding another type of plastic in order to decrease our carbon footprint. It never hurts the bottom line to be a bit more eco-friendly."

"Sounds like a marketing campaign I'd like to work on, but I hear a question in your voice."

"There are pluses and minuses to this plastic. It doesn't always match our client's specifications. It requires very detailed explanations of what it can and can't do." He watched as Gabe took some notes. "I'd like to hear about your most recent marketing campaign."

"Well, I worked for a coffee company based in Texas. They had a patented type of roast with notes of pecan and cocoa. It began in a small town called Calvert and became known as *the* place to stop on the way from Houston to Waco. We created a short video featuring the company's ice cappuccinos and mochaccinos, along with the slogan, 'Pecan on your way by.'"

"Is there anything you'd change about the campaign?"

"I would have recommended that they franchise their operation in order to expand into other districts. The grocery shelf wasn't a hit."

"How does accounting fit with marketing?" He wanted his company to adopt sound business practices that would stand up to scrutiny.

"Some clients want benchmarks so they can compare their costs and revenue against similar companies. It creates efficiencies and identifies unnecessary expenses that can be eliminated to increase profitability."

Phil leaned back in his chair, debating whether to ask the next question. "Your resume mentions that you took several courses in forensic accounting. Did you ever think about becoming an auditor?"

"Actually, yes. I wanted to follow the money and catch criminals like Al Capone and mafia gangsters!"

"Some of my favourite movies," Phil said, smiling. "It's possible I may need the services of an auditor, as it happens."

Gabe's gaze sharpened. "You have concerns about your company?"

"Yes, I do. Some of our suppliers say they haven't received payments on time, yet I know the dates on which we mailed the cheques. The invoices and cheques balance each other."

"I've done work on behalf of clients who suspected embezzlement. I've worked with police investigators and acted as their marketing consultant as a cover."

"Bob's my acting partner. Ever since he's been given more responsibility, things haven't been the same. My cashflow is getting squeezed."

"I see. What kind of remuneration will I receive?"

"Salary-based, but I've thought of another possibility that might add to your financial gain."

Gabe leaned forward, but before Phil could say more the door opened and Erin stepped inside.

"Bob's here," she said.

"Send him in." Phil almost laughed out loud when he saw Bob's sportscoat buttoned unevenly. When did Bob ever wear a sportscoat in the warehouse?

"Bob Harrington, meet Gabe Michaels," Phil said. "Gabe Michaels, Bob Harrington."

After shaking hands, Phil slid Bob his notes from the interview, withholding the last page.

Bob scanned them. "I love the benchmark idea."

"It impressed me as well," said Phil. He gazed at Bob, trying to communicate his desire to hire Gabe on the spot. "Good marketing recommendations, too."

"Gabe, did Phil talk with you about potential remuneration?" Bob asked.

"Partially."

Bob nodded. "Gabe, would you mind stepping outside and chatting with Erin for a bit?"

Gabe pushed himself out of the chair and ducked through the door.

"Here are my thoughts," Phil said, leaning in close to speak to Bob in a low voice. "We give Gabe a base salary. We offer his marketing services to our clients and they pay him to develop their campaigns. That way, he continues to grow his reputation."

"That's a great idea. Less financial pressure on us to pay him what he's worth, but it still entices companies to pursue working with us. Love his ad campaigns. Where did you find him?"

"Would you believe my pastor's son and Gabe were groomsmen at a mutual friend's wedding? They hit it off and stayed in touch over the years."

"You discuss our company's business with your pastor?"

Phil watched Bob shift in his chair. *Keep your cool, Phil. Don't give him any reason to think you're on to his tricks.*

He breathed in for four counts and out for eight counts before answering.

"I told Pastor Brad how much I missed Samantha's input. I was trying to figure out how to make work and home balance out."

"Well, I can see why your pastor might have suggested him," Bob said. "Sorry if it seemed like I was jumping down your throat about it."

Phil clenched his armrest. *I should be jumping down your throat about the way you've been abusing your privileges as a warehouse manager.*

"No worries," he offered instead. "It's tough trying to stay up to date. Anyway, let's hire him. I'll make the job offer happen, but right now I need to go get Cami from school."

Bob smiled and stood up. "Sounds good. Thanks for including me."

"Can you send Gabe back in here?"

A few minutes after Bob left, the door opened again and Gabe strode inside.

"Gabe, thanks for coming in today," Phil said. "Bob and I have a few more things to discuss, but we're really intrigued by what you'd add to our company. You'll have our formal response tomorrow."

"My pleasure, Phil. Great meeting you!"

With that, Gabe left.

Phil stood up a few minutes later and walked back into the main office. "Erin, please write up a formal job offer to Gabe Michaels." He passed her a post-it note with some numbers scrawled onto it. "Here's the base salary."

"Certainly," Erin said. "It'll be in your inbox by 4:00 p.m."

"Thanks, Erin. See you tomorrow."

Sixteen

A New Normal?

Phil dashed out the door and jumped into his car. He made it to the school pickup line with two minutes to spare. Cami was waiting her turn, the teacher directing students to wait behind the bright orange line as parents pulled up to gather their exuberant kindergartners.

"Hi Daddy! I made this for you! I made one for Mommy too! Can we take it to her today?"

She'd forgotten the long drive already, even though the echo of her cries still haunted Phil's mind. He wasn't sure he wanted to repeat that family visit so soon. He had thought Samantha would be different now that she was at the rehab centre instead of the hospital. He'd worked hard with the lawyer to make that opportunity happen. But Samantha had behaved so oddly.

"Well, can we go?" she asked.

"No, not today."

"But I need to, Daddy."

She waved two creatures made of pom-poms in his face as he doublechecked to ensure that she had buckled up properly.

"What should I name it?" he inquired.

"Thing One, just like in *The Cat in the Hat*. Mommy can have Thing Two."

"Well, we'll have to find a special place to put things you want to show Mommy when we go visit. But right now we're going to get burgers."

He glanced in the rearview mirror to see if his answer upset her, but she was already engrossed in her own little world with Thing One and Thing Two.

Dodged a bullet there.

Phil pulled out of the carpool lane and merged into traffic. He steered towards Cami's favourite fast food place, hoping the kids play area wouldn't be too crowded. He also tried not to think about the magnitude of germs lurking on every surface.

When he pulled into the restaurant parking lot, he shut off the engine.

"We're here, kiddo. Time to unbuckle and have some fun!" He looked into the back seat and saw that she had completely zonked out in the fifteen minutes it had taken to travel here. Poor kid! Those night terrors were taking their toll. If he hadn't already booked the playdate with the neighbour kids, he would have just gone through the drive-thru and headed home.

"Wakey-wakey, sleepyhead. It's time for lunch."

Cami opened one eye.

"I think I just saw Kristina and Bella go inside. Are you ready for chicken nuggets?"

Now Cami opened both eyes and started tugging at her seatbelt. Smiling, Phil helped her out of the car. Cami tugged at him to walk faster.

Before letting her into the playground, Phil got her to sanitize her hands. Meanwhile Mary Ann waved at him to go order, signalling that she'd watch the girls while he got food.

After picking up their burgers, chicken nuggets and fries, he found an open table close to the playground and called for Cami to come down the slide to eat. A minute later, Cami, Bella, and Kristina were munching their chicken nuggets and fries, chattering about kindergarten and other things.

"Phil, how are things going?" Mary Ann asked. "Good job on the playdate planning."

"Pretty well overall, but Cami's been waking up with night terrors two or three times per week. I talked with Pastor Brad and he suggested art therapy might be a good fit for her. So I booked an appointment for Thursday afternoon."

"Add a little extra magnesium to her diet. That assists with deeper sleep. Some other mom mentioned it to me the other day."

"Thanks for the tip."

"How's Samantha? You saw her, right?"

"Yeah. We didn't have much time at the hearing to talk, but we had our first family visit on Sunday. She seemed excited about a horse named Star and introduced Cami to her."

"How did Cami like the visit?"

"She had a good time petting the horse. Leaving, not so much."

He didn't want to get into the details with Mary Ann. It felt wrong to be sharing personal stuff with another woman.

"Transitions are an artform," she remarked. Her empathy reminded him of Samantha's stories about her students. "Just when you think you've figured out a good way to sidestep the meltdowns, the little creatures come up with something new to cry about."

"I couldn't agree more, but I'm a little new to dealing with it on a daily basis."

"I've wondered how you're going to balance work and your home life. You weren't home a lot during days before, were you?"

Had his neighbours noticed how little time he'd spent at home? What else had they noticed?

"I plan to work while she's in kindergarten and stay home in the afternoons," he said. "She and Kristina are in the same class, right? With Mrs. Poirier not Mr. Carson?"

"Yes, they're in the same class. Randy and I thought we might help you out a little, by the way. We were thinking Cami could come over two afternoons a week to play with Kristina. Mondays and Wednesdays would work for us since Kevin doesn't have soccer practice then. I thought it might help you out while Glenda's in recovery and Samantha's getting treatment."

"Wow! That's so generous of you. Let me talk it over with Samantha first. I'm sure she'd agree, and I don't think Cami will mind at all. The timing couldn't be better."

"Kristina would be over the moon. She's such a social creature that she even misses her big brother during the afternoons."

"I find that hard to believe, especially after seeing those two in the van last week!" Phil laughed. "Do you often have Bella over at your house as well?"

"No, I offered to pick her up earlier because her little brother had a doctor's appointment today. When you invited us for the playdate, I'd already committed to picking Bella up from school on the first day of kindergarten."

Phil tucked that piece of information away in case Samantha asked him how many kids were at Randy and Mary Ann's on Mondays and Wednesdays.

While watching the girls go up and down the swirly slide a dozen times, he thought back to the old slide he used to play on at Herbert Ferry Park. Camping there had given his mother fits, so certain she'd been that he would fall off the slide.

He glanced at his watch and saw that it was almost 1:30 p.m. Probably time to give the ten-minute warning.

He walked over to the slide and waited for Cami to come down next.

"Boo!" he said when she reached the bottom. He put on his scariest ghost voice. "Theees is your 10-minute vorning. Ve haf to leaf in ten minutes. Make dem count."

"Aww, do we hafta go?"

"Yes, ve haf to go."

"Daddy, you're silly!"

"Vy, don't you see how many times you girls can go up and down in ze last few minutes?"

The giggles trailed off as she raced back up the stairs. "Let's see how many times we can go down in the last ten minutes!" she shouted to her friends.

"At least quiet time will be easy today," said Mary Ann.

Phil nodded. "Maybe I'll get something done off my giant to-do list on the home front."

"Good luck with that. When I get serious about my to-do list, something always seems to interrupt me."

Phil shrugged off Mary Ann's comment to review what he'd jotted down on the new notebook app he'd found for organizing. Ah, there it was! Take out the chicken. Prep the noodle casserole. Pull out the old annuals from the flowerbeds.

He sounded like his mother.

"Philip, I need help with the garden," his mom called. "Since your father's gone, you'll have to come home right after school. I can't do this by myself."

"No problem, Mom."

Volleyball practice would go on without him. It's what Dad would have done.

Phil wondered what the coach would say. This was the fifth practice he'd miss because his mom needed him. The auction and sale of the horses and land had knocked his mother's work ethic into overdrive. He couldn't deny her anything since he still blamed himself—well, his inaction—for his father's death.

Would her to-do lists ever end?

———◦•◦———

Phil stepped out on the back deck, happy that September was still warm and dry for the farmers trying to bring in the harvest. Cami's first week of school was going well.

He left the door open and the screen door latched in case Cami called to him from her room. He blessed Glenda and Samantha for having set up this period of afternoon quiet time. He looked forward to the opportunity to be alone with his thoughts.

Had Bob delayed payments on purpose? Did Bob think Phil was so engrossed in the situation with Cami and Samantha that he wouldn't notice how much money the company had lost?

He'd just promised Samantha on the weekend that he would devote all his afternoons to Cami. Would this undo the fragile bridge of connection he'd tried to establish?

Sunday had been exhausting. Samantha had been so distant. Cami wouldn't stop hugging her. He'd trailed them both around the barns, surrounded by the musky scent of horses. It had pulled up memories of Buck.

He missed those afternoons of solitude back home in the pasture, with nothing above but puffy clouds and blue sky. He remembered those afternoons spent with his father in the tack room. And the corral, the death trap waiting to happen.

And he could never forget the sound of the ambulance siren in the distance. It didn't do anything to silence the voices that echoed in his mind...

———◦•◦———

"Dad, you all right?"

Phil's dad patted his shoulder. "Yeah, son, might've cracked a rib or two, but I'll be fine. Just let me lean on you a bit while I catch my breath."

He supported his dad as they walked towards the barn.

"I'll rest here while you go catch the colt and unsaddle him."

"Shouldn't I get Mom?" Phil asked. "She'll want to know what happened."

"Just deal with the horse. Your mother knows the drill. Horses come before people."

Phil didn't like how pale his dad looked. The sheen on his face spoke volumes about the pain he was in, but he obeyed. He'd watched his dad fly through the air and hit the top rail of the corral fence. That had to have caused more than just broken ribs.

He picked up the lead rope he'd dropped after his dad became airborne and coaxed the colt to follow him to the barn.

He glanced back at his dad. "How're you doing? Are you sure I shouldn't call Mom down here to look at you? I'll just tie the colt up in the stall and call Mom. Maybe she can persuade you to get looked at."

"Go on. Get him settled and then I'll go into the house to talk to your mother."

His dad braced himself before he took another breath. Sweat dripped off his face—and when he shifted his body, his face grew even paler.

An uneasy feeling snuck into Phil's heart. His hands flew into motion, removing the bridle and saddle at lightning speed.

Hearing a sudden thud, he raced out of the stall to discover his dad lying on the floor beside the bench where he'd been sitting. He ran to the barn phone to call 911. When the dispatcher got on the phone, he gave her the necessary information.

But the moment he heard his dad make a sound, he dropped the receiver and ran over to help, despite dispatcher's request for him to stay on the line.

"Help me lie flat, son."

Phil supported his dad's head.

"You can call your m..."

At that moment, his dad lost consciousness. Thinking fast, Phil pulled his dad's cell phone from the holder on his belt.

"Mom, it's Dad... he's... he's hurt bad. Come quick."

He ran to the barn phone and filled in the dispatcher on what had happened. He then hung up and punched 911 all over again, this time on his dad's cell.

Phil stroked his dad's hair until the sound of sirens filled the air.

—◦◦—

Phil gazed up at the clear blue sky. A neighbour was mowing the lawn next door, but he tried to shut out the sound. He propped his feet on the deck railing. If anyone walking through the back alley saw him, they'd think he looked very relaxed. But his fingers twisted his shirttail into a tightly wound rope of material.

If only he'd held onto that lead rope further away from the corral fence. He could have used his dad's wisdom right about now...

Phil didn't want to underestimate the pain Samantha or Cami were in. He'd made that mistake with his dad. But he wasn't sure he could wall off his own pain anymore. He'd sacrificed himself on the altar of his mom's needs. Could he do it again for Samantha's?

Seventeen

Horse Therapy, Take Two

"Good afternoon, Samantha," said Janet. "Which horse would you like this morning?"

Samantha looked around until she spied Star in the far corner of the paddock. "Star?"

"Certainly. Just grab a lead rope from the wall in the barn."

Samantha glanced around the barn but couldn't quite figure out where Janet was pointing.

"They're on the wall," Janet said when she noticed Samantha's confusion. "Behind the cubbies."

Samantha swapped out her shoes for cowboy boots, then took a multicoloured lead rope off the hook and went to get Star.

Meanwhile, Janet set up two pylons about three meters apart.

"Today, lead Star in a figure-eight around these pylons. Remember not to loop the rope around your left hand. Just gather it, okay?"

Unsure, Samantha led the horse towards the other side of the paddock. Star veered towards the fence and stopped to grab a mouthful of grass from the other side.

Samantha's eyes burned. Would she ever get the hang of this? Was she doomed to be led around by her circumstances?

Star swung her head around as if to ask, *"What are you going to do about it?"* The lead rope slipped out of Samantha's hands, much like the thin edge of control she still had over her emotions.

"Star, you naughty thing," said Janet. "Stop fooling around and giving Samantha a hard time."

Janet reached for the rope and placed it firmly in Samantha's left hand. She then guided her right hand to hold the rope directly beneath the snaffle ring of the halter.

"Let's move her into the centre of the corral," Janet instructed. "Keep holding the lead in your left hand and write words on her flank... words that convey how you felt when Star went over to the other horse and tried to eat the grass."

Samantha printed all sorts of words: frustrated, helpless, angry, upset, out-of-control, hopeless, anxious, dumb, stupid, hurt, worthless...

Her shoulders dropped and her breathing deepened. The decrease of tension with each letter surprised her. It was getting easier. The wetness on her cheeks testified to the action's significance.

"You seem calmer," Janet said. "What's going on?"

"The horse twitched as I wrote the words. I didn't even know all those feelings were in there."

"Now just erase the words by stroking the horse's flank."

The weight on her chest eased as she concentrated on erasing those feelings. The velvety softness of Star's coat reminded her of the afghan that had been wrapped around her so long ago.

"Samantha, I want you to choose one of those words and write on the horse any other situations that make you experience that same feeling."

Samantha wrote. Her on-again, off-again relationship with her mom frustrated her. Her mom seemed to think she could be her parent again after having remained clean during Samantha's college years. That had frustrated Samantha.

Phil had taken her mother while planning for their wedding and asked her to step away and just be a guest. Her mom had left Saskatchewan shortly after the wedding and sent a Christmas and birthday card every year.

But for someone who'd stepped out of her life when she was a child, her mom sure seemed to have a ton of advice. Maybe it had been her mom's way of making up for lost time.

Her grip on the lead tightened and Star fidgeted.

Samantha had never felt pressure around her grandmother, though. Gran had always found a way of releasing her from expectations, freeing her to explore life at her own pace.

She paused. Was she taking on her mom's expectations? Hmm. Was it true the failing to meet expectations produced frustration?

Do I feel frustration in the same manner when dealing with Phil? she asked herself.

Mouth dry, Samantha swallowed. How had she felt when Phil had tried to make up for lost time with Cami by buying expensive gifts?

Star moved away, as if sensing the anger bubbling beneath Samantha's fingertips.

Or how had she felt when Phil had made excuses about not making Cami's first dance recital or ignored her need for physical touch before intimacy?

Janet encouraged her to verbalize some of what she'd written on the horse. As Samantha shared, she twisted the lead rope repeatedly until she'd wound it around her hand. She looked down and realized that she'd better undo the knot before Star bolted.

"Samantha, what are your strategies for dealing with your frustration?" Janet asked. "Do you ever express it? Do you do something physical or verbal? What most frustrates you?"

"It's... me. I'm most frustrated with myself."

"Tell me more."

"I guess... the fact that I'm trying to meet expectations. It makes me feel like a failure because... I don't know... well, I didn't know I felt frustrated by everyone else's expectations of me."

"Write that on the horse." Janet waited until Samantha finished. "Do you need a little more time?"

Samantha shook her head.

"Before we repeat the exercise, use your hand as a giant eraser. As you erase all your frustrations, concentrate on letting go permanently."

Tears streaming, Samantha wiped off the frustrations that had choked her for so long.

"Now, Samantha, I want you to lead Star through the same set of pylons," Janet said. "Remember that you've got the lead rope. You're in control. Assert where you want her to go. If you feel tentative inside, project confidence. The horse can sense your hesitancy."

Moving with determination, Samantha led Star around the pylons and then even made a second figure-eight for good measure. Pleasure seeped in after she completed the course without knocking down a pylon in the second attempt.

"Good work, Samantha. I'm going to add a few more pylons. I just want you and Star to weave among the pylons. Go all the way down the corral and then come back through them again, weaving in the opposite direction."

As her confidence grew, Samantha led Star around each pylon, realizing that the horse was tracking with her, not fighting her. It was an amazing feeling.

"What are you smiling about, Samantha?"

I'm smiling?

"She's tracking with me and not fighting me," Samantha said.

"Let's stop and write about other situations when you felt that others followed your lead without argument."

Seeing Cami copy Samantha's blown kiss to Phil. Phil's satisfaction when she'd arrived with a picnic basket the day after he received the keys to the warehouse. Negotiating a better deal on a new car than her grandad thought she'd get. Joining her friends on a boycott of the English teacher who had insulted her. Starting a petition for lower tuition and getting it signed by hundreds of students.

A strange feeling rose inside her as she wrote. She couldn't quite name it. A bubble of hope? Courage? Power?

"Samantha, erase her flank again and then bring her to the lawn chair. You get to reward her by feeding her. Here's an apple and a couple of carrots. You can hold these in your hand if you'd like, or put them in the bowl. Stroke her nose and tell her what a good horse she is."

While feeding the horse, Samantha couldn't help but giggle. Star kept whiffling and snuffling all over her.

Later, after the session, she unfastened the lead rope and gave Star a gentle tap on her flank to let her know that she was free to go. She hung up the lead rope with the others.

"Don't forget to change shoes before you go," Janet told her.

Samantha waved her acknowledgment as she left the corral.

She felt much better. How could just two sessions shift the darkness inside her? Could equine-assisted therapy be the lifeline she needed? The dance between herself, the horse, and the counsellor felt so intimate and heartfelt. It felt natural.

God, is this how You put the colour back into my life?

After journaling about her experiences with the horse later that day in her room, she tackled an assignment given to her by Dr. Andrews: to write a letter to her husband and ask him questions about his fear of losing her.

Dear Phillip,

I saw the look in your eyes as you were trying to keep me alive. You kept your promise to come home early that day, and I was furious about it. I would be dead if you had done what you usually do.

Why did you come home early? Did you feel guilty about how much time you had spent at the office lately? Maybe you had a meeting to go back to. Maybe you just thought you'd sneak in a few minutes with your favourite girl. And I didn't think the favourite was me. I thought it was Cami.

You came to the hospital right after I got there. You held my hand and squeezed it. Even when they put the tube down my throat with the charcoal slushy, you stayed. I was so shocked. I couldn't believe it. You... the squeamish one?

You were in the courtroom as well. That lawyer is expensive, too. I looked her up and saw the kinds of fees you paid. Even when I refused to see you, you still fought for me.

You would completely rearrange your schedule for Cami's sake. I wish you would have done that for me, but I'm thankful Cami has you for a dad. I wish you could be a dad to so many more children. You deserve it and so do they.

I thought you viewed me as a failure when you hired Glenda and set Cami up in daycare part-time. I thought you had no time for me, but really you were just trying to help me find time to heal. You were trying to take the pressure off, like Gran did. I didn't see that before. Thank you,

your Samantha

Gratitude overwhelmed her as she put down the pen and gazed at the multicoloured afghan. Who had Phil gotten to repair it?

Just before suppertime, the orderly came to her room. "Would you like to join the others in the dining room today?"

"Yes, I think I'm ready."

Thinking over her letter on the way to the cafeteria, she wondered what else she wasn't seeing about herself and those around her. Was it possible that horse therapy was helping her reframe what she had assumed about others?

She sat across from a petite, dark-haired woman. Taking a big breath, she decided to take a risk.

"Hi, I'm Samantha."

"I'm Cassidy," the woman replied.

"For an institution, these meatballs are pretty good."

"Yeah, though I'm usually not a fan of pineapple in my food."

"My husband would probably agree with you. Can I ask you something?"

"Sure."

"Have you tried to call anybody yet? I'm going to try tonight and check in with my daughter's first day of kindergarten."

"No, I haven't. Tough missing those firsts, isn't it?"

"Yeah. Nice meeting you, Cassidy."

The phone rang and rang. Finally, the screen changed and a breathless Phil appeared.

"Hi Samantha. Cami's out of the tub. She's getting her jammies on. I'll go back to her room to see if she's dressed. Sorry it took me so long to answer. I left my phone in our room for safety's sake!"

Samantha smiled. She knew her daughter was wild in the tub.

"Yes, I used to do the same thing," she said. "I'll wait while you check in with her."

She could hear murmuring in the background. It only took a minute for her daughter to bounce into view.

"Hi Mommy!" shouted Cami, her hair completely wet and tangled from the bath. "Can you teach Daddy how to braid my hair while it's wet?"

"I can try, but I think he'd better try brushing it first."

Phil piped up. "I've got the brush for wet hair, Samantha. You just chat with Cami while I try to work through this mess."

"It's not a mess, Daddy. it's my beauuuuuuuutiful Rapunzel hair!"

"Just don't ask me to sing the song while I brush it."

Samantha smiled at their banter. "Cami, how was kindergarten today?"

"Um, we sat in a circle and listened to a story. It was the same book Daddy and me read last week! Can you give me a kiss on my hand when I come see you?"

"Sure, honey. What else?"

"I built Rapunzel's tower with blocks today. The boys were mad 'cause I used up all the blocks."

"Mmhmmm."

"I played frozen tag in the big gym."

"Where did you have lunch today?"

"Daddy took me to get chicken nuggets and I gotted a playdate with Bella and Kristina."

"That sounds like fun!" Samantha gave her husband a thumbs up as he slogged his way through their daughter's hair.

"I thought those girls would never stop giggling," Phil said. "Do you think her hair is ready for the braiding lesson?"

"Do you want double braids or one braid?" Samantha asked Cami.

"Two, just like Kristina's."

"Okay, Phil, you need four pony elastics. Then you're going to take a comb and part her hair down the middle."

Phil walked out of view for a minute, presumably going into Cami's bedroom to find the tools he needed.

"After you part her hair, draw the comb down to the nape," Samantha instructed when he got back. "Now sweep the hair away on the right side of the neck. You're going to work with the hair on the left side first. Take the comb and move it upward from the nape of the neck to just above her left ear. Now take the comb and brush it down and up from her forehead over the top of her ear. Centre the cluster of hair above the ear and use your hand to hold it close to her head. Brush through the hanging hair with a comb. Pick up a ponytail and twist it around the hair twice and pull it gently so it's snug. Do the same thing on the right side."

Phil completed the task amidst cries of "Ow, that hurt!" as a squirmy Cami kept making silly faces at her mom.

Samantha talked Phil through the braiding process until he had finished. "Not bad for a beginner."

Phil grunted.

"Mommy, can you read me a story?"

"Not this time, honey. It's time for mommy to go to a class."

"Isn't it nighttime, Mommy? How come you have to go to school now?"

"It's time for bed for you, but Mommy has to go to school to learn to get better so she can come home."

"Okay, Mommy. Love you to the moon and back!"

"I love you more."

The sound of knock at the door distracted Samantha.

"Sorry," she said. "The orderly is knocking. I need to head out."

"See you Sunday?" Phil asked.

"Yes, see you Sunday."

She ended the call.

How had it felt to tell Phil that she'd see him on Sunday? Peace wrapped around her like a warm blanket on a frosty night. Her honesty with Star was making a difference.

Eighteen

After putting Cami to bed, Phil's thoughts turned back to work. He walked into his home office and glanced at the phone. Should he call Gabe and tell him he had gotten the job?

He clicked through his work emails until he saw the one from Erin with the formal contract. He skimmed it to make sure nothing had been missed. Flawless as usual.

Well, why shouldn't I just call Gabe and offer him the position? he asked himself. *I'll be further ahead tomorrow if Gabe accepts.*

"Hi there," he said after dialling Gabe's number. "It's Phil Camden. I don't normally call people in the evening, but I wanted to let you know that we'd love to give you the job. You can start tomorrow morning at 8:30 a.m. if you're still interested. I just sent you an email which breaks down your salary. Let me know if that meets with your satisfaction."

"I'll open it right now," Gabe said. "Give me a minute."

Phil drummed his fingers on his desk while he waited.

A few moments later, Gabe came back onto the line. "The remuneration is acceptable. Just to be clear, you want me to do a deep dive into your financials to check for discrepancies. And you want me to cover the marketing?"

Phil spun around in his chair. Did he really want to start down this road?

"Yes," he said. "If we're going to gain the attention of another venture capitalist, we have to go over everything with a fine-toothed comb. We need absolute transparency." He hesitated for a moment. "But I need to have your complete confidentiality in this. Our cashflow hasn't gone up to match the increase in work we've gained since my television appearance. Until the reason becomes clear, I don't want any hint of this conversation leaking to my operations manager and acting partner."

The meaning was clear: *Don't tell Bob what you're doing.*

"You have my word."

"Thanks. I'll see you tomorrow morning. Welcome aboard!"

After hanging up, Phil found that he couldn't wait to tell Samantha that he'd finally found someone to handle the marketing. He hoped she'd approve of Gabe.

He opened his laptop and started typing an email to Bob containing the employment contract, as well as the news that Gabe had accepted the job. His neck protested and he rolled his shoulders back a few times.

What would happen if Gabe found evidence of mishandled funds?

You could always talk to Noah, he told himself.

A ping announced Bob's reply. In the email, Bob offered to donate his unused whiteboard to Gabe's new office.

Phil sent the signed contract to Erin with a request to start Gabe's orientation the next morning. He added a note about finding a desk and chair for the empty office next to Bob's.

He doubted the company had any extra laptops kicking around, he suddenly realized. They'd most likely have to order one. But that wasn't such a bad idea anyway.

Question after question occurred to him. Would Gabe prefer a certain type of accounting software? Or a certain app for graphic design? And of course he would need a temporary login, especially since Bob might not come to the office in the morning. Maybe Gabe could use Bob's login credentials to view the full list of suppliers, their invoices, and the shipping fees...

<hr>

Something had awoken him, but he didn't know what. Phil listened. Hearing Cami's cries, he threw back the rumpled covers and trudged to her room.

"Hey, what's going on?" He knelt beside her bed and took her hand in his.

Cami hiccupped. "I had a bad dream, Daddy. Dragons were chasing me."

"That sounds scary." He pulled her towards him. "Want me to stay here for a while?"

She nodded her head against his chest.

Phil decided that he'd rather deal with bad dreams than night terrors. He held her in his arms and wished that Samantha would share which dragons were chasing her. He only knew about the dragons of grief and loss they'd experienced together.

In the early years of their marriage, she had fought those dragons alone. Her fortress of solitude had projected the illusion of security and safety; he hadn't known the dragons had breached the walls and endangered her life.

He'd built his own fortress to keep the dragons at bay with Glenda and work. Then he'd invited Samantha to join him at work, hoping to protect her as well, but she hadn't found his fortress secure.

Samantha had also never shared the significance of the multicoloured afghan with him, but he'd often found her wrapped in it before they lost Micah. It had been in her dorm room at college and had never left their bedroom until she tossed it into the nursery when she returned home after recovering.

That is, until he'd found her unravelling it after the last miscarriage.

Realizing that Cami had fallen asleep, he tucked her in again. He crawled back into bed by three o'clock.

He later awoke to the chirping of birds flying around his head and realized after a moment that it was actually his alarm. He showered and got dressed as quickly as he could. Thankful that she was still sleeping at 6:15, he headed downstairs to prep breakfast and coffee. But he didn't think any amount of coffee would compensate for the level of sleep he'd lost.

———◦———

Phil sat across from Gabe at the new desk Erin had set up for their new hire. After walking him through the initial details of the job, Phil was ready to tackle his accounting suspicions.

"I think…" Phil shook his head. "I can't believe I'm going to say this, but I think Bob's manipulating vendor payments. Either that or he's overbilling our clients for raw materials."

Gabe nodded. "I'll have Erin pull invoices from the last three months and check with your suppliers to confirm cost contracts."

"That sounds good. Bob's giving me a detailed expense and income account for this past quarter. You can check his numbers against your findings." Phil moved on to Gabe's principal task. "I'd also like you to create a marketing pitch for this green plastic. Highlight the benefits and drawbacks. Look at our existing clients and see if any of their products would be good candidates. We'll then set up an informational meeting to pitch them on it. I want our 3D printing to be the best, most eco-friendly service available. It'll help us attract new clients."

"Have you considered using a customer relationship management system?"

"Is that a type of software?"

"It's a platform that links your different departments. It connects marketing to sales to customer service. Every person who uses it has access to notes, activities, and metrics that help coordinate across departments. It allows you personalize each customer's experience."

"Sounds helpful, but wouldn't it be better for a larger company?"

"I can give you a summary of the different types of software that are available. If you're interested."

"Gabe, that sounds like a great idea. Let's involve Bob. If we can agree on a software package, we'll install it on your work laptop as well."

"Should we ask Erin to coordinate a meeting at the end of the week?"

"Friday should work for Bob. Most shipments go out on Thursdays, and raw materials come on Friday afternoons."

Gabe jotted this information down on his agenda. "You could do a cost analysis for each type of software and judge for yourself what would be the most efficient or beneficial."

Phil looked at his watch and realized it was eleven o'clock. He had more paperwork to get through and another client to meet before leaving to pick up Cami.

"I've got to get back at it, Gabe. See you tomorrow." He stood up. "Oh, and email me if you have questions. I'll get back to you tonight after I put Cami to bed."

After setting his phone's timer for twenty minutes, Phil powered down on the paperwork. He then talked through some design difficulties with a client, suggesting that they add two more layers with more pronounced tapering in order to give the product both improved functionality and attractiveness.

When the timer went off, he packed his laptop, checked his phone messages, and headed to the school. It was too bad Cami didn't attend a full day kindergarten program.

He picked up Cami and made it home in short order, then made some ham and cheese sandwiches, placed some carrot chips and cherry tomatoes in a container, and grabbed juice boxes. He assembled everything on a tray; the weather was still nice enough for an outdoor picnic.

He poked his head into the living room. "Cami, can you wash up? It's time for a picnic lunch."

"Okay, Daddy."

Leaving her puzzle partially done on the coffee table, Cami trotted off to the washroom.

Phil had laid out a picnic blanket on the grass. When Cami sat down on it, he stuck the straws in the juice boxes. Both munched contentedly until a wasp started buzzing around the remains of Cami's crusts. She bolted to the back door, screaming, while Phil tried to rescue the veggies.

The wasp kept circling. So much for his plan to have Cami help with the yard work after her quiet time! But maybe she could assist him in making a wasp trap so she'd feel better about playing in the yard again.

Eventually Cami settled down and he cleaned up the remains of their picnic. As she settled down in front of a movie, he searched online for wasp traps. It turned out all he needed was vinegar, juice, and an empty pop bottle.

When the movie was wrapping up, he called her over and explained that they were going to make something to catch those pesky wasps.

"Thank you, Daddy. My friend Bella is allergic to wasps, and she had to go to the hospital. Her arm was really fat after it stinged her!"

Ah! Now he knew why she'd reacted so strongly.

Phil cut the soda bottle in half and Cami helped tape the two halves together. He watched his daughter as she poured in the juice and added two tablespoons of vinegar. How had Samantha always dealt with the constant surprises parenting brought her way?

Nineteen

Acknowledging Loss

The knock on the washroom door reminded Samantha of her lack of privacy.

"I'll be right out," she called.

The truth was that she would much rather have been outdoors. If this confrontation with grief was to be mandatory, she didn't want to feel boxed in by walls.

"Coming?" the orderly asked.

She left the washroom. "Sorry. I just felt a little squirrelly, you know?"

Why was she so afraid of tears? No, it wasn't tears. She feared losing control in public. But why was she so afraid of losing control?

She hesitated before entering the conference room, then saw that only four other women were there. Make that five; she gave Cassidy a small smile of welcome.

There were no tables to hide behind, so Samantha chose a burgundy armchair.

As she tried to get comfortable, a woman with long black hair pinned up in a messy bun entered. Her jeans and long cardigan eased Samantha's worries. It didn't look like this would be a formal lecture.

She followed the woman's invitation to stand up, stretch to the ceiling, then lower her arms and focus on deep breathing. The woman had them repeat the exercise several times.

"Take a seat. My name's Bonnie Hartley. We share the grief of pregnancy loss."

Samantha pressed deeper into the armchair, seeking sanctuary from the difficult topic. Her protective arms clasped over her womb as if to shield it from further impact.

Bonnie continued. "As a nurse practitioner, I knew all the medical reasons behind a miscarriage. But I had little understanding of the emotional complications that pulled me under into a dark and dismal place. Raise your hand if you felt abandoned by the medical system after your miscarriage."

Like choreographed dancers, the women all raised their hands. Samantha slid her trembling hand up to join them. The solidarity was comforting, yet disconcerting. For the last thirteen months, Samantha had camped on the idea that her pain was unique. Instead their upraised hands unified them, from the petite dark-haired woman to the runway model lookalike. A miscarriage left no one untouched.

She risked another glance at Cassidy.

Bonnie looked around the room, holding each woman's gaze for a moment. When Samantha held Bonnie's gaze, she found deep compassion there.

"Pregnancy loss often gets brushed off." Bonnie turned to a slide being projected onto the wall. "You hear all sorts of phrases. Like, 'There was probably something wrong with the fetus' or 'You can try again' or 'You lost it so early. Good thing you weren't attached.' You may also hear the statistics, like one out of four women miscarry. If you're over forty-five, it's fifty percent. These factual statements are accurate, but do they help us cope with our loss?"

The women shook their heads in unison again.

"When you met with your physician, did he or she discuss acute stress disorder, or ASD?" Bonnie asked. "It's possible you were experiencing these symptoms. I'm going to pass around a handout. Please check off any symptoms you experienced after your pregnancy loss."

Samantha's mouth dropped open as she skimmed the list of symptoms.

A sense of numbness or lack of emotion? Check.

Feeling dazed? Check.

Unable to recall details of the trauma or event? Check.

Reliving the event through recurrent thoughts, dreams, or flashbacks? Check.

Avoiding anything that's a reminder of the miscarriage? Check.

Persistent edginess plus distress? Check.

Around her, a chorus of pencils marked the applicable statements. Each one seemed to absolve them of guilt and grant relief. The truth was finally chipping away the lies. Samantha hadn't been able to say anything to Phil or Glenda, or even Cami. She had felt trapped in a cage of silence.

Bonnie's voice broke in. "Sometimes women who have experienced an early pregnancy loss, late-term loss, or complications meet the criteria for PTSD. With no intervention, twenty-eight percent of women meet the criteria after three to six months post-event. This next exercise will help you identify whether you belong to those twenty-eight percent."

She looked to her left. "You three, please stand on that blue line of tape." Then, to her right: "And you three, stand on the line of red tape. If you've experienced the symptom I read out, I want you to walk over to the black taped line in the middle and then return."

Samantha looked across and saw that Cassidy was standing directly opposite her. The other woman kept her eyes on the floor and waited.

"Have you relived the pregnancy loss over and over?" Bonnie began.

Samantha stepped forward, then back to the red line.

"Have you had nightmares about the hospital drive? The place you were when the labour or cramping began?"

Again, she stepped forward, met Cassidy's eyes, before returning.

"Do you avoid new moms, hospitals, or doctor's offices?"

Samantha remained where she was this time.

"Have you had difficulty sleeping, been more irritable, or suddenly felt jumpy when startled?"

Samantha stepped forward.

"Any anxiety or panic attacks?"

Samantha stepped forward.

"Feel untethered to reality? Like you're just floating in a perpetual sea of fog?"

Samantha stepped forward. When they both reached the black line, Cassidy reached out and touched her arm. Samantha covered her hand and squeezed it.

"As you can see, many of you meet the criteria of a PTSD diagnosis related to the trauma of pregnancy loss," Bonnie said. "You're not alone."

Their rhythmic stomps towards the black line and back had solidified the commonality they shared. And when Samantha looked up at Cassidy, she saw that her new friend had tears in her eyes.

Samantha raised her hand.

Bonnie gestured to her. "Do you have a question?"

She took a deep breath. "So what you're saying is that our symptoms came from our pregnancy loss. Those symptoms could happen to anyone. Our doctors should have picked up on this when we had our two-week follow-up appointment."

"Yes, that's exactly what I'm saying. Would any of you like to commit to joining a grief therapy session that addresses this specific type of loss?"

Samantha didn't want to miss any therapy time with Star, but suddenly she didn't want to miss these sessions either. Maybe she could talk to Phil about it. Perhaps it would help her open up and tell him about the repetitive thoughts and flashbacks she'd been experiencing lately.

Samantha cleared her throat. "Um, Bonnie, may I keep this handout? I think it might help my husband to understand me a little more. I sometimes have a hard time communicating what I'm thinking. I lose my train of thought."

"Sure. Would anyone else like to keep theirs?"

Cassidy nodded and a few others raised their hands.

As they prepared to leave the room, Cassidy walked slowly over to her. "Samantha, are you headed to the gym? Wanna work out together?"

Samantha smiled. She looked forward to having some debriefing time.

———◦————

When Samantha arrived at the barn that afternoon, the overcast sky and breeze hinted at cooler days ahead. Both Star and Duke stood in the corral, saddled.

"Do you feel like riding today?" Janet asked.

"The last time I rode, I was seven."

"Star's used to being ridden, but not since she foaled. She didn't fuss while I saddled her, which is a good sign. However, I'm not sure if her previous riders used a mounting block."

Samantha frowned. "Aren't mounting blocks used for people who don't have any upper body strength?"

"It puts less stress on the horse's back. The wrenching done by inexperienced riders can leave a horse vulnerable to saddle sores." Janet stepped closer to the hoses. "Today we're going to learn all the parts of the saddle. So if I give you an instruction, you'll know what I'm referring to, okay?"

"Okay."

She indicated the saddle on Duke. "First, this is a Western saddle. The main difference is the horn. English saddles just have pommels. Cowboys use the horn to help them rope cattle. If they had a saddlebag, they would attach it here as well. The seat is where you sit. The cantle is in the seat's rear. This Western saddle has a breast collar. There's a front cinch and a back cinch, or flank cinch."

"I didn't even know two types of saddles existed."

"We're also going to learn how to bridle a horse today. I'm holding the bridle by its crown piece. This slips over the horse's head and behind her ears. The brow band rests comfortably just below the ears. These long bands are the cheek pieces. I've attached the reins to the bit. This is the nose band. And here is the curb strap."

Heart pounding, Samantha felt tentacles of anxiety take hold of her throat. This was a lot to take in.

She made no move towards the bridle Janet held out to her. Paralysis gripped her limbs as she struggled for a deep breath.

"You've got this, Samantha. First, let's practice just holding the bridle. Grasp both cheek straps below the brow band in your right hand. Place your thumb and index finger of your left hand on either side of the bit. That's it!" Janet patted Samantha on the back. "Now comes the fun part. Hold the bridle over Star's face. Rest your arm midway against her head on the right side so the noseband's right in front of her nostrils. Stick your thumb in Star's mouth behind the bottom back teeth. You might have to wiggle your thumb a bit in order to get her to open her mouth."

Samantha felt the rough wetness against her thumb and quivered.

"Now slide the bit in. Hold on to the crown of the bridle with your left hand and gently bend the horse's right ear forward to slip it under the crown."

The velvet of Star's ears caressed her hand.

"Good! Now hold the crown with your right hand and use your left to slip the left ear under the crown. Fantastic work! Loop the reins over the horse's neck. I'll hold Star while you get the mounting block near the gate."

With a shiver of pride rippling down her back, Samantha shook out her arms and practiced deep breathing as she trotted over to pick up the mounting block.

She wiped Star's saliva on her pants before attempting to pick it up. Wincing, a little, she readjusted her hold so the block wouldn't rest against her inner arm on the left. Though the stitches were gone, her arm was tender in certain spots. Surely this counted as light exercise.

Samantha placed the block and took the reins from Janet in her left hand and reached for the horn. She used her right hand to steady the stirrup while she put her left foot in.

"Great job," said Janet. "Push off with your right leg and straighten your left. Then swing your right leg over the horse."

Samantha sat in the saddle with a little support from Janet. She wiggled her right foot into the stirrup and squirmed to find a more comfortable position.

"Let's check your stirrup length. Get balanced and hold on to the horn if you need to, and then slide both feet out of the stirrups. The bottom of the stirrup should hit your anklebone."

Samantha complied. The stirrups were exactly where they were supposed to be.

"I knew we were similar in height," Janet said. "So I adjusted them to fit me."

Mounted on Duke, Janet leaned over and released Star's lead rope from the post. She wound the lead rope around her saddle horn and both horses sauntered towards the far end of the corral.

"Today we'll walk around the corral. Then I'll unclip the lead rope so you can walk Star around by yourself."

Despite the grey tinge to the clouds, Samantha's spirits were high. She was proud of herself for conquering her anxiety. She focused on the rhythm of the horse's legs and swayed to the motion.

Janet unlatched the lead rope. Just like that, Samantha was on her own.

"Let's increase the difficulty and have you practice changing direction using the reins as the guide. It's not unlike steering a car. Pull on the left if you want to go left and pull on the right if you want to go right."

After the third change in direction, Samantha steered Star into the stall indicated by Janet. Once through, Janet latched the door behind her.

"Okay, Samantha, now you're going to dismount. Use your left hand to hold the reins and grab the horn. Stand in your stirrups and lean towards the horn. Disengage your right foot from the stirrup and swing it behind you, over the cantle. Now grab the rear of the saddle with your right hand and lower yourself to the ground."

Samantha's thighs ached, but she felt great.

"Great job for still holding onto the reins. Slide the crown piece over her right ear and then her left. Now ease the bridle off her nose. See, she let go of the bit. Don't let her bowl you over. That's it. Hang the bridle up on the nail beside her head."

After Janet's inspection, she snapped on the lead rope and looped it around a post at the front of the stall.

"Time to unsaddle her," Janet said.

Samantha's fingers felt clumsy, like the day she'd first dressed her newborn girl to come home from the hospital. When she unbuckled the breast collar, it felt like the first time she'd unfastened all the buckles on Cami's car seat.

Funny, she thought. *I haven't thought about that hospital experience in years.*

She refocused on Janet.

"Bring it over the right side of the horse and over the seat," Janet instructed. "Buckle it into the stirrup nearest you. Next, undo the front cinch slowly so it doesn't hit Star's legs. Now take your latigo and double it up and loop it through the tug. Take the end and wind it around the doubled latigo, pulling it up through the tug and down just like you were doing your husband's tie."

Those words evoked a sharp memory. She recalled her attempts to fix Phil's tie outside the chapel where her grandmother's memorial service had taken place. Her tears had made it impossible to see, and the repeated attempts left Phil feeling exasperated. He had said the tie looked like a first-grader's attempt.

"Place your left hand on the top of his rump. Now walk around to the other side. You want to place your cinch facing up so it dries properly. Just put the ring over the horn."

Samantha followed each instruction. She pulled the saddle off and hefted it onto the saddle horse, but only after she'd hooked the stirrup and cinch over the saddle horn.

"Now get her saddle blanket. Flip it over and place it on the saddle."

Perspiration clung to Samantha's forehead and the back of her shirt stuck to her like gum in a two-year-old's hair. Leaning against the stall wall, she studied Janet's technique of picking up each hoof and checking Star's legs for any bumps and scrapes. Janet used a hoof pick to clean Star's feet. Next, Janet picked up a currycomb. Motioning for Samantha to come closer, Janet showed her how to use the comb in circular motions against the grain of the hair.

"Be mindful of the bony areas and don't press too hard. Always monitor a horse's legs. Sometimes the flank or belly is ticklish to the horse."

Janet's instructions landed on another memory Samantha had forgotten. During a massage class they'd joined, she'd gotten the giggles when Phil's pressure tickled her. When had they stopped doing things like that as a couple?

"Samantha, I'd like you to try currying the other side of Star," Janet said.

Samantha finished Star's other side and combed out her tail as well.

"How much time did all that care for Star take?"

"Almost an hour," Samantha replied.

"After an intense emotional experience, do you allow yourself time to do the things that replenish your energy, your spirit, and your body?"

Her daily routines provided the framework for her day, but how would she find a rhythm that allowed her to process deep emotions? Caring for Star would take time, but it felt worth the effort. And if Star deserved her time, then so did her relationship with Phil.

This would be an interesting conversation.

Phil, we need to talk about our calendars and look at them from an emotional expenditure point of view, she thought. *Who would have thought I could apply business principles to healing our relationship?*

Twenty

Reorganization

The knock on the door interrupted Phil in the task of reorganizing his office at work.

"Enter at your own risk," he called. "My sample shelves need sorting. Clients like to see examples of our products... especially those who are just starting the 3D printing process."

Phil watched as Gabe edged into the room, careful not to trigger a domino topple of all the products precariously stacked up on the floor. He picked his way to an area free of clutter.

"Mind if I take a few of these samples?" Gabe asked. "I'd like to examine them more closely. Could help me craft some wording around each type of material. I need to capture their best qualities."

"That's an excellent idea. Plus it creates more room on my shelves!"

"Do you have the specs on each of the materials? I could use them in marketing campaigns. Individualized for each client."

"Erin can show you."

Narrowly avoiding a stack of plastic mugs, Gabe turned to leave the room, but at the last minute he pivoted. "Could I create a generic form to help me get to know clients and their needs? I'd like you to fill it out as well."

"Hmm. A new service we offer to our clients and links back to our website?" Phil asked.

Any additional income stream would be welcome. The latest legal fees had depleted his personal savings account.

"I think the idea has potential," Gabe said. "We could try it with five of your key clients and see how much revenue it drives their way with a targeted campaign. Consider it a pilot project to gauge whether it broadens your market reach."

"That sounds promising. What kind of questions would you want to ask?"

"What pain point does your business solve? Describe your solution in two sentences or fewer. And what does success look like?"

What does success look like? Phil thought he had that figured out, but now he wasn't so sure. A year and a half ago, he'd thought he had it made. Now success looked like making it through the day as a functional single dad and paying the heating bill on time.

"It's a very compact survey," Phil mused. "Yet it could generate a lot of useful information. Well done!"

Just then, Bob stuck his head in the door. "What's well done? Are we having steak for lunch? I like mine medium rare."

Gabe swung around to face the new arrival. "Oh, you didn't tell me Bob was a stand-up comedian!"

Phil smiled. "Actually, Bob, that's an excellent idea. Steak or ribs, Gabe?"

"Both are favourites. But I've got a lunch date with a client today. Another time?"

"You bet," chorused Bob and Phil.

As Gabe went back to his desk, Bob manoeuvred around the stack of mugs and napkin holders.

"Our latest employee is no slouch, Phil." Bob held out a printed sheet of paper. "Here's that report you asked for. Doublechecking invoices, material amounts, and cheques... you wanted it before Thursday, correct?"

"Thanks."

Phil scanned the report. He saw that everything appeared to balance. And yet the bank statement he'd seen earlier didn't correspond to these numbers. He hoped Gabe could help him discover where the money had disappeared to.

"No problem," said Bob. "Just doing my job."

Right, Phil thought. *Knocking me into the poorhouse.*

He gripped his armrests to keep from blurting out his suspicions. He leaned forward as if looking for something he'd dropped. Eventually the heat in his cheeks faded.

"What do we know about the supplier of that new eco-friendly plastic?" asked Phil.

"They're called Ecotough. It's completely non-toxic and biodegradable. One of the toughest PLAs on the market. Do you remember what it's made of?"

"It can't be sugar cane."

"Field corn. It's made in Canada. It never ceases to amaze me how many uses corn has..."

Phil sighed after the meeting ended and Bob closed the door. The man could banter, crack jokes, and still wreak havoc.

When his phone chimed, he looked down and saw that it was a text from Samantha. She wanted to talk about a new seminar she'd been taking called Grief Share.

He called her back. "Hi! Thought I'd give you a quick call and chat in person."

"How come you're not heading out to pick up Cami?"

"Mary Ann offered to get her on Monday and Wednesday afternoons."

"Oh..."

He winced as he heard the disappointment in her voice. She obviously wished he hadn't been working this afternoon.

"Like I said, Mary Ann offered. I didn't ask. Kristina was having a hard time being by herself without her brother."

Samantha was silent for a long moment. "Does 9:00 p.m. work for us to talk? Or will you still be working?"

Phil heard the edge of sarcasm but kept his own tone neutral. "Nine will work. Talk to you then."

"Yes... we *will* talk."

He hung up. Despite Samantha's doubts, he knew he'd made the right decision about taking Mary Ann up on her offer to have Cami two afternoons a week. Hopefully he could help Samantha understand, but right now every moment he spent in the office helped keep the business afloat.

His stomach suddenly rumbled and he remembered all that talk of steak and ribs.

Before he could get out the door, though, Erin passed him a message. It was from the defence lawyer he'd hired to represent Samantha. Something about "recent developments."

His heart dropped when he read these ominous words and Erin made herself scarce.

Phil went back into his office and closed the door. He took a deep breath and returned the attorney's call.

"Phil Camden here," he said when the call went through. "You left a message for me? About recent developments?"

"Yes, Mr. Camden, that's right. I've heard that Glenda Henderson is now recovered enough to answer questions. The police have scheduled an interview."

He gripped the soft leather of his office chair's armrests hard, his nails digging into them. At first he didn't quite know how to feel.

Then a swell of gratitude ran through him, choking off his larynx reducing his replies to monosyllables.

"Oh my."

The lawyer paused. "I'm not sure when it will be happening, but it's soon."

He fumbled with his phone to mute it while he reached for a box of tissues to staunch the emotional swell of tears.

"Oops, sorry, I'm back," he said after he'd dried his cheeks. "Wow... so she's really well enough to talk?"

"Yes, according to the doctor."

"Does this mean she's going to give a full deposition?"

"More than likely.

Phil's knees moved up and down like the needle on a sewing machine as he ended the call. This was very good news. It meant manslaughter was off the table!

Energy was zipping through him and needed to be released. If he felt this good, he could only imagine how Tom felt.

He headed out to the warehouse, grabbing a set of noise-cancelling headphones as he walked in. He started by chatting with the printer operators and asked if they had any difficulties or concerns to discuss. Supply issues? Unexpected downtime? They didn't seem to have noticed anything unusual.

As his burst of adrenaline settled, his hunger pangs returned. He glanced at his watch. One-thirty already? No wonder he was hungry.

Realizing that Bob should be almost back by now, he walked over to the small office in the corner of the warehouse and phoned Erin.

"Is Bob there or is he still out at lunch?"

"Still out."

"Can you text and ask him to bring ribs from the restaurant before he heads back?"

"Sure thing, Phil."

On his way back to the main office, he saw something coming out of one of the printers that didn't resemble any product he'd verified. Was that a Glock frame?

He moved closer to look at the shape of the product being made. He stopped cold. On first glance, it definitely did resemble a Glock frame. But that couldn't be right. He had always insisted that no weapons parts would ever be manufactured here. Samantha had been especially passionate about this, since she'd gotten involved with an organization that sought to bring healing and restitution to victims of violence. She had made him swear never to get into the gun business.

He examined the product more closely, though, and realized that his first instinct had been right. It *was* a Glock frame.

Phil's shoulders slumped as he returned to the office. He wanted to pull up the paperwork on the client behind that order. He'd have to put a stop to it.

And where was Bob? He definitely should have returned by now. Maybe he'd had a doctor's appointment? Even if Bob showed up, Phil no longer had any appetite for the ribs he'd requested.

But before he could look into it, Gabe came out of his office and interrupted his train of thought.

"I created that survey we talked about. Do you want to test-drive it before I email it out to clients?"

Phil nodded. "Yeah. Let me fill it out using the company's own information."

Gabe went right back to work as Phil disappeared into his office to check his email. He couldn't get his mind off Bob's absence, though. Should he confront his acting partner about the Glock order? Should he do it by text? Or wait until he saw him next in person?

He decided that it would be better to do it in person.

Gritting his teeth, he grabbed a pen and began filling out a paper copy of the survey Gabe had sent him.

He filled out everything he could think of regarding Tailor-Made's operation from budget to marketing needs and risks. Soon he got to that big final question. *What does success look like for you?* It was complicated to answer.

So far, the fall season had brought one hiccup after another. Sometimes Phil wondered whether success was still a possibility. Could he scrape together enough money to hold it together? Was Bob sabotaging the business?

One way or another, he would have to get to the bottom of it.

Twenty-One

Home Again, Home Again?

"Daddy, Daddy, you're back!" Cami flung herself into Phil's arms and squeezed with all her might.

Phil gave his daughter a tight squeeze in return.

"Thanks for inviting us over for pizza, Mary Ann," he said as his neighbour came out of the kitchen. He turned back to Cami. "How was your day, punkin?"

"Come see," she said. "We painted pictures today and made a giant fort out of blankets."

Cami tugged him towards the basement stairs in order to get to the rec room. Phil dutifully oohed and ahhed over his daughter's artwork and even crawled into her fort.

"There's hardly enough room for a daddy," he remarked.

"It's not built for daddies. Just girls."

"Oh," said Phil as he wriggled his way back out.

He looked up from his partially prone position at the sound of Randy's hearty guffaw. Kristina let out a delicate giggle that bounced about the room.

Phil pushed himself to a standing position to shake Randy's hand in welcome.

"You beat me home today," said Randy.

"Yes. A shower and comfortable clothes were exactly what I needed before indulging in a pizza and game night."

"Pizza's here. I just came to tell you both to wash up and join us at the table."

A few minutes later, Phil and Cami had wedged themselves in the back corner of the banquette.

"Lord, bless this food," Randy said, opening in prayer. "Thanks for our guests and pizza places that deliver. Amen."

As Randy lifted the lids on the pizza boxes, Mary Ann started serving slices onto plates.

"Can I have ham and pineapple, Daddy?" Cami asked.

"You bet, honey. One slice coming up."

Phil longed for more conversation like this, punctuated by girlie giggles, instead of tense whispers, tears, and sombre silence. He couldn't remember the last time conversation had flowed this way at his family's dinner table.

"Daddy? Daddy?"

"What, sweetheart?"

"Randy asked you a question."

Phil looked at Randy. "You did?"

"Nothing profound," the man said. "Just a question about whether you wanted the last slice or if you were ready for dessert."

"Dessert sounds good."

"Good. Okay, everyone, let's rinse our plates and forks and put them in the dishwasher. After that, wash your hands. We're gonna walk to the corner store for ice cream. And Phil's buying!"

Phil smiled. "Okay, okay. Serves me right for forgetting to pick up dessert at the bakery on the way home."

He went with his daughter to help her wash properly before heading out with the rest of the group. An hour later, after ice cream, Phil reluctantly corralled his daughter and walked her home for their usual bedtime routine, complicated tonight by sugar and overtiredness.

It was almost nine o'clock before Phil finally got Cami settled. He then stopped for a cool glass of water and listened for the little voice asking for water as well.

Much to his amazement, he heard nothing.

He hustled down the stairs and grabbed the phone when it rang, swiping it before Samantha could hang up.

"Sorry about that," he said. "I just checked to see if Cami was asleep before you called. She had a big day. Playdate, pizza, and ice cream."

"Sounds like fun. Where'd you go for ice cream?"

"Just down to the corner store. I went with my usual."

"Rocky Road?"

"Nailed it."

Samantha knew him better than anyone. He couldn't lose her.

"How's Cami doing with all the changes?" she asked.

"Mostly okay, but the night terrors are taking a toll. Her kindergarten teacher asked me what time she usually goes to bed. She mentioned that Cami was lethargic at circle time and very sleepy during storytime."

"She's still having her night terrors, huh?"

"Not every night. Some nights it's twice and other nights it's just a nightmare or bad dream." He hesitated. "I've got her booked with an art therapist tomorrow, so I'm hoping that works. She doesn't say much to me."

Samantha's heart sank to hear how much the events of the last month were affecting Cami. She put her phone on speaker and declared war on the internal voices saying, *"Hang up. This is too painful. He's the reason you wanted to bail on life. Way to create mental health problems for your daughter."*

She reread the goal she'd written in block letters on her ADL list: *Be present, listen, and respond.* Where had the counsellor said to start? With empathy.

"Lack of sleep is rough," she finally said. "Like when Cami was a newborn. Sleeping over two hours felt miraculous. Art therapy sounds like a fantastic idea. It'll feel fun for her rather than scary since she's so creative."

"I'd forgotten those days," Phil said. "You took the brunt of the sleepless nights so I could put in eighteen-hour days trying to find clients."

"And I was grateful when you took off Sundays so I could nap."

"I can't remember the last time I did that. Forgive me?"

Samantha focused her unexpected anger at the long overdue apology into straightening up her tiny bathroom. She folded her towel with great precision.

"So what about you?" she said once she'd calmed down. "Are you having any flashbacks or anxious moments? Are you seeing a counsellor?"

"I've been meeting with Pastor Brad. Not a counsellor, per se. No big anxious moments since being at the hospital. I have to watch myself for anger when situations are tense, or when I feel powerless to change a situation."

"Are you angry at me, Phil?"

Her soft tone broke through the wall of self-control Phil had erected around his emotions. Awash with heat, his breathing rate increased as his brain flooded with all the feelings he'd repressed over the past few months.

"Am I angry?" His voice crackled with tension. "Yes, I am. I'm angry at you. Me. That I have to divide my time between the business and Cami. I'm angry at Bob's funny accounting. At delegating the investigation to a new employee I just met. At what's happened to Glenda."

Phil pushed away from the kitchen table and paced around the small island.

"I'm angry that I even think these stupid thoughts. Why didn't I see the signs of how low you felt, your desperation? Why didn't I get help? I'm angry that my sons died. We needed help and I..."

He ran his hand through his hair and sank back down into the kitchen chair.

"I'm angry at God for letting us go through this. I'm angry that our little girl wakes with night terrors, that she cries and misses you during the day and night. I'm angry 'cause I can't make any of this go away and it will always be part of our story."

Phil took a ragged breath, his heart and head pounding as all the emotion poured out of him.

"I'm angry because I don't know what to do next, and it scares me, Samantha."

Phil's vulnerability gave Samantha the courage to share her own journey.

"Phil, I'm angry, too. I'm not the wife I think I should be. I'm angry with my body because I can't carry a male child full-term. Why labour and delivery for a child who was already dead in my womb?" A sob shook Samantha, and she wrestled for control. "I hurt Cami when I shut down and disappeared emotion- ally. You spent more time with Bob than me and Cami. I'm angry you couldn't even spend an entire weekend with your family without checking on work. And you ignored my concerns about Bob. I'm angry that I needed Glenda to do laundry, cook meals, and take care of Cami. And I still can't believe I was the person who put her life at risk. I..."

Remorse choked Samantha with self-loathing.

Phil was silent for a moment, but then he chuckled. "Ve haf a lot of anger. Maybe ve should invest en some punching bags."

If Samantha could have thrown her hairbrush through the phone, she would have.

"Phil, every time we get into a serious conversation, you crack a joke. As if you're trying to stop us from going deep. Why is that?"

The silence that ensued screamed in Phil's mind and he nearly buckled under the tension. He strained to put his thoughts in order. They swarmed about him, each demanding to be heard.

He'd just shared his own struggles and been vulnerable about his anger. Now Samantha's anger threatened his hedge of self-protection, threatened the fragile truce they'd forged.

Why couldn't he make a joke? Why did he have to contort himself in order to make his wife happy? What had he done to sabotage all the progress Samantha had made? Could he choose to be brave through all this? To face the conflict head-on?

"Humour's my failsafe," he acknowledged. "It protects me from drowning under everything I'm carrying right now. I heard you. I need time to process this, to understand how I've hurt you. I keep falling into the trap of self-protection."

Phil took a deep breath and held it.

"I want to defend myself, too. You don't know how I'm feeling. Yes, it sounds completely self-absorbed, but how can I be honest with you when I think it might sandbag the progress you're making? We've danced around the issues so much so that we've forgotten how to be honest about our true thoughts and feelings."

He let out a sigh and decided to unbutton one aspect of his closed-off heart.

"You want to know how I see myself? This is it. I'm a guy who fails everyone around him. Your depression stems from my inability to father a healthy child with you. Jailtime awaits you, no matter how hard I try to fix it. You even look at me as if everything's my fault. But I try to wall off those thoughts and feelings and keep going."

When the call ended, Samantha's eyes filled with tears. Her husband's words had pierced that which was cloaked and hidden, undoing years of compromise and passive acceptance of one another. Could such brokenness ever mend?

How could she keep sharing if the weight of what he also shared felt equal to hers? She wanted to dump everything she carried in his lap and let him handle it, but he seemed to push it right back onto her. Maybe that was why the doctor had suggested family therapy. How could two broken individuals ever hold on to a marriage, much less a family? Would the truth break them apart?

Giving up would be so easy.

After blowing her nose, she reviewed her goal: to tell Phil about the constant flashbacks she'd been having since Micah's stillbirth.

She had to call him back, and this time she turned on the video feature.

"Phil, can you please hear me out a little while longer? Stuff has been happening to me that we need to talk about."

She waited for Phil to turn his video feed on. Gazing into his red-rimmed eyes, framed with dark circles, she carried on.

"Remember the first checkup after losing Micah? You took me to that appointment. Remember on the way home afterward, when I asked you to pull over so I could get out of the car? I needed some air. I kept hearing the ultrasound technician say, 'Get the obstetrician in here, stat!' Four weeks later, it happened again. I went by myself to St. Joe's and pulled into the parking lot. All I could hear was the squeaky wheel of the empty isolette being wheeled out of the labour and delivery room.

"I never go down Twentieth Street anymore. I was supposed to go back to St. Joe's to see the obstetrician for this latest pregnancy, but my hands shook so hard that I could hardly steer. That's why I insisted that Cami never come with me to appointments. I was terrified I'd get into an accident. It got to the point where I could hardly drive myself anywhere. I never knew when that feeling of utter terror would hit me."

Phil had a look of surprise on his face. "Is that why you asked if Glenda could do the grocery shopping these past two months?"

"Yes. Glenda was perfect for me and I can't believe I hurt her. In my haste to end it all, I pushed her. I didn't want her to follow me up the stairs. I was so intent on making the pain stop."

"And now?" Naked sorrow peered out through his eyes.

Samantha took a deep breath. "I've had a couple of sessions with the equine wellness instructor, and I've noticed a difference. I thought I was just a piece of deadwood, but now I feel tiny shoot of hope budding inside. Can I email you some of the things I learned at our grief seminar? I learned some facts about

PTSD and miscarriages I didn't know before. I thought it might help you deal with your grief, too. I... hope you can..."

Samantha swallowed the lump back down.

"I know it's getting late," she said. "That email might explain what's been going on in my mind more coherently than I can. I wish I could say I've made substantial progress, but for now this is all I can give you, Phil. I hope it's enough."

———◆●◆———

Phil was quiet for a few moments. When was the last time she had offered her thoughts and pushed past his anger? She hadn't offered her opinion about anything in a long, long time. Could he remove his wall of self-protection and be vulnerable, too?

"We've got a start, Samantha. Thank you. But it's almost eleven o'clock now and you and I need to get a few hours' sleep. Can I... pray for us?"

Samantha raised her eyebrows but nodded.

"God, thank You for bringing us together in marriage. Thank You for blessing us with Cami, Micah, and our other little one. Help us forge a fresh path together. Amen."

Phil opened his eyes and stared at Samantha for a moment.

"Good night, Sam I Am," he whispered.

———◆●◆———

Samantha ended the call and blew out a huge breath she hadn't realized she was holding.

Then she allowed herself a smile. Sam I Am. An old endearment from better days. She clung to that.

When had she and Phil ever prayed together? Despite the prayer being simple and short, he had said everything that needed to be said.

Twenty-Two

When I Wake

Nothing about this Thursday was going well. Clothing choices, spilled milk, and cereal all over his outfit...

As Phil wrestled the keys out of his pocket, his elbow flew into the water bottle Cami was holding, knocking it to the cement in the garage. The bottle cracked.

Then a flat tire on the minivan two vehicles ahead of them snarled the carpool lane.

When he finally got back on his way to work, a detour on the primary artery delayed him another ten minutes.

No sooner had he come to a full stop in front of the offices than Bob waylaid him in the parking lot.

"One of the 3D printers quit reading the digital file properly," Bob explained. "The computer tech said the hard drive's shot. It's a big order and our client needs it filled by tomorrow."

"Great," Phil mumbled. "Just great. This day just gets better and better!"

He seemed to have lost his ability to filter his disappointment. Frustration roared out of his mouth.

"By the way, I was in the warehouse yesterday afternoon and you weren't around. Since when do we take clients who produce weapons?"

Bob looked aghast. "What do you mean, weapons? We don't have any clients making weapons. I met the rep from Ecotough yesterday, though. Wasn't sure their product would work with our existing 3D printers. That's why I was out of the warehouse. I wasn't neglecting my duties, if that's what you were going to accuse me of doing."

"That's the least of my concern right now! One of the new clients you signed up is making Glock frames. Didn't you examine the digital file they sent over? We have a zero-tolerance policy for gun parts. What if he's selling them to criminals?"

Bob opened his mouth, then closed it and swallowed. "I think I know what you're talking about. It's a company that makes lookalike toys. They're water guns! Get off your high horse, Phil. I wouldn't go against company policy."

"Like it or not, I've asked my friend Noah to come down and take a look." Phil said. "He's the deputy chief. I want him to check on that client to see if they have any known connections to crime. In the meantime, shut down production for today please." He moved a step closer, folded his arms against his chest, and stared Bob down. "Admit it. You didn't look closely at that client's digital files, did you?"

Bob shifted his gaze away and shrugged. "I was just excited to have a new client after all the bad press you'd been getting. I guess I didn't examine it closely enough. I took the client's word for it."

That glib answer grated against Phil. His jaw twitched as he tamped down the red-hot lava of anger flowing in his veins.

"Next time, do your due diligence. The press doesn't need another reason to come after us." Phil rolled his shoulders to release the tension that had built up.

"Do you really have to share this with Noah?"

"I don't have a choice. Even a lookalike Glock is a problem. We need to get ahead of this."

Bob sighed. "And they were a good-paying customer, too. Back down to the warehouse I go."

Phil watched as the man disappeared into the warehouse. Was he just a talented actor, ignorant of what a client was doing? Or was Phil being sold a bill of goods? Maybe Bob was in it up to his neck.

It was nine-thirty before Phil made it into the office. Erin raised her eyebrows but said nothing.

He sat down in his office chair, closed his eyes, and leaned his head in one hand. "God, he whispered, "give me grace to make it through the day without completely losing my mind."

Then he pulled his agenda out of his briefcase and looked at his schedule for the day.

Erin knocked on his door a few minutes later. "Good morning, Phil."

"It's still morning. That we can agree on. Good is debatable."

Erin handed him his messages. Phil rifled through them and noticed one from Tom Henderson and another from Pastor Brad.

"Thanks, Erin. How are you today?"

"Doing fine, but you look like you could use a couple of espresso shots right now."

"Too bad we don't have an espresso machine in the office," he said, holding up his thermal mug. "Guess this will have to do."

He wanted to follow up on those messages, but the printer malfunction had to take precedence. Thank goodness he had a secret IT weapon in Blair Compton, the best tech he'd ever hired.

"Can you get Blair in here?" he asked.

Erin nodded, then went back to her desk.

It didn't take too long for Blair to peek his head in the door. "You need something, Mr. Camden?"

Phil smiled. He had never been able to dissuade Blair from calling him Mr. Camden, no matter how many times he'd insisted on the use of his first name.

"Morning, Blair. Sounds like you have your hands full in the warehouse."

Phil leaned back in his leather chair, nodding as Blair went through the problem point by point, spewed out all sorts of technical language about what he thought had gone wrong with the equipment.

"When you have a moment, why don't you swap out the printer that's not working with the one that was making the Glock lookalikes?" Phil suggested. "The machine is smaller, but we should still be able to meet our deadline if we start right away."

"No problem, sir. I'll get it done."

"Thanks, Blair. You make my job easier!"

"Thanks, Mr. Camden."

Next, Phil checked his email. Gabe had sent over a new social media ad which would start running on Monday. He emailed Gabe about a few tweaks.

Finally, the time came for him to call Noah. Phil drummed his fingers against his armrest while he waited for Noah to pick up.

"Noah speaking. How may I help you?"

"Hey. It's me, Phil. I've got a potential nightmare on my hands. I went down to the warehouse to check on things yesterday and found a lookalike Glock frame coming out of one of my printers."

"That's a problem. How'd it get past all your policies?"

Phil's drumming stopped. "I blew it, Noah. I let Bob do a contract on his own when I was... taking care of Samantha. I should have been paying closer attention."

"I'm glad you called me right away. I'll send an officer to come down and collect the pertinent information we need. This might be the break we're looking for in one of our cases."

Phil's drumming resumed. "I could email you the digital file, as well as the contract. That is, if it would speed things up for you."

"That'd be great."

He hesitated, then asked the big question that had been gnawing at him. "Noah, could Bob be involved at a deeper level?"

"Involved in what, specifically? How much do you know about his personal habits?"

"Not much. We don't spend much time together outside the office. I deal with an occasional complaint about inappropriate comments, and I know he frequents happy hour on the weekends. That and his humour really annoys Sam."

"We might put some surveillance of him, provided I can get the proper paperwork. He may not be involved with anything criminal, though."

"Thanks, Noah. I better get back to work here. I really appreciate your attention to details."

"Take care."

Phil decided that he had no time to stew over this. After taking care of a few more emails, he took the time to call Pastor Brad.

"Good morning," Phil said. "You left a message to call?"

"Yes. Just following up on our conversation about Cami. I felt led by God to check in on you."

"Art therapy's been great for her."

"And you? Have you started any type of counselling?"

"Well, I wanted to, but... well, things have been busy at the office. I've cancelled every appointment I made." Phil cringed at his excuse.

"Phil, during the nights when Cami sleeps through, are you asleep or awake?"

"Restless. There's so much going on at work right now. Conversations with Samantha have been pretty intense. I'm getting hammered on all sides. Finding the time to do even one more thing feels... well, it feels impossible."

"So what happens to your relationship if you don't work through some of these stressors?"

"I see your point," Phil said. "When we first met, you told me to pursue professional counselling. I didn't know I'd be dealing with more than one crisis."

"Sometimes professionals can help you see where patterns cross over between our professional and personal lives. We need to break those patterns in both worlds."

"Thanks for the call," Phil said. "That jives with what I discussed with Samantha last night. Or rather, what we argued about. Thanks for the advice."

Phil hung up, taken aback from hearing Pastor Brad say that God had nudged him to call. *Thanks, God, for the push.*

He had head knowledge about the things Samantha was working through, and the things he himself needed to work through. He'd kept his equilibrium despite the nagging sadness that weighed him down at the strangest moments. For instance, seeing Randy ruffle Kevin's hair before he left for work. That had left him choking back tears.

It was time to stop ignoring these moments and process them instead.

Last but not least, he keyed in Tom's number and waited.

"Good morning, Tom. It surprised me to get your message."

Phil put Tom on speaker while he stretched, hoping to rid himself of the tension that threatened to bring on a whole new level of headache.

"I thought you'd like to know that Glenda's making progress," Tom said. "She's being moved to City Hospital where they have a rehab facility. She needs physiotherapy and occupational therapy to restore lost muscle function since she's been in a coma for so long."

"That's wonderful news, Tom. Thanks for letting me know."

"Want to say hello to Glenda? She's right here beside me."

He waited a moment for Tom to put the phone up to his wife's ear.

"Hello, Glenda," Phil said. "I'm happy that your hospital bed will soon be a thing of the past."

He didn't say anything, but he also held on to a secret hope that Tom would drop the charges against Samantha soon. At least being able to have this conversation was promising.

"Me too, dearie. How is m—m—my little p—p—p—poppet doing?" asked Glenda. "I... m—m—miss h—her."

The halting tones of her speech concerned Phil. Had her language centre been part of her original injury? Or maybe it was the result of medication.

"She's doing all right," he assured her. "Some days she comes home with more sparkles on her face than on her craft, but she's enjoying kindergarten. Would you like to see her? I know she'd love to visit you again."

"The wee d—d—dear came to see me?"

"Yes, she brought you a sparkly purple card and those pansies in your room."

"I would l—l—l—love... to see her. I b—b—bet she... has grown. How is S—S—S—Samantha... healing?"

"Her wrists have healed. After the conversation I had with her last night, I would say that she's making progress on all fronts."

"I am g—g... glad to hear it."

Glenda handed the phone back to Tom.

"The nurse is here," Tom said. "Take care, Phil."

"After Glenda gets settled at City Hospital, I'll bring Cami by on a Thursday afternoon. Text me a time that's not busy with physio or OT."

"Will do."

Phil thought that Thursday afternoons would work well as a regular outing for Cami—that is, until he remembered that he'd set up three art therapy sessions on three consecutive Thursdays starting this week.

Me and my big mouth, he thought. *I have to learn to consult my daytimer before making promises I can't keep.*

He shot Tom a text: *Will have to be Tuesdays, not Thursdays. Hope that still works.*

Phil looked at the time on his phone and realized that he had fifteen more minutes until he had to thread his way back past the detour to pick up Cami at school. He spent that time emailing documents to himself for review.

How was he going to juggle visits to Glenda and therapy—not to mention, sort out the mess at work?

Twenty-Three

A Safe Space

With Cami's hand tucked in his, Phil led his daughter into the waiting room of the art therapist's office. As he checked in at the reception desk, Cami tugged on his hand.

"Look, Daddy, look."

Wide-eyed, she pointed to paintings hung on the wall.

"And over there."

She pointed to a sculpture. All the art here had been created by children for children.

Just as they were about to take a seat, a woman dressed in a flowing peasant skirt and sweater entered the waiting room from the office.

She smiled. "You must be Cami. I'm Margareta Collins. Nice to meet you."

Cami ducked behind Phil.

Margareta held out her hand to Phil. "Mr. Camden."

"Hello. Nice to meet you."

"Cami, would you like your dad to see where you and I get to play today?" Margareta asked.

Cami slowly stepped around Phil and nodded.

The therapist motioned for them to come in and see the art space.

"Over here we have paint. Here we have modelling clay and playdough. We have different chalks and pastels in this drawer. We have chenille wire and other types of wire to make sculptures in these bins. Here is our collection of magazines and catalogues to make collages."

With her eyes shining, Cami declared, "Oh Daddy, this is the bestest place ever!"

Margareta and Phil exchanged a smile.

Phil bent down. "Can you play here while I go back to the waiting room?"

Cami nodded, and Phil quietly exited.

He stopped at the receptionist's desk and asked if someone could explain to him how art therapy worked. Nodding, the receptionist dialled the number of another therapist who was free for the next twenty minutes. A client was running late.

Soon she introduced Phil to Genny. Phil told her about how night terrors had been affecting his daughter's daily function.

"Your daughter's stuck in a feeling state, which means she's operating out of her brain's right hemisphere," said Genny. "When we use our hands to make art, we signal our left hemisphere to come back online. It's like we're making an internal emotion into an external piece of art. This can be very helpful."

"Can you give me a concrete example of how it works?"

"Sure. If kids are struggling with anger, we have them create an anger monster. Then we ask them to picture an anger monster and draw it on paper. This gives the anger an identity. Together, we find out what the monster needs. This also works well for other emotions, like fear or sadness."

Phil nodded, trying to understand this. "What do you mean by what the anger monster needs?"

"Sometimes we're angry because we're tired, so the monster needs sleep. Other times it's lonely and needs a friend to listen."

"Ah, that makes sense." He looked around at the various doors leading off the main hallway. "Do you have other counsellors practicing from this office?"

"Yes, we do. Is there a particular issue you would like to explore with a counsellor?"

"Lately I've been triggered by the same events that have affected my daughter. It's impacting all my relationships. If possible, I'd like to schedule appointments for the same times that my daughter is in art therapy."

She gave the request some thought. "I think it might suit Stefan Reid to work with you. He could also facilitate joint therapy sessions for you and your daughter, along with Margareta."

Well, that sounded promising!

Phil sat on one of the leather couches in the waiting room and pulled out his laptop. Now he could answer a few more emails and make a to-do list for the next day, not to mention a grocery list.

Half an hour later, he heard the door open and he quickly closed down his laptop.

"Daddy, Daddy, look what I made," Cami exclaimed.

She held up a shoebox that had many distinct elements ranging from sparkles to cotton balls.

"Wow, that looks amazing. Can you tell me about it?"

"It's my safe space, Daddy. It's pretty and comfy and it's the best place to read stories. It has a comfy chair and a blanket to hide me from the bad guys. You know, like Mommy has."

Phil's heart tightened. A blanket to keep her from the bad guys? What bad guys?

He tuned back in to Cami's words.

"Over here is a light, so I can read my books. Oh, and I made a spot for you to sit on pillows in case you want to read me stories, too."

"Mr. Camden, Cami and I had a wonderful time creating together," said Margareta. The therapist bent down and placed a hand on Cami's shoulder. She pointed to a small table in the waiting room. "See the books on that table? Would you like to go read for a few minutes while I talk with your dad?"

Cami looked from Margareta to Phil.

"Go ahead, honey," he said. "I'll be right here."

"Don't take too long, Daddy. I wanna make this today!"

Phil and Margareta exchanged smiles.

When she'd gone off to look through the books, Margareta gave Phil a handout. He looked down and saw that it explained the concept of the safe space and offered some ideas about how to create one with a child. The steps seemed simple enough.

Now if only he could create a safe space with Samantha. What would a safe space look like in their marriage? Would it work both ways? Sometimes he wished he could snuggle under her multicoloured afghan and remember what it had felt like to be significant in her eyes.

⬤◦⬤

As the video call opened, Samantha glimpsed the dark circles under Phil's eyes. "Hey, good to see you."

Phil covered a yawn with his hand. "Likewise."

"Cami wearing you out?"

"You could say that. We made a safe space in her room tonight."

"Oh, what's that?"

Phil lifted a diorama in front of his phone's camera. "This is the model we used to make a bigger replica of it. I acted as her gopher and contractor."

"I take it that's her art therapy project?"

"Yeah."

"What did you make it from?"

"Remember the shower curtain that didn't match the rest of the bathroom? I used the rings and an old hula hoop to build the fort. I attached your scarves and belts to the hook that used to hold her stuffed animal net and then linked it to the hula hoop."

"Genius!"

"Next I went downstairs to the basement for accessories."

Samantha winced as she thought about him exploring the rec room. There were Christmas totes stacked haphazardly in one corner and boxes of clothes marked "Age 1–3," "Age 4," and "Age 5" in the other. She imagined he'd kicked stray blocks and winter boots out of the way. She hadn't tried to clean that area in months.

"What was Cami doing during all this?" she asked.

"Tub time."

"Good strategy."

"Remember that pink low rocker you got from your aunt when Cami was moving to a toddler bed?"

"How could I forget? I spent so many hours in that chair while she was learning to stay in her bed and go to sleep."

"Well, I finally found it behind the artificial Christmas tree. But not before my feet tripped over the requisite number of blocks. I can't remember the last time Cami and I played down there."

"I can. You had finally taken a Sunday off so I could catch a nap before the baby came. That was about two weeks before everything unfolded."

The burst of anger zinged out of her mouth before she could filter it. She clapped her hand over her mouth as she watched Phil stiffen in front of her.

"You know what I was up to," he said defensively. "I certainly wasn't trying to get out of family day. With you stepping back from the company, there were more demands on my time. I was trying to create some space so I could be with you when the baby—I mean, Micah—arrived."

Samantha choked down her natural response and waited. The silence ballooned and pushed everything except the spectre of Micah's death out of the room. She watched Phil struggle to maintain control.

"You know what Cami wanted to talk about when we got the pillows in the right spot?" he continued. "Her brother in heaven. At that moment, the safe space felt anything but safe to me, Sam. Was she... was she like that with you?"

Samantha could tell Phil was working hard not to lower the temperature of the conversation. Still, its g-force pressed her deep into the chair.

"Yes," she acknowledged. "The first time it happened, I backed away and said 'Mommy's too sad to talk about it please.' Then I escaped to the bathroom and locked the door."

"Was that... was that when you, um, started... leaving her to, uh, play in her room more?"

Well, at least he's trying to be kind. What kind of mother am I anyway?

She twisted her hair up into a bun, giving herself time to feel those emotions. "Yeah."

Confessing her withdrawal further weakened the barrier she'd erected. It was time for it to come all the way down.

Before she could say anything, Phil backed down. "I've got to go check on Cami."

As he left, Samantha twirled a strand of hair that had escaped the bun. Guilt poked her in the ribs like an overbearing friend.

"False alarm," he said, returning to the screen. "She's sleeping."

Samantha smiled at the relief in Phil's eyes. "I'm glad. I don't want to keep you up much longer, so is there anything more we need to talk about other than the fact that our dear daughter ties us up in knots with her questions?"

"I think I've found a professional counsellor for myself. Also, Pastor Brad phoned to encourage me this week." He paused for a minute. "Is it hard? You know, to talk to someone?"

"It is. I think that's why I like the horse therapy. Once I'm honest with the horse, it's easier to go further with a psychiatrist."

"Well, this counsellor works from the same place where I take Cami for art therapy. He's going to start art therapy for me, too, so I can picture the emotions that have been closed off since..."

"Since your dad died?"

Phil nodded.

"I hope it will help you sleep better," she said.

"Me too. Speaking of sleep, I'm dead on my feet. Good night, Sam I Am. I love you."

"I love you too."

Samantha wondered what would happen once Phil started opening up to the counsellor. Would he become more aware? Would he push away from her? Would he stop trying to take care of everyone to get circumstances under control?

Twenty-Four

Anniversary Grief

Pulling out her journal, Samantha reread the journal entry she'd written right after having the hardest conversation she'd ever had with Phil.

Dear Diary,

Wow, that was intense. Have we ever communicated that much anger without blaming one another? I didn't know Phil carried that much inside. I wonder what a counsellor would say about some of his stuff? He spouted off so much, but it surprised me to hear him say that Bob was embezzling money from the company. Does that mean our company is in trouble financially? How was Bob doing that? How could he even pull that off?

Phil looked exhausted. No wonder he jumped at Mary Ann's offer to take Cami. Maybe I shouldn't jump down his throat. It must be so hard for him to be fully present when Cami's in his care with all of that running around in his head.

The big question is this: do I believe Phil about his use of humour? If he uses it as a safety valve, that's a good thing. More of an upside than a downside. It breaks the tension. If he uses it like a shield, that's a bad thing. It prevents him from being vulnerable and dealing with issues honestly.

Note to self: ask my psychiatrist about developing a series of cues that say "Stop discussion now. Roadblock ahead." I need to do that better, maybe go on more outdoor outings and take time to smell the flowers. I need to stop judging his use of time.

It's almost been a year since we lost Micah. How is that possible? I want to erase that day from my memory. I miss his sweet face. Will Phil and I ever get past the hard part? I see bits and pieces of progress, but then it feels like mountains get in the way.

Those dark circles under his eyes reflect the toll of Cami's night terrors. She was always such a good little sleeper, even during teething.

Picturing her at nine months, Samantha remembered her little legs scrunched up and her arms wrapped around her favourite blanket.

A tap on her door reminded her that it was getting late. The rhythm of daily routines was significant here.

She doubted that sleep would come easily tonight. But as she pulled the covers up, she whispered a prayer for the second time in two years.

"God, I know it's been a long time since You and I talked about everything that's been going on in my life, but the Bible says that You're near to the brokenhearted. Draw near to my sweet girl, Cami. Help her to know she's a treasure. Keep the bad dreams away. Wrap her in Your peace. Cradle her in Your love. Make us a family again, a genuine family, not one in name only. And help Phil figure out what to do with the business. Keep Bob from wrecking it. Lead Phil to the right therapy for Cami. Protect him from getting too busy and absorbed in the business. Thank You for listening. Amen."

<hr />

In the morning, Samantha realized that the date mocked any progress she'd made.

I come around to this every year, again and again, she thought. *Just when I think I've regained balance in my family life, I'm reminded of everything I've lost.*

Her eyes blurred with unfallen tears that suffocated the life of a thousand dreams. One moment she felt joy; the next, heartbreak. Then came the agonizing minutes as she remembered what it had felt like to wait for the doctor. Her memory reel included visions of the injections they'd used to induce labour, the invasion of stripped membranes, the pain of the epidural line, and her final grunt of exertion upon expelling the silent, perfectly formed baby.

With that, the curtain fell on the irrevocable final act of *The Empty Womb*.

Once, she had thought she was God's favourite, such as on the day she'd walked into Gran's house, leaving behind food insecurity and neglect. But now? She couldn't see the stars behind the clouds.

She willed the orderly to ignore her, to just let her have this one day to mourn rather than process and dialogue.

But you can't bury anything in a mental health facility. Exposure equals healing.

With the orderly's encouragement, she slid out from under the covers and got to her feet. She began her daily routine. She took a shower and got dressed. Next thing she knew, she'd eaten a muffin, drank some water, and was on her way to ADL check-in. Today she added an item to the list: *Talk to Dr. Andrews about Micah during process therapy.*

Samantha worked out in the gym but couldn't make herself chat with the other women. At least, until Cassidy came up to her.

"Hey, what's going on?" Cassidy asked. "You look rough."

"It's an anniversary day."

"'Nough said. I get it."

Cassidy squeezed her shoulder as she went back to her workout.

Samantha grabbed a snack at the cafeteria and her coat from her room before heading over to Dr. Andrews's office. The walls leered at her, mocking her decision to work through this day. The increase in her pulse pulled her heart up to her throat, choking her with anxiety. Memories hit her like flashbangs, making it hard to focus. She almost didn't hear Dr. Andrews's invitation to sit and speak.

Finding her voice, she managed, "Any chance we can go outside today?"

She sat down, rubbing her hands up and down her thighs.

"What's on your mind?" Dr. Andrews probed. "What edge are we going to explore that has you so uptight? It's a pretty chilly fall afternoon."

"Today... is the day. The anniversary of the day... I lost Micah. I can't handle being in a small room. It's too full of triggers." Samantha's words rushed out in a heap.

Dr. Andrews's eyes shone with compassion. "All right, let me grab a coat. I see you brought one."

A few minutes later, they were both walking outside the doors and falling into step beside each other along a pathway that wound its way through the trees.

"Tell me about Micah."

Samantha swallowed, her mouth dry. "The name Micah means 'Godlike,' or 'gift from God.' That's why we chose it. We thought it would work for either a boy or girl." She looked up at the trees and enjoyed the fresh breeze on her face. "We made it past the five-month marker, then seven months. We were confident the pregnancy would go full term. Just like it did with Cami."

"That's a beautiful name. Go on."

"I went in for another ultrasound, to confirm the gender since the original ultrasound wasn't clear. I didn't feel good that day. I just felt off. The baby hadn't moved much lately, but I assumed it was because we were due soon. I wasn't really worried... until the ultrasound technician hollered over the phone for the obstetrician to come. The technician probably didn't actually holler, but the fear I saw in his eyes made everything seem louder."

"What happened next?"

"They moved me to labour and delivery at St. Joe's. By this time, my fever spiked and I wasn't progressing, so they stripped my membranes." Samantha shuddered as she revisited the shock of that event. "Two hours later, they gave me an epidural. Four hours after that, I gave birth to a stillborn baby boy. He was almost five pounds. When they cleaned him up, the nurse wrapped him in a receiving blanket and offered him to me to hold."

The imprint of that memory swelled and overflowed Samantha's cheeks. She swallowed and then lowered herself onto a park bench.

"I... I held him for a while. His perfectly formed limbs were hardly thicker than a finger. Phil stroked his head and his cheeks while I held him. He was so tiny, so light."

She fell silent as they walked on in silence. She recalled the sensation of the soft downy skin of Micah's head as it rested on her arm. She looked down at her arm now, positive that she'd see him there.

She shook her head. Was she losing it?

"Samantha, what's happening?"

"Um, the memory of him in my arms. It's so real. I could almost feel him in my arms just now."

"That's not surprising or unusual. Is there anything else you would feel free to share about that day?"

"I started feeling dizzy and shaky. And before I knew it, there was a flurry of activity around me. Phil said... Phil said, 'Honey, something's wrong.' A nurse leaned over to pick up Micah. It all happened so fast. I let go of my baby and... I... never saw him again." Samantha hugged her middle. "I guess I almost died from sepsis. When I regained consciousness two days later, I asked Phil if they could bring Micah to me so I could nurse him. I didn't remember that he was dead. It was as if my mind refused to believe what had happened."

Samantha rubbed the outside of her arms, trying to warm herself up.

"How did Phil respond?"

"His face just went white and he looked at the floor. Then he raised his head, took my hands in his, and said, 'We lost him, sweetheart, and then we almost lost you. I... I'm so glad you didn't leave me, too.'"

Dr. Andrews sat down next to her on the bench. "If you could change the timeline of those events, what would it look like?"

"I'd stroke his downy hair and kiss his sweet cheek and tell him I loved him beyond measure and that I'd see him again in heaven." Samantha shifted her feet. "I just felt robbed of that time with him compared to some of the other moms who've had stillborns."

"A beautiful opportunity," he said softly. "We're getting better at caring for those who are grieving stillborns or miscarriages, but we've a long way to go. I'm sorry your experience didn't reflect all that it could have been."

Feeling validated, Samantha quivered. At long last, something deemed her longings and desires valued and significant. His words settled something deep in her spirit.

"I didn't get that chance with either of the babies I lost," she said. "Is there anything I can do now?"

"Yes, there is. It will take some time, though. Why don't you close your eyes while I list some options? Something will resonate with you as a fitting closure."

She closed her eyes as he continued.

"Some moms write poetry, or a letter. Others remember the anniversary by lighting candles and releasing their hopes and dreams. Some go to a special place and cry, scream, or shout about their loss."

Samantha suddenly began to sway. "Do you need anything, Samantha? Perhaps a glass of water?"

"Yeah, maybe. I feel a little overwhelmed right now."

"I'll text someone to bring you a water bottle out here." Samantha pondered what Dr. Andrews said while the doctor completed the task.

"You can create a grief ritual, like a birthday cupcake in memory of Micah and your other child."

Samantha clenched her fists and felt every muscle scream out in agony as she fought to rein in her wild desire to open her mouth and insist that for nine years she'd never been honoured that way, so why should her unborn babies?

She sensed Dr. Andrews's gaze on her and forced herself to exhale and drop her shoulders.

"Did something I say trigger you, Samantha?"

"I didn't experience that when I was young, so it doesn't have any significance for me."

"I'm sorry that wasn't part of your story. Should I go on with other possibilities?"

"I'd like to find one that really reflects who Phil and I are. At least, I hope we can find something that connects with both of us."

"A memorial service is another idea. One friend of mine miscarried four times. She named each baby and created a beautiful headstone that she set up beside a favourite tree in their yard. Close friends came, and they sang a few songs and said a prayer or two."

Samantha sat back on her bench, absorbing all these different ideas. What would she do to memorialize her boys? She thought about all the little boy things she'd imagined they'd do with Phil—bike riding, playing ball, rock climbing in the mountains. She'd decorated the nursery with blue stripes and a wallpaper border with teddy bears wearing baseball uniforms.

Maybe they could create a sports scholarship at Phil's company for underprivileged boys. That thought made her smile. She wanted her losses to count towards something good in this world. She didn't just want to long to be reunited with them in heaven.

"Samantha, can you share your thoughts?" Dr. Andrews asked.

"Phil and I both enjoy baseball. Cami played T-ball last year, but morning sickness prevented it this year." A pang stabbed Samantha's heart.

"Go on."

As Samantha pulled multiple tissues from her coat pocket and wiped her eyes, she wondered if her tears would ever stop.

"I always imagined that we'd go to the park on Sunday afternoons and play catch, all four of us. Phil had already bought a nerf bat and ball for Cami as an early Christmas gift. How I wish we would have gotten that chance. Maybe a sports grant for underprivileged kids in their names?"

Dr. Andrews caught her eye as she lifted her head. "Me too, Samantha. Sounds like a good idea, and one that fits your family."

"I hope so."

"Did you ever name the baby you just lost?"

"Phil's walls were up from the moment I conceived. His dad's name was Matthew, and I wanted one of our children to bear that name. Phil didn't warm up to the idea."

"Have you thought about recording their names or placing their ashes somewhere you could visit?"

"I just had the same idea while you were talking. And I've thought about stitching their names on our baseball gloves. The ashes of both are in the nursery closet right now. We avoided the discussion about what to do with them."

"Well, it needs to be discussed. It's important to hear what you and your husband each need in order to heal. How do you think Phil's dealing with his grief?"

"Not well."

"Why do you say that?"

"If he's home, he focuses on stuff around the house, like the lawn or the vehicles. I don't think he feels the loss the same way I do."

"What do you mean?"

"He never talks to me about it. And if I bring it up, he says I should focus my energy on the child that's in front of me."

"What do you think?"

"Talking is how I process things. I tried to ignore what I was feeling, and it just got worse. A never-ending cycle that tightened its noose around my heart until all feeling disappeared. Being shut down by Phil, I..."

She shook her head.

"Okay," said Dr. Andrews. "Now that you've realized this, what new goal should you make to have a healthy outlet for your thoughts and feelings rather than burying them?"

At the sound of footsteps, Samantha turned her head and took the water bottle handed to her from the orderly. She smiled her thanks, grateful for a little more time to think about Dr. Andrew's question as she sipped the contents.

Samantha was quiet for a while, then declared, "Even if it's uncomfortable, I need to share what I'm thinking and feeling. Without in-depth communication, our marriage suffocates from the pain we feel."

"Great work today, Samantha. Today was significant. You used the anniversary of Micah's death to move towards healing. And you also took a step to consider involving Phil and Cami in that healing."

"Thank you, Dr. Andrews."

Samantha stood up from the bench and began walking back along the path towards the building. Would Phil notice the difference during their call this evening? Or would the call set them back?

Twenty-Five

Evidence that Convicts

Phil looked up as Gabe entered his office with several folders in hand. Lines had hardened around Gabe's eyes; his lips pressed together.

"You are not bringing me good news, methinks." Phil sighed and then buzzed Erin, asking her to hold all calls, including any from Bob.

"It's worse than I thought." Gabe spread out the sheaf of papers in front of Phil. "Take a look at the client bills and compare them to the receivables. As near as I can tell, he's charging fifteen percent more and depositing the extra… somewhere else. He's doctored the cheques to suppliers and underpays them just enough so they continue sending supplies. Your credit rating is dropping. Could be he had a duplicate line of cheques made."

Phil looked at the papers and then compared them to the ones Bob had given him earlier.

"According to your calculations, we owe almost $150,000 to suppliers," Phil said, "and we're overcharging our clients by almost another $100,000, but none of that money is going to the company. I won't have money to make payroll in two months, maybe even less."

"That's correct. I'd like to get the police involved."

"How long has this been going on?"

"It started about a year and a half ago." Gabe cleared his throat. "I think you need to call the police today and show them this information immediately. Talk to your bank manager as well and sign a waiver of access for the police to track what's going on in your accounts. The police need time to access Bob's financial records in order to see where this money is going. Where's Bob at the moment?"

"I don't know."

"Make the call. I'll stay in the outer office and talk to Erin about the marketing campaign. If Bob comes in, I'll head him off."

Once Gabe left, Phil found himself staring at the spreadsheets. He was one month from disaster, including bankruptcy.

He picked up his cell phone and called Noah. When he was unavailable, Phil left a voice message and waited for the receptionist to come back on the line to book the earliest possible appointment.

Next he called Mary Ann and asked if she could pick up Cami from school.

Then, needing prayer cover, he left Pastor Brad a message: "I covet your prayers for the business right now. Please pray. It's bad."

Gathering the papers Gabe had brought to him, Phil placed them in an envelope. He called the bank manager and made a phone appointment for 3:00 p.m.

Next on the docket was talking to a lawyer. Phil called his corporate lawyer, a man with whom he'd had very little involvement since incorporating, and set a meeting.

Briefcase in hand, he headed out to his car, where he met Bob in the parking lot.

"Ask Erin about the marketing campaign," Phil said. "I'll see you tomorrow."

"Anything wrong, Phil?"

"Nothing I can't handle. Gotta go. My meeting starts in fifteen minutes."

Not only was he frustrated with himself for missing the discrepancy in his books, but he hadn't listened to Samantha in the first place. He should have exercised greater caution before making Bob an acting partner and giving him access to the bank accounts. Any misstep now could completely sink his fledgling, once profitable business.

His phone rang just as he was backing out of his parking spot. It was Noah.

"Hey Noah," Phil said. "Looks like you finally get to put your commerce degree to work. We need to figure out the mess Bob's made to our cashflow."

"Well, you're in luck. They didn't make me deputy chief just for my good looks. How can I help?"

"I'd like to show you what my new employee discovered. He's a whiz like you."

"If you come now, I can fit you in."

About a half-hour later, Phil was pushing open the door of the station. Noah met him and offered a firm handshake. The warm welcome bolstered him. He was doing the right thing.

Noah led him to a conference room where two white collar crime investigators were already waiting. Phil laid out the spreadsheets on the table and gave them the gist of what Gabe had uncovered.

"Phil, do you have a financial contingency plan to stay operational?" Noah asked. "These sorts of investigations can be slow."

Phil shook his head. "I'm maxed out, to be honest."

"Okay. We'll work hard at this for two weeks. I'll see if I can swing some resources to keep tabs on Bob in case he runs."

Phil felt a wave of relief wash over him. "When can we confront him?"

"If the judge comes through on the warrant in the next two days, it's possible to bring him in for questioning by the end of October."

Phil wondered whether his creditors would give him a bit of grace. "And is there anything I could do to alert my creditors about the situation?"

"I need you to just sit tight for the next two weeks. Don't say anything. Don't do anything. After we pull Bob's financial records, we'll have a better idea of what's going on. We'll need to meet with each supplier and verify their accounts payable."

Maybe Noah was right. Even though he wanted to get this taken care of sooner rather than later, waiting was probably the better idea.

While waiting to meet with the lawyer, Phil checked in with Mary Ann and thanked her for picking up Cami.

"Is it too much trouble for you to also get her to her art therapy appointment? I should be able to pick her up afterwards."

After Mary Ann reassured him, he relaxed. He had just started mulling supper plans and come to a point of decision when the lawyer opened the door to her office.

Phil tried to make sense of the legalese in the contract between him and Bob, wishing he had brought along a dictionary. The big question was whether he could sue Bob in civil court if the criminal case went awry.

With his lawyer holding a second set of spreadsheets illustrating what was going on, Phil felt a little more confident. He could hold disaster at bay a little longer.

From the lawyer's office, he alerted his bank manager about the situation and let him in on the police investigation. The banker suggested putting longer holds on outgoing and incoming cheques to slow down the amount of money disappearing from the account. It turned out Noah had already contacted him before Phil called.

As Phil drove to art therapy, he called Pastor Brad.

"Turns out your instincts were spot-on. It's going to be a rough go, but now it's in the hands of the police," he said after offering a brief explanation of what was going on.

"Sorry to hear that. Let me know if I can help. I still have some clout from my corporate days."

"Thanks for the offer. The bank seems willing to cooperate, so hopefully the police collect enough evidence to end this."

As he walked to the front door of the building, he breathed a prayer of gratitude that despite the dire circumstances God was walking before him into each situation.

He'd barely sat down in the waiting room when the door opened and Cami came running towards him with clay figures in her hands. She set them down on the coffee table in the reception area.

"Hi Daddy! Look what I made. It's you and me and Mommy."

The clay figures looked like game pieces. It was unlike any game he'd ever played. He didn't know the rules or how to win.

"Oh Sam, am I ever glad to see you tonight," he said from his home office later that evening. "It's been a day. Let me tell you."

"Me too. I wasn't sure I felt like getting up. I've been working through some stuff regarding this day."

Phil felt puzzled. Were they talking about the same thing? He checked his desk calendar.

Oh... oh no.

How could he have forgotten?

"Um, you won't believe this, but Cami made little sculptures of us today. They look like board game pieces. You know, the ones from our favourite game? She loved sending us back to start over and over, didn't she?" He paused. "I think we were playing that game the day before you went to the hospital…"

"Weird. I didn't think she was old enough to have memories about that day."

"Well, can you think of the last time we both played a board game with her?"

"No, not really. Did we stop playing games for a time?"

"I know I did. When we lost Micah, I started avoiding home after work."

"She might not have a specific memory, but that period sure affected her connection with us," Samantha said. "Do you think we're doing enough to help her?"

"She asked if we could play more games together today."

"Maybe you should bring those sculptures with you next family visit day."

Phil felt like he'd dodged a bullet. He'd gotten away with not having remembered this all-important anniversary. Could he risk now sharing what his own day had been like?

"I met with Noah today," he said after a few moments of silence.

"Oh? Anything to do with the cashflow issue?"

"Yeah, as a matter of fact. Gabe thinks he's figured out how Bob has been working the accounts."

"So now what?"

"Noah is working on it." Phil blew air through his teeth. "Hopefully he finds enough evidence to make an arrest."

"I can't believe that happened today, of all days. On the anniversary…"

"Yeah. But it kind of took my mind off it."

"As in, you forgot about the anniversary completely until I brought it up."

Her tone zinged straight to his heart. He had no defence.

So I didn't get away with it, after all.

"Just because I don't remember every date and every hour doesn't mean I don't care," he said, his anger rising. "It doesn't mean I've forgotten either. My day starts and ends with Cami. I can't afford to mope around every time I look at the calendar and see every loss I've ever experienced."

"You think I'm just moping around? You think that's what my depression is?"

Phil slammed his hand against the desk. "This isn't why I called. I wanted to share my frustrations, too. It's too much for me to take in. You're a partner in the business. I need you and all that you bring to make things better. After I lost my dad, you were the person who brought joy back into my life. I don't know where that person is..."

He slumped down on the desk and put his head in his hands. After a few moments, though, he finally raised his head to look at Samantha's face and saw tears streaming down her face.

"Aww, Samantha, I'm sorry I lost my temper. I've got nothing left in the tank. Please forgive me."

"I'm sorry you're going through all this on top of my absence. Maybe we should take our tired selves to bed and leave this topic for another day. Good night."

The screen went dark.

The weariness in Samantha's voice convicted Phil. Great! Now he'd wonder if this would bring on a setback. Why couldn't he have remembered this day's significance?

Then again, now it was all he could think of. And it didn't just involve the loss of Micah. For Phil, the most devastating memory had been hearing the doctor's ominous pronouncement: *"We're doing everything we can, but your wife may not survive."*

Twenty-Six

It's Friday, but Sunday's Coming

Phil leaned back in his home office chair. Although his bed called, sleep eluded him. He might as well work.

Maybe Samantha's still up. Maybe she can help me switch off the workaholic mode I've sunk into these past two weeks.

With little energy left, he dialled Samantha's number. Her face popped on the screen.

"You look awful, Phil."

"Everything's falling apart at work."

"Oh?"

"Yeah. Suppliers have been phoning the office. I feel like I'm lying all day long. And Noah asked for more information about the company that was making Glock frames."

She seemed puzzled by this. "Phil, what do you mean? Glock frames?"

"You mean I haven't told you? Bob signed a contract with a company that makes lookalike Glock frames."

"How did that happen on your watch?"

"It was the week our hopes went up in flames, you know."

"Have you had any sessions with your counsellor yet?"

Phil hung his head. The thought of opening up to someone made him feel physically sick. It would mean revisiting something he never wanted to talk about again. Not ever.

"What about talking to Pastor Brad?" Samantha's soft tone dispatched his excuses before they could even leave his mouth.

"No... I've been so focused on saving our income that I haven't been able to sleep. Sorry to say, Cami and I have subsisted on restaurant fare, meaning pizza and chicken nuggets. My stomach's in knots."

Not to mention, I feel like an unanchored hot air balloon, lost in the clouds.

"Look at me, Phil. I'm sad that you haven't taken time for yourself, but I know you're trying to do the best you can. You didn't ask for Bob to undercut the company. You didn't ask to deal with the shock of a suicidal wife. But I want you to remember this: you are a brilliant businessman. Focus on your strengths and let Noah handle everything else."

The warmth of her encouragement softened the blow of disappointment he'd read in her eyes. How he missed her at work! She had a way of sorting through the noise to help him find the right direction. But would she ever be whole enough to come back?

"I found this quote by Francis Chan," she said. "'Our greatest fear should not be of failure, but of succeeding at things in life that don't really matter.' Isn't that great? I know I've focused on my failures, but now I want to focus on you and Cami."

"I think I need to write that quote down. That's an excellent motto. Maybe it will help me sleep tonight."

As she repeated it, he scratched the words down in his journal.

"Look, Sam... I feel like I'm in a circus, only I'm the ringmaster, the circus clowns, the trapeze artist, and the lion tamer all at once. I'm juggling more roles than ever."

Phil rolled his shoulders, took a deep breath, and then broke the code of silence he'd been keeping ever since her suicide attempt.

"I've just met with the banker," he said. "He knows what's going on, but I'm scared I won't have favour there anymore after this. Will he trust my judgment in the same way he used to?"

She didn't say anything but nodded for him to continue.

"I've also met with the lawyer. I'm being as helpful as I can, but I can't help but wonder whether she suspects I'm in on this scheme with Bob."

Samantha snorted. "As if you would ever hurt the company. Or use a Glock, for that matter. Tell this lawyer to talk to me if it seems like she's going down that rabbit trail. I'll set her straight."

Phil smiled at her feisty response. She could never resist stepping in if she felt there was a sliver of injustice.

"Thanks, honey. That means the world."

He watched her shoulders straighten at his encouragement. It felt good to know that his words could bring strength.

"How is your client recruitment going?"

"Gabe's been recruiting."

"And how are you fitting in all these meetings?"

"Well, I have taken them in the car."

"Wait. Does that mean you're having meetings when Cami's with you in the vehicle?"

"Are you kidding? That would be impossible. She's like you. She requires my undivided attention."

Phil enjoyed seeing Samantha smirk.

"By doing all this, you're teaching her what's important," she said. "Phil, seriously, you're taking on too much. Just promise you won't cancel our next visit. You need a break from work—and soon."

"Yes, I plan on making it. And we all need a break. Cami broke down the other day at bedtime. She told me, 'I like Mommy's voice, but I need her arms, too.'" Phil brushed away his own tears. It mirrored Samantha's reaction. "She and I are really looking forward to seeing you."

"Hearing her pain is hard, Phil. I think I'm making progress, but sometimes I don't think it's fast enough for her and..."

"Hey, it's only a few more days until we see each other. Buck up, little soldier, and chortle."

"I haven't heard you say that since university days. Well, it fits for both of us. So right back at you."

"Guess we'd better hit the hay."

Phil kept his smile pasted on until Samantha hung up. He rubbed his cheeks and wished his jaw didn't ache. What if he couldn't buck up and chortle? Would she be there for him if he couldn't turn the business around?

He got up and paced around his home office. What if he said the wrong thing or got mad at the wrong time? Would Gabe or Erin end up losing their jobs because he couldn't make payroll? Would he have to go back to work in the warehouse if they cut technicians?

After triple-checking locks and lights in his house, he pulled out his Bible and flipped through the first few books until he landed on Psalm 18. He read the passage aloud in order to drown out the doubts and guilt shouting at him. Maybe he could practice what Pastor Brad had preached this past Sunday: how to use Scripture as the basis for one's prayers.

> I love you, God—you make me strong. God is bedrock under my feet, the castle in which I live, my rescuing knight. My God—the high crag where I run for dear life, hiding behind the boulders, safe in the granite hideout.
>
> I sing to God, the Praise-Lofty, and find myself safe and saved.
>
> The hangman's noose was tight at my throat; devil waters rushed over me. Hell's ropes cinched me tight; death traps barred every exit.
>
> A hostile world! I call to God, I cry to God to help me. From his palace he hears my call; my cry brings me right into his presence—a private audience! (Psalm 18:1–6)

Phil got up and started walking around his bedroom, repeating the tenets of the verses he had just read.

"God, thank You. You've made me strong. You're the bedrock that steadies my feet. The two of us were on the precipice. You're bringing each of us into the safe fortress of your love as we process and grieve for our beautiful boys." His voice broke as tears trickled down his face. "Thank You for nudging me to go home early on that horrible day. Glenda is getting stronger all the time. Thank You that Cami didn't witness everything."

Phil sat down on the bed.

"Thank You for sending Gabe as a support while Samantha heals and awaits her trial. God, You saw that I was drowning in the flood of hurry and avoidance of pain. It was strangling our marriage, my family, and my business. Oh God, forgive my arrogance for thinking I could just use my strength to make it through. Forgive me for thinking I didn't need You, that somehow my daily life was mine to take charge of instead of relying on You. God, I thought therapy was for the weak." He stood up again, his volume rising. "Fill me with humility and the ability to be honest instead of hiding my devastation." He shook his fists up in the air. "I wanted to be a dad to those boys... why couldn't I have that chance?"

He fell on his knees, buried his face into the mattress, and sobbed like a child. The dam had broken.

As his tears lessened, he felt a blanket of peace steal over him. Maybe now he could sleep.

Phil got up, washed his face, and settled into bed. He awoke to Cami shaking him.

"Daddy, Daddy, it's time to get up."

He peered at his clock, which read 7:15. Then he looked at Cami.

"You're already dressed for school!" he exclaimed. "I better get cracking. Can you go down and pick a cereal or yogurt cup for breakfast?"

"Okay, Daddy." Cami pattered out of his room and down the stairs, singing softly to herself.

After a two-minute shower, Phil towelled off and dressed for work in record time. The blanket of peace felt like a comfortable old sweater draped around his shoulders. He strode into work carrying a coffee and breakfast wrap.

"Good morning, Erin!"

"Good morning. You sound chipper today."

Phil smiled. "I am. Any updates or emails I need to get on top of right away?"

"One of your suppliers would like to meet this morning. Bob then wants to see you at 9:30, and Gabe's already in your office."

"Thanks."

Phil entered his office. Gabe stood up to greet him.

"Here's the social media ad campaign we've been working on," Gabe began. "These ads will be featured by a bunch of accounts, including some 3D printer manufacturers. Isn't that fantastic?"

The best part was that campaign wasn't going to be costly. Getting the word out about Tailor-Made would be like free advertising for these manufacturers.

Before leaving the office, Gabe paused at the doorway. "About that other matter... anything happen between yesterday and today that I should know about?"

"God."

Gabe smiled.

Only a few minutes later, Bob was standing in that same doorway.

"Good morning, Bob. I just need a minute..." Phil typed like a madman, then hit send on the email he was composing and turned his full attention to Bob. "How's everything going in the warehouse? Anything out of the ordinary? You look a little stressed."

"Rough night, I guess. My girlfriend was furious because I stayed at work late instead of going to the bar with her. She blew up at me."

"Not fun."

The rumpled state of his clothing and his uncombed hair underlined Bob's agitation. "Everything's under control at the warehouse, but I have a question about the bank. Didn't you get the hold policy waived for deposits? I think they're putting holds on the account again. Would you mind looking into that?"

"I have a meeting with the bank manager on Monday morning. Is that soon enough?"

"I guess it will have to be. Also, there's an upcoming symposium in Toronto on all the latest developments in 3D printing. Are you and I going, or will you send me with Gabe instead?"

"What are the dates again? I remember thinking it would be great to attend, but my circumstances have changed."

"It starts on November 12 and ends on the sixteenth."

"Check with Gabe. He may want to broaden his understanding of the industry. The networking might be helpful."

Bob nodded. "Okay, I'll talk to him. But what would you think about me bringing my girlfriend? It would go a long way as an apology for last night."

"If you foot the bill, sure."

Phil couldn't believe how relaxed he was with Bob. He could see the opportunity for everything to go wrong. This could give Bob a chance to flee the situation, and even disappear, if he suspected anything. And yet Phil felt no need to control the situation.

Thirty minutes later, Phil gave Erin a sheaf of notes to type up into a new formal agreement—and this time he took care to eliminate Bob's access to the payments and invoices.

"Erin, I'm going to take the afternoon to be with Cami, since yesterday's plans got squashed."

"I'll mark you as unavailable."

As Phil packed up his laptop, his cell phone rang. He looked at the call display. Noah.

"Hello, my friend," Phil said. "I just talked to Bob, and he seems really stressed about something. I'd like to meet next week. How's Tuesday?"

"Tuesday works, but only in the morning."

Phil hung up the phone and marvelled at the speed of the investigation into Bob's mishandling of funds.

God, You were waiting for me to quit trying to do things on my own terms, he silently prayed.

Still, there had been that odd request about Bob wanting to take his girl-friend to Toronto. Maybe he should have asked Noah about that.

But regardless of Bob's plans, Phil's next step was to simply keep putting one foot in front of the other. And that meant taking Cami to the bowling alley this afternoon. She needed to learn the tradition that had first brought he and Samantha together.

Twenty-Seven

Family Day

Samantha paced in the common area. Twenty more minutes and she'd get to see her family.

She peered out the door to see if they'd gotten to the parking lot yet. Phil was usually early, so she hoped today was one of those days.

Spying an SUV turning in the lot, she turned to the orderly. "They're here. May I go out to the parking lot to greet them?"

As soon as the orderly nodded, Samantha zipped up her coat and met Phil and Cami as they were getting out of the car. Cami leapt into Samantha's arms and wrapped herself around Samantha's neck. Phil kissed her softly, then gently held them both in a hug.

They all stood there for a moment, revelling in the joy of simply being together.

Samantha looked from Phil to Cami. "Ready to head to the riding arena?"

"What's an arena?" Cami asked.

"It's a place where you can ride horses."

"Daddy, you didn't tell me we were going to ride horsies! I don't have any cowboy boots."

"Guess again!" Phil opened the back of the SUV and pulled out a pair of pink cowboy boots. He helped her balance as she wiggled out of her runners and tugged on the boots.

"All set, Mommy!"

Samantha and Phil exchanged smiles over their exuberant daughter and headed to the arena where Janet met them. Together they headed for the corral.

"The wind's a little brisk today, so we'll do everything in the barn or arena," Janet said. "Phil, today you're going to do a trust walk. Samantha tells me you have been around horses in the past."

"Yes, my parents had horses. I grew up riding."

"That's great. Cami, have you been around a horse at your grandma and grandpa's place?"

"It's just Grandma. I don't gots a grandpa at the farm, just Grandpa Tom, but he lives in the city with Mrs. Henderson. I only gots to pet their noses over the fence when Grandma and I bring them treats."

"What treats, Cami?"

"Um, carrots and apples."

"I have a special job for you at the end of our session then." Janet looked at Samantha, who nodded her agreement.

Phil cocked his head and looked at Samantha with a question in his eyes. She dismissed his worry by giving him a thumbs up.

"It's all good, Phil," said Janet. "We won't let anything go awry. Today's group lesson is going to be on trust. Phil, let's get you blindfolded. Samantha's going to guide you through an obstacle course while you lead Duke. Do you remember how to hold a lead rope?"

"Hold it below the snap ring with your right hand and gather the rest with your left, like a figure-eight."

"That's correct. Can you let Cami know why we don't wrap it around our left hand?"

"Cami, we don't wrap it around our hand to keep us safe in case Duke gets scared by a piece of paper or a loud noise," Phil said. "He might want to run away. If I wrap it around my hand, I might get pulled around."

He shivered. This was bringing back the terrible memories of that last day in the corral with his dad.

"That was a great explanation," Janet said. "Samantha, are you ready to blindfold your husband?"

"Here goes." She tied it into place and tugged to make sure it was secure. "No peeking, Phil. Can you see anything?"

When Phil shook his head, Janet placed the lead in his right and the extra length in his left hand.

"Now I'm going to set up the pylons to weave around," Janet said. "You'll walk between some poles without knocking them off. A platform to cross, up and over. Also, you'll pick your way through a series of poles on the ground."

Samantha watched Janet rearrange the obstacles in a different order than had first been visible when they entered the ring.

Samantha nodded her readiness and took a deep breath. "Phil, complete a quarter turn to the right and lead Duke in a forward motion. Take five or six steps. Now stop, do a quarter turn to the left. Now go forward again..."

—◦—

Phil nudged Duke with his shoulder to get him moving, then turned his body a quarter turn and started walking forward. "That's a boy, Duke."

"Okay. Stop and turn a quarter, then turn to the left."

When Duke planted his feet, Phil tugged the halter closer to his body in order to manoeuvre the horse. "Am I in the right spot, Samantha?"

"You're going to be stepping over some poles now. Edge closer... now take a step over the first pole. Keep going. There are two more poles to step over."

"Come on, boy, that's it," coaxed Phil. He then waited for the next set of instructions.

"Okay now, just keep walking forward until I tell you to turn one hundred eighty degrees."

Phil and Duke walked slowly. He felt a little unsure and reached out to stroke Duke's neck.

"Now stop and turn a quarter turn to your left," Samantha shouted. "Then another quarter turn to your left."

He executed those turns, walked forward, then sprawled flat on the ground when his foot hooked the first pylon.

"Oops, sorry. I should have told you to wait before letting you go forward."

"Are you okay, Daddy?" Cami asked anxiously.

"Just fine, honey." Phil brushed off his pants and gathered up the lead. "Okay, I'm ready."

"You found the first pylon. Go around it and move to your left. Walk forward. Now go to your right and move forward. Um, next move to your left and go forward."

Phil proceeded with more caution than before, but he successfully carried out Samantha's directions through the pylon-weaving exercise. She directed him to go forward before turning one hundred eighty degrees to the right. She then warned him that he'd have to coax Duke over and onto a plywood step.

"Let's go, Daddy, let's go! Let's go, Daddy, let's go!"

Phil felt the edge of the step, then skirted to the right of it in order to centre Duke and coax him over the obstacle. The sound of Duke's hooves on the plywood echoed in the arena, making it hard to hear Samantha's next instructions.

"What was that? I couldn't hear over Duke's clopping around."

"Nice work, Phil. We're on our last obstacle," explained Samantha. "You've almost made it through the course. Go us!"

Hearing her encouragement produced unexpected emotions in Phil. Had it been that long since Samantha had encouraged or complimented him? Or had he been so caught up in his own world and loss that he'd missed opportunities to spend time with her? Phil swallowed hard and waited for Samantha's last instructions.

"Phil, there's a set of poles about four feet wide. You and Duke have to walk through them. The poles are at chest height, so hold the lead in your right hand so your left can feel for the pole."

Letting the lead rope out until he was only holding the end, Phil took small steps, allowing Duke to follow. He hoped to prevent Duke from shying away from the obstacle, so he walked ahead in order to discover where the poles were.

"Move to your left, Phil, or you'll miss the obstacle completely."

"Okay, Sam."

Phil found the end of the pole and sidestepped until he found the other pole on the right. He turned and stood in the middle of the two poles, tugging on the lead rope until Duke was in front of him. Then he pivoted and took Duke and himself through the parallel poles.

"You did it, Daddy! Way to go! Is it my turn now?"

Janet and Samantha exchanged smiles. "Not yet. Daddy still has some work to do."

"Okay, Phil, you may take off your blindfold," said Janet. "Your blindfold is damp. Were you sweating or struggling with some emotions? Can you share them with us?"

"Samantha's compliment. It brought up a loss I wasn't aware of until today."

"Are you ready to describe this loss yet?"

Phil wasn't sure about having Cami hear his confession, so he made a motion in his daughter's direction. Janet drew her over to the side and gave her some pictures to colour in the barn.

Once they'd gone, he drew closer to his wife.

"Samantha, I really miss your encouraging words about how I'm doing as a father and business owner and husband. Tailor-Made wouldn't be the company it is today without your input. But after we lost Micah, we drifted. How could you encourage me? I avoided our home. You wrote... in that letter, you said you were a burden. Since we stopped sharing our struggles, my own burdens have been much heavier. I forgot to include you. I also forgot the way you could find the positive in almost any frustrating situation. Samantha, I was wrong to neglect you and leave you alone in your grief. You were right about Bob. Forgive me for ignoring your wisdom and insight."

———◦◦◦———

The sound of Duke's breathing echoed in the arena, overpowering the thundering in Samantha's ears. The horse swung his giant head over Phil's shoulder as if to say, *What are you going to do about Phil's words?*

As Duke stared her down, dared her to receive the heartfelt words, Samantha just stood immobilized. At first, she opened her mouth to speak and then closed it, terrified to discover what might come out. How could a simple encouragement have impacted him so much?

Phil's longing for words of affirmation stunned her. He thought she had been right about not trusting Bob? It had only been a gut instinct.

Mind whirling and realizing she needed to acknowledge Phil's apology, she took a few steps until she stood in front of Phil.

"I forgive you, Phil. There was nothing I could give you. I was so caught up in what we'd lost that I forgot about what I had—you and Cami. Forgive me for blaming you for everything and for not being there for our family. I used it as an excuse to believe you didn't need me in our relationship anymore."

"Samantha, we lost our boys. An enormous loss. And then I almost lost you. We should have gone for help together. I think the reason you felt like quitting was my own avoidance. It made you feel less confident, less secure in what I thought of you." He reached for Samantha. "You weren't secure enough in my love to be confident to keep pushing for what you needed from me. The business has been losing money these past eighteen months, and now we're on the verge of bankruptcy. You talk about a relationship based on performance. All I could think about was that I could no longer support you and Cami, that I had failed you as a husband and Cami as a father."

"What... how...? You spent so much time at work. And the number of clients... how could bankruptcy even be possible?"

"I wasn't productive at all. Like you, I felt like I was stuck in neutral. I took the loss of Micah pretty hard. Even more so when you were sick and the doctor said you might not survive the infection. I distanced myself because it scared me. I didn't know how to deal with your depression, so I avoided it. And I avoided my own grief by escaping to the office and pretending to work."

"You called him by name," Samantha whispered, tears rolling down her face. "I didn't know you felt anything at all for losing Micah. You didn't talk about him at home."

"I talked to Pastor Brad about it once. I know we should have made time to talk about him. Seeing the closed nursery door next to our bedroom has always been painful. And when we lost our second, I thought I was being punished by God for not being home more."

"Wait, you thought you were being punished by God?"

"Yes."

With a deep breath, Samantha opened the last secret door of her heart.

Twenty-Eight

A Secret Revealed

Phil longed to erase the lines on his wife's forehead. It foretold the coming of a headache. He waited, wondering how much soul-searching either could take before collapsing in exhaustion.

"I thought I was being punished by God for what happened in college," she said.

He reached out to take her hand. "What happened in college, Samantha?"

"I... I had.... an abortion."

His hand dropped from hers like a hot potato. Feeling gut-punched, stomach acid burned the back of his throat like wildfire. Pictures of Micah's ultrasound flipped through his mind, and he found himself imagining a perfectly formed miniature baby at five months.

"Was it around the middle of our third year?" Phil asked, still sifting through memories of their college days. "After we crossed the line that one time, just before I headed out for my cross-cultural business internship?"

"Yes, the new year's kiss that didn't end at midnight."

Samantha's quiet answer shook him. Another child lost. He'd attributed her dark cloud to his going away for six months. Between the pace of summer jobs and her own upcoming student teaching practicum, was it any wonder he had missed the deeper issue plaguing her?

A smouldering ember of anger darkened Phil's face. This was not the first trial his wife should face. He felt the familiar red heat creep up his neck. He rubbed his rigid neck muscles to soothe himself, to hold back the fury.

"When we got pregnant with Cami, I thought I could forget our firstborn, but I couldn't," she added. "Then I knew I was being punished by God, because we lost Micah later. I should have told you. I'm sorry."

Phil's urge to yell, curse, and slam something—or even someone—terrified him. Tossed about by anger, he clamped his jaw.

"Samantha, I don't want to say the wrong thing. Could you get Janet back here, please?" His terse words clipped her fragile wings.

She went over to the others, then remained with Cami while Janet approached him alone.

"Phil, what's going on? How can I help?" Her voice rang out like a clear bell, piercing his tornadic thoughts and disrupting the downward spiral.

Unsure whether Janet knew the truth, he wanted to protect Samantha's confidence for the moment, and his own.

"I just found out something that infuriates me. I need to process it, but not here. Somewhere else. And I certainly don't want to drive home feeling this way. Can you help me figure out a safe way to release this anger?"

"Want to go for an actual ride on Duke? You could head out on one of our marked trails. You'll just need to wear one of our riding helmets as a safety precaution."

He had stopped riding when his dad passed away. Losing his riding companion and the man with whom he'd talked through all his problems had also meant he quit talking. They'd sold Dad's horse to cover the funeral costs, although a friend had agreed to board Phil's horse until they were ready to bring him back.

His mom still found herself short of cash, though, and used that money set aside for his postsecondary education. Selling Buck had enabled him to pay for his first semester of tuition at university.

And that was the end of riding for Phil.

Well, it was more than that, but he couldn't go to that place right now. He had no dad to turn to, no friend to stand with, and now a second betrayal by the woman he loved.

The agony over this new loss levelled the walls he'd built.

"Yes." It was all Phil could muster amid the thoughts pummelling him.

This explained Samantha's mercurial mood swings and the distance he'd struggled to bridge.

Ten minutes later, Phil had Duke fully saddled. Leading the horse by the reins, Phil followed Janet as she headed to the back of the arena and opened the gate and then pushed open the tall doors.

"If you head that direction," Janet pointed east with her right hand, "you'll find the marked trail. It heads towards a clearing and a small slough before looping back towards the arena."

Phil swung his leg over the saddle and settled into the seat. He urged Duke into a pace faster than a walk. Duke's trot soon shifted into a canter and he disappeared into the clearing.

———⚫—

"Where's Daddy going, Mommy?" Cami's worried eyes peered up at Samantha.

"He's going for a ride."

"I thought I was going to get to ride today."

"When Daddy comes back, maybe you can ride in front of him on the saddle."

Janet nodded when Samantha turned to look at her to confirm that possibility.

"Cami, which horse would you like to meet?" Samantha asked.

Cami pointed to Daisy, who was contentedly munching some oats in the arena's corner. Janet grabbed a riding helmet from the wall of the arena and then let Cami pull her towards Daisy. She helped Cami fasten the chin strap on the helmet and adjusted it to fit securely. She then loosened the lead rope from the post and placed the gathered part in Cami's left hand. The lead rope went into the girl's right hand.

"Now it's your turn to go through the obstacle course, but you don't need a blindfold or your mom's instructions. Daisy loves kids."

Cami clucked to Daisy as though she had been around horses all her life and led her confidently over the three poles on the ground. She chattered to Daisy while leading her to the correct place to start the pylon-weaving. Watching her was exactly the distraction Samantha needed; it was something to focus on other than the fear gnawing at her. Would Phil forgive her?

"Come on, girl," Cami said. "You've got this. Nope, not that way, Daisy. Come over this way. Yikes, Daisy, you're going to knock that one over. Oops."

"Don't worry if you knock one over, Cami," Janet called. "You're doing awesome!"

Cami got Daisy turned around in order to tread over the wooden box on the ground.

"See, you just step onto it like this, Daisy, and then you go off it like this."

She tugged Daisy onto the box and then off it again, straight into the parallel poles. She led her through like a pro.

Samantha couldn't have been prouder and wondered where this confidence came from.

Cami patted Daisy's neck and stroked it, murmuring into Daisy's ear.

"You did a great job going through the course," Janet said to her. "Should we give Daisy a treat to thank her for working with you?"

"Oh, yes! I love giving treats to horses."

Samantha walked over to Star and inscribed each of her fears about Phil's response to her most painful secret. She wept into Star's mane, grieving her abortion, grieving for her child and the potential she'd ended, the relationship she might have had.

Star grew antsy and Samantha released the clip of her lead rope, letting her go. She watched Star gallop away and roll in the soft dirt of the arena, then get up and shake herself off and do a few more laps. She wished she could shake off what she'd done as easily.

Then came a quiet whisper.

"You can." It was her grandmother's voice, singing as she tidied the kitchen. *"What a friend we have in Jesus, all our sins and griefs to bear. What a privilege to carry everything to God in prayer! O what peace we often forfeit, O what needless pain we bear, all because we do not carry everything to God in prayer!"*[2]

When Star came back to Samantha, she whispered, "Oh God, I can't carry this load anymore. Please forgive me for harming my child and for keeping it from Phil. I choose to leave whatever happens next in Your hands. Please heal our family and help us find home again."

Janet came up beside her. "You might as well groom Star and reflect on your day."

Soon Cami drifted towards them, too, and Samantha welcomed the warmth of her tiny body pressed against hers.

But the love she longed for was Phil's. She looked out towards the trail Phil had taken and hoped he'd come back to her.

---

[2] Joseph Medlicott Scriven, "What a Friend We Have in Jesus," 1855.

———◦○◦———

Phil slid off Duke, drew the reins over his head, and led him to a fallen log in the clearing. He took a seat, surrounded by dry grass and barren trees bereft of their leafy glory.

"My heart feels like those trees, God, naked and stripped bare. I don't have words. I want to wrench back time to that moment when I asked more of Samantha than I ever should have. My anger scares me, God. She knew I loved her, didn't she? Why didn't she tell me about the pregnancy? I could have stopped her from making that decision. Why didn't You stop her from taking that life? Another child! Three children, God? She didn't even give me a chance! Why?"

In his agony, he crushed the pile of leaves against the log, pulverizing them with his feet, grinding them into the dusty pasture grass. The wind whistled and branches hissed their condemnation. The cold air penetrated his fall jacket and he flipped up the collar to keep the wind from sliding down his back.

After he swiped angry tears off his face, he tugged Duke a little closer by choking up on the reins.

"God, forgive me for putting Samantha in a place where she even thought our future together would be better off without our child. I went outside the boundaries of Your design. God, I give You my anger towards Samantha and my anger at myself. I don't know how to deal with the hurt."

Although the wind hinted at the season to come, the faint aroma of a campfire swirled with memories of a camping trip they'd taken at Pike Lake. Echoes of Samantha's teasing laughter floated through his memory. They'd debated who had the best toasted marshmallow for s'mores.

It reminded him of the companionship they once had, proof that their love existed despite the secret Samantha had buried in her heart.

What carried us at the time? Did You, God?

Duke nudged him with his nose and Phil reached up to scratch his neck. The horse whiffled Phil's hair with his breath.

"You're a character, aren't you." He smiled despite all the baffling emotions competing for his attention. He looked at his watch. "You're right. It's time to head back."

He needed to work through his anger. He would make it a priority to find time in his schedule to see Pastor Brad twice a month for the next three months.

Phil pulled out Stefan Reid's card and stared at the number. After a minute, he dialled it and immediately booked four sessions, each one to take place while Cami was in art therapy.

His heart, although saddened by Samantha's announcement, now felt as though it could go on beating. He looped the reins around the saddle horn, tucked his left foot into the front stirrup, and mounted Duke. It was time to collect Cami and head home.

He hoped he could communicate the process he'd just gone through with God without adding to Samantha's stress. Although the day had been painful, Samantha had demonstrated that she wanted to change—and it was time to make some of those changes himself.

He settled Duke into an easy lope back towards the outer corral.

When Phil arrived back at the arena, he circled around to the barn, slipped off Duke's back, and pushed open the sliding doors to encounter the sound of merry chatter and contented nickers. The empty stall beckoned, right across from where Samantha and Cami were busily grooming Star.

He cross-tied Duke and started untying the back cinch. Then he deftly unsaddled the horse and set the saddle over on the sawhorse before returning to the left side to remove the bridle. Still unnoticed by Samantha and Cami, he picked up a currycomb and began working his way down the left side of Duke.

———◦◦◦———

"Look, Mommy, Daddy's back!"

Samantha's brush crashed to the stall floor. Keeping a hand on Star, she bent down and picked it up. She then carried on with the last remaining patch of Star's coat.

Cami had slipped in beside Phil to help him groom Duke. Glad of the distraction Cami's chatter provided, Samantha rinsed out the combs and brushes and left them in the pail to dry.

Janet came into the stall with some feed for Star and Samantha took the pail and dumped it into the trough. Afterward she followed Janet out of the stall to get hay for Star.

Once they'd finished watering and feeding Star, Samantha stood on the edge of Duke's stall and waited for Phil to look up and notice her. Her longing was palpable, at least to her.

However, the invite came from Cami instead.

"Mommy, Mommy! Daddy said I could help him, too! I just love horsies. Can I get a horsie? Can we go visit Grandma soon?"

Samantha edged in behind her daughter and wrapped her arms around her.

As she raised her head from kissing the top of her unkempt braids, her eyes met Phil's. Dark sorrow had deepened his hazel eyes to an almost emerald green. Then he winked, a signal that contained a small measure of hope.

He looked back at Cami. "Next, you're going to want an elephant and a hippopotamus, Miss Cami. Let's finish making Duke feel like a king. Then it will be time to eat and drive home."

Phil handed Samantha an extra brush and together they finished taking care of Duke's needs. Although unspoken, it felt to Samantha as if they'd built a bridge. Perhaps they were ready to care for each other's needs together, too.

Twenty-Nine

Wrestling with Grief

Phil sat on the edge of the seat which Stefan offered him. The art on the walls intimidated him. He kneaded his thighs in anticipation of what was to come. Could he begin with art? He wasn't like Cami or Samantha in this way.

Stefan leaned back in his chair. "You look a little nervous, Phil."

"Well, um, do you have to be artistic to do art therapy?"

"No, not at all. No skill necessary."

"That's good."

"When you filled out the questionnaire about your hopes for these sessions, you mentioned a desire to break down the walls between you and your spouse. Is that still accurate today?"

"Yes."

"Based on that, I'm going to invite you to create the wall that you feel surrounds you." He indicated the stack of blocks on the carpet in front of them. "I've also left you some clay so you can make an image of yourself. Then, a little later, I'll have you use post-it notes to list the experiences you think led you to build that wall."

Stefan stepped out, having given Phil ten to fifteen minutes to work with the blocks and clay. He looked around, not sure where to start.

He began by constructing the blocks into a simple fortress. Then he grabbed the clay and fashioned a stick figure. How was this beneficial?

Next, he grabbed the pile of post-it notes.

Well, God, it's you and me. Where do I start?

An image wormed its way into his mind: his dad flying through the air and crumpling onto the corral fence. He scratched the words "dad's accident" on the first post-it. On the next, he added "the surgeon in the doorway."

More images came to him. His mom sitting at the table, entering invoices into the computer, tears streaming down her face. "Financial troubles," "worry," and "fear" all found their way onto paper.

On another note, he sketched a picture of a horse beside a trailer. His stomach churned upon remembering the day Buck had left the yard.

"New Year's Eve," he wrote.

He drew a map of Canada as well as a series of stick figures to show the distance between him and Samantha.

"Her practicum."

"Her weight losses."

"Micah."

"Miscarriage."

"Bob."

"Suicide attempt."

And then the worst of all: "abortion." What an ugly word!

To cut short, to cut off, to terminate. That's what all these notes had in common. They'd cut short his communication with his dad, with Samantha, with Micah, and with the two other little ones.

"So what's your wall telling you?"

Phil jumped. He hadn't heard the door open.

"Sorry, didn't mean to startle you." Stefan looked at the words and pictures Phil had produced.

"Every one of these things cut me off from someone," Phil said, gesturing to the post-it notes. "To protect myself, I built an invisible wall in order to stop communicating, having already lost too many relationships. I thought if I didn't communicate, if I didn't express my emotions, my relationships would be okay."

"What are some ways you built the wall?"

"I hoped that if I provided people with financial stability, it would make them stay with me. My mom kept talking, her words wrapping around me like a hug, bringing comfort despite the pain of my dad's death. I had to make it up to her, since it was my fault she had lost her best friend."

"How old were you when that happened? And why do you think it was your fault?"

"I was sixteen. I should have shortened the lead rope so Dad was further away from the corral fence, but I got scared of the horse's unpredictability."

"Accidents happen. Did your dad die in front of you?"

Phil grimaced. "No. He got up and walked around, breathing kind of shallow. We caught the horse, got it unsaddled, and brought it into the barn before he collapsed. That's when I called Mom and 911."

Stefan rearranged the blocks so that an opening appeared in it. "What about New Year's Eve?"

"Samantha and I conceived a baby that night," Phil said, his eyes landing on that particular post-it. "Our relationship changed after that. By having sex before marriage, I felt like I killed something in her."

"Not everyone would agree that's wrong. Why was it wrong for you?"

"My dad always said that marriage was a covenant, and that sex was a symbol of that covenant. He urged me to respect and cherish the woman I dated by not using physical pleasure to satisfy my own needs. I felt like I let him and Samantha down when I didn't cherish her in that way." He took a deep breath. "I didn't know until recently that Samantha had an abortion, but every time I saw her she had her multicoloured afghan wrapped around her. Samantha's grandmother told her that the blanket was a picture of God's love for her. After everything that happened, I always wondered whether she wore that blanket because she doubted God's love."

Again, Stefan rearranged the blocks, creating another hole. "Who's Micah?"

"Our son." Phil twisted the corner of his shirttail into a tight roll. "He was stillborn. Sam almost died." When the shirttail was unrolled, Phil's hands went limp.

"How long ago?" Stefan's voice held notes of empathy and kindness.

Phil looked up. "A year and two weeks."

The counsellor gestured to another spot in the wall. "Perhaps you'd like to add a window here."

Obediently, Phil removed a couple of blocks.

"What would it feel like for you to build a doorway?" Stefan pressed. "Imagine walking outside your wall and looking at it from the other side."

This suggestion punched through Phil's brain like a sledgehammer. *Could I? Could I go outside?*

"Why did we make these openings in the wall?" Phil asked.

"Let me ask you this: what's the purpose of a window?"

"To let you see what's going on around you. Or to give you a way out." Phil stood and started pacing around the small art studio. He paused at the window and looked out over the bare-limbed shrubs into the courtyard.

"I'll let you come to your own conclusions for our next session." As he spoke, Stefan pulled off the next post-it and began writing a single word. "I want you to look at this next post-it as food for thought."

Phil took the paper and looked at the word. *Grace.*

———◦◦———

Snowbanks glistened along the walking trail, but the brief chinook invited exploration. Samantha and Cassidy bundled up to enjoy the respite.

"Tell me about your journey," Cassidy asked.

She had invited Samantha to go for a walk along the trails. Both women had forged a friendship over the past few weeks.

"Well, I had a rocky beginning with my mom, but my life smoothed out when I started living with Gran," said Samantha. "Then I met Phil. We had a blast at university... that is, until I got pregnant. I thought my life was over. My mom was a high school dropout and drug addict, so I thought I'd have to drop out just like she had. I couldn't imagine having a baby and completing my practicum at the same time. So I dealt with it."

"What did Phil say?"

Samantha let out a long sigh. "I didn't tell him. He didn't even find out until last week."

"Whoa!" Her friend looked shocked. "And how did he react?"

"Let's just say he started counselling this week."

"What about you? Abortion... it just doesn't sound like something you'd do, now that I know you. How did it affect you?"

"I struggled with longer bouts of depression. When Phil proposed, it kept the darkness at bay. But I lacked focus. My grandmother revelled in planning our wedding, so I just let her take over. We got married the final weekend before Christmas, at the end of my practicum. I had zero time."

Cassidy shivered. "I can't imagine being a teacher. All that hormonal angst? No thank you. Give me a research lab and a microscope."

"On my first day, I watched a sixteen-year-old eviscerate a veteran teacher. That made me think. Why would I ever want to subject myself to that kind of behaviour?"

"I'm *so* glad I'm not that age anymore," Cassidy said. "Too hard."

"However, the fact that I pursued a degree in secondary education meant I could avoid the grief of having to take a university math requirement. Every elementary education degree demands it."

"Really? I lived for math and science classes."

Samantha shuddered. "Phil loved math a lot, too. He really helped me stay organized during my practicum. He came up every weekend to encourage me to keep going. Thank goodness my cooperating teacher had an extra bedroom he could camp out in!"

"How long was the drive?"

"About two and a half hours from Saskatoon."

Cassidy frowned. "I thought he was still taking classes at U of S at the time."

"Yup. He even rescheduled a final exam so he could come up for the winter festival pageant. That took place two days before our wedding."

"And this whole time he was working on the business plan for Tailor-Made?"

"Before you think he's some kind of superhero, his final year was part co-op, part class. The guy he interned for in California encouraged Phil to develop a full-fledged business plan. He connected Phil with an innovative ag tech company in Saskatoon, and the time spent with them gave him the courage to launch Tailor-Made."

"Does he ever stop and relax?"

"He used to relax when he met me. I made him."

"And now?"

"Now I'm not sure if he'll ever relax around me again. I mean, how could he? I just sprung the worst possible thing he could ever imagine. If he searches online for anything about the increased possibility of miscarriage after an abortion, he's going to blame me for Micah and Matthew's deaths."

Samantha bent a branch back that had sunk over the trail, weighed down by the recent snowfall. She blinked at the brightness of the sun as she turned to make sure Cassidy didn't get hit by the branch.

"And when are you going to stop blaming yourself? You had no problem with Cami's pregnancy. Didn't you tell me you almost died of infection with Micah?"

"Yeah. I'm not sure where I picked up E. coli. The doctors said only four percent of stillbirths result from that."

"So, girl, why do you still think his death is your fault?"

"Well, I guess I don't, really, if you put it that way."

"I think you're looking to blame yourself because it makes you feel better, and because it justifies your suicide attempt."

"You're like a guided missile today."

Samantha halted when Cassidy touched her arm. They stood together, breathing in deeply and admiring the purity of the snow that covered the towering evergreens. Samantha felt the weight of her friend's words expunge the guilt she felt over the abortion.

"I don't mean to hurt you," Cassidy said. "I just see a friend who's stuck. You've helped me by being honest. Now I want to help you move past the shame and blame game."

"Thanks, I think. You've been a good sounding board this week."

"Well, when we get sprung from this place, we're still gonna be friends, right?"

"Spa weekend, it is!" Samantha looked straight at Cassidy. "Women of Forest Acres, unite!"

With that salvo, Cassidy reached down, made a snowball, and chucked it at Samantha. The ensuing battle helped Samantha work off the nervous energy that had been building up over the course of their conversation.

"Truce!" Cassidy raised her hands in surrender.

They both laughed, brushed the snow from each other's hair, and headed back inside.

Samantha wondered whether Phil would be okay if she made room in her schedule to take regular weekends with friends. She hadn't invested in her friendships since Micah. Now she needed to spend more time with people who understood her pain and would walk with her as she moved forward. But would a weekend away set Cami back?

Thirty

A Reprieve

Tuesdays had taken on a life of their own. Phil and Cami had a ritual breakfast of chocolate chip pancakes and strawberry shakes. Cami then went to school and Phil went to work. However, on his way to pick her up from school Phil would pick up a couple of hamburgers, which they'd eat in the parking lot of the city conservatory. They'd admire the flowers there before heading to the hospital for the rest of the afternoon.

They had gotten to call these Terrific Tuesdays.

On the second to last Tuesday of October, Tom stopped Phil and Cami before allowing them to enter Glenda's room.

Tom motioned back towards the elevator. "Come this way."

Phil and Cami walked hand in hand into the elevator, where Cami enveloped Tom with a big hug.

"Guess what Mrs. Henderson has for you today, Cami?" Tom asked.

"I dunno. Do I get to ride in the wheelchair again?"

"No. Guess again."

"Um, jump on the big mat?"

By this time, they were walking towards the physical therapy room. Tom stopped them before they got to the door.

"I'd like both of you to close your eyes."

Phil and Cami scrunched their eyes shut and let Tom lead them inside.

"Okay, you can open them now."

Standing before them, Glenda held onto a cane. She took a few steps and stopped beside her husband.

"You can walk! You can walk!" Cami exclaimed, bouncing up and down.

Weeks of being told not to rush Glenda for a hug went out the window as Cami moved to throw her arms around the older woman.

Tom put his arm around his wife to prepare for the onslaught.

"Wow, you've made some amazing progress this week," Phil said. "How long until they release you?"

Phil gave her an embrace of his own, gently nudging Cami away from Glenda's cane.

"Well, dearie, both therapists said there's no reason I can't continue therapy on an outpatient basis," Glenda told them. "I go home tomorrow. Isn't that grand?"

Tom smiled. "Bathroom renos are complete and home care signed off on them. We've banished all area rugs... for now." His eyes danced with excitement.

Cami's shoulders drooped and she let go of Phil's hand. "So Terrific Tuesdays have to stop, Daddy?"

Her uncertainty melted Phil's heart. He was proud of the way his daughter had encouraged Glenda every Tuesday to go a little farther.

"Pish-posh, poppet. Grandpa Tom said you can come visit me at our house for craft and puzzle Tuesdays." Glenda reassured Cami with a soft squeeze around her shoulders. "I've got to practice me dexterity with the best teacher I know, luv."

"Oh, goodie."

Tom waited until his wife and Cami walked over to the parallel bars. "Phil, we've dropped the charges of assault and battery against Samantha."

Phil breathed a sigh of relief. He reached out and shook Tom's hand. "Thank you, Tom. You don't know how much that means to me, and how much it will mean to Samantha. She's been making huge strides at the rehab centre and this just takes an immense weight off both of us."

"Well, you and Cami have made a tremendous difference in Glenda's recovery. Cami's visits have always inspired her to try harder, so she'd have something new to show Cami."

"Can you clear up a mystery for me?" Phil asked, changing the subject. "After Samantha miscarried, I caught her unravelling her special blanket. When I went to pack Samantha's things for her stay in North Battleford, I then discovered it in Micah's room, looking like it always had."

"Glenda took it home and put it back together. She likes to keep busy when she's watching TV, you know. Anyway, she returned it to the room the day she got hurt."

The timing of the blanket's return wasn't lost on Phil. He couldn't wait to tell Samantha!

"Anyhow, I just wanted to say thank you for bringing Cami by every week," Tom added, "no matter what was on your plate at work."

"Honestly, Tom, it's become one of my favourite days of the week. I can forget all the rigmarole of work and the stress of trying to be both Dad and Mom and just enjoy time with Cami."

Tom gave Phil a playful tap on his belly. "I'm thinking you might need to eat fewer chocolate chip pancakes."

"That's where you're dead wrong, Tom."

Cami waltzed over. "What are you laughing about, Daddy?"

"Grandpa Tom thinks I'm getting fat from too many chocolate chip pancakes. I told him not a chance. Terrific Tuesday pancakes will give anyone who eats them superpowers. Right, kiddo?"

Phil swung Cami up over his head and settled her on his shoulders.

"Right, Daddy!"

They headed to the occupational therapy room for a board game. The therapist had said that moving the game pieces around would help Glenda become more adept with her pincer skills, using her thumb and index finger.

Phil knew better. The real reason they played was so Cami could boast about beating her dad and Grandpa Tom.

———◦———

Samantha felt proud of Phil's efforts to keep Cami connected to Glenda with Terrific Tuesdays. Could she build the same relationship she'd had with Glenda before putting her life in jeopardy? Would Tom allow her to make amends?

She paged through her journal to find an entry she'd written in response to a prompt called "do-over wishes."

Dear Diary,
As I sit here wrapped in the afghan of promise, I'm reminded of Glenda's words.

"Dearie, you've got to take off the blinders and see the bigger picture. When we fix our eyes on the mistakes we've made, we miss the beauty of sunrises and sunsets. It reminds us that there's Someone greater who's in charge.

"This blanket of yours, the one you've kept close, is a reminder of that beauty. Joseph didn't see the complete picture when he was stuck in a cistern, nor when he was in prison or ignored by someone who might have been able to put in a good word for him. He held on to the promise given him by his father about a plan for their family to be a blessing to many and that one day they'd return to the land given them by God.

"Did you know he even made a plan for his bones to be carried back to the home the Creator had promised his people? 'Cause, luv, the universe isn't dependin' on you to run it. It won't fall to pieces because you did something you regret. The Creator above made a way to redeem our errors. You've just got to believe for yourself. Your story is part of a bigger story. That promise of a hope and a future isn't a fairytale."

I wish I'd never hurt Glenda. I wish I could have a do-over with so many parts of my life. Creator God, do You really make new those who are broken? No matter which roads we choose, will we still find our way back home? Can You restore, recreate, and redeem that which I can never undo?

———•○•———

Snow stuck to the dining room windows. Phil picked up the suitcases in the hallway and brought them back upstairs to unpack. He scanned the highway report and saw nothing but trouble for his trip to see Samantha.

The lights flickered.

"Daddy, I'm scared."

"It's okay, honey. I don't think we're going to see Mommy today. Old Man Winter is a little grumpy this morning. Do you want to help me find our camping lanterns in case the power goes out?"

She nodded and slipped her hand in his.

He headed down into the basement and flipped the switch for the gas fireplace. The lights dimmed and then powered up again. He hoped those lanterns were easy to find!

The rec room was still a complicated jumble of totes, boxes, and toys.

"I found one, Daddy!"

"Good girl. How'd you know where it was?"

"Mommy and I played camping once. I found it under the blankets we used for a tent."

Phil kept searching for the other set of camping gear. He'd just opened the last box when everything went black.

"Daddy? Daddy!"

"I'm here, honey. It's okay. The power just went out. I found the other lantern, but it needs batteries. Keep talking, honey, so I can find you. Can you switch on the lantern?"

Phil knew the rec room was a landmine of disaster, so he edged forward carefully. Suddenly, a small flicker of light lit up Cami's tear-stained face. Had she been crying silently in the dark?

"Hey, looks like your lantern needs batteries, too. Let's go upstairs and find them in Daddy's office. You're so brave, honey." He scooped her up with his free hand and climbed the stairs to the kitchen. He kissed her tousled hair. "Let's light the candles."

"They're so pretty!"

"Should we go hang out in your safe space and pretend it's a camping day?"

She shook her head.

"Okay, what should we do today?" he asked.

"Call Mommy?"

"That's a great idea! Let's go get the batteries. Then we'll see if Mommy's free to call us, okay?"

Phil flipped her onto his shoulders. Her giggles made him feel like he'd conquered Mount Everest in the dad department.

Soon he and Cami were snuggled under blankets in front of the fireplace, waiting for Samantha to answer their video call.

"Hey, you two!" Samantha's smile lit up the screen.

"Mommy, I gotted scared in the dark!"

"You did?"

"Daddy finded me and gived me a piggyback ride on the stairs to get batteries."

"Is the power off, sweetie?"

"Yeah. Daddy says the weather is grumpy today so we can't come see you."

"Oh, honey, I miss you, but I'm glad you're safe at home instead of on the roads right now."

Phil wished he could reach through the phone and hold her close. "Hey, Sam, you look good."

"Did you find the lanterns?"

"Yeah, but we're saving them for later. We were looking in the basement when the power went off and..." Phil motioned his head towards Cami. "She got a little anxious. But the windows are letting in enough light for now."

Samantha searched Phil's face. He no longer had those dark circles underneath his eyes. Something seemed different, like a barrier had disappeared between them. She wished she could ask him how the last few weeks of counselling had gone, but Cami was in plain view and within earshot. She knew he'd kept his word about going despite the extra pressure at work. She couldn't imagine an adult taking art therapy, but maybe it would help unlock some of Phil's inner pain.

"You'll need ski pants on Monday, Cami," she said. "It's going to be cold. Are you gonna help Daddy shovel some snow today?"

Phil butted in. "Where would I find those?"

"Probably in the winter gear box in the basement."

"I'll look for those later, when the power comes back on." Phil turned to Cami. "Do you want to talk to Mommy while I go outside and shovel the front steps?"

"Noooooo! Stay here, Daddy."

"Wanna play a board game with us, Sam?"

Samantha nodded and Cami clung to his side when he pulled the box off the shelf, then propped his phone on the holder. Old Man Winter wasn't getting in the way of family time—not if he could help it!

When they finished the game, Phil made Cami put it back on the shelf. He seized the chance to say something in private.

"Hey Sam, I just wanted to let you know that Tom dropped the charges. No more trial."

Samantha clutched her throat. Her mind went fuzzy as she thought about what she'd just read in her journal. Was this the beginning of restoration?

"Sam, did you catch what I just said? Did the connection cut out?"

"Yeah, Phil, I heard you. Just speechless, I guess."

"By the way, Glenda fixed your blanket. She returned it on the day she got hurt. Isn't that amazing? I think the Creator is sending you another message."

"Really? I didn't realize she'd found me out!" She paused for a moment. "What message do you hear Him saying?"

"He knew what was going to happen and made sure you wouldn't forget His message about the hope and future He has for you, even if you tried to destroy that message."

Rocked by his words, Samantha grabbed hold of the bedside table. She glanced down at her blanket. In her darkest day, the Creator had left her a sign of hope.

"Take care." Phil winked at her. "I better go. Someone's hungry."

Samantha stared at her darkened phone. Did she deserve this reprieve? Or was this the part where she needed to take the blinders off and look at the bigger picture?

Thirty-One

What About Bob?

Sweat drizzled down Phil's back as he shovelled the alley in front of his garage for the third time. Thank goodness Cami was occupying herself, for the first time since the power had gone out. Did watching TV count as occupying oneself? How did Samantha ever get anything done?

He trudged up the steps and opened the back door. "Honey, it's time to get dressed for school. We gotta go. Come get your ski pants on."

He watched her struggle to get the pants on.

"Daddy, I can't get it zipped up and my toes feel funny."

Phil looked down and saw the space between the top of the boot and the bottom of her pant leg. He reached down and pushed on the toe of her boot.

Ah, today is a definite Monday, he thought.

"Okay, here's what we're gonna do. Since it won't be that cold, you can wear your muck boots and splash pants. I'll go get an extra sweater, and you can wear your fall coat over that."

At least it turns out that the mitts and toque fit.

After delivering Cami at school, he arrived at work and found, to his relief, that the parking lot had been cleared. He stamped his feet on the office's welcome mat to knock the snow off.

When Gabe and Erin met him in the lobby, Phil felt the hair on his neck stand up.

"Good morning. What's up?"

"Bob hasn't shown up for work today," Erin said. "He's usually here before me on Mondays and gives me Friday's and Saturday's production numbers to enter into the computer."

"Did anything unusual happen on Friday that I don't know about?"

"He seemed a little irritated when he brought in the invoices for me to send out. He said he was dealing with a customer complaint about the discrepancy in pricing."

Phil's heart sank. One client or supplier must have slipped up and mentioned something, despite their careful plans to keep Bob in the dark.

He hurried to his office and Gabe followed.

"Gabe, I need you to head out to the warehouse. Log on to the computer and check to see how everything's going down there." Pulling a card out of his Rolodex, he handed it to Gabe. "Here are Bob's login creds. I'm going to call Noah and let him know. The police said they were monitoring his credit cards starting last week in case of something like this."

When Phil called Noah, he had to wait for dispatch to put him through.

"Thought you might call, Phil."

Caught off-guard, Phil asked, "Why?"

"One of my detectives got an alert Sunday night that Bob had used his credit card to purchase a charter flight to Jamaica, leaving at 10:00 a.m. this morning."

"Bob doesn't have holidays coming and we don't have shipments of material coming from there. Unless it's something new. Regardless, I didn't authorize the trip."

"We figured that out and alerted airport security. He's been in the longest security line and been selected for a spot check."

"So now what?"

"We're ready to press charges of embezzlement. There's a money trail, documentation, and now an attempt to leave the country. We've already collected evidence and presented it to the crown prosecutor. We notified him about Bob's presence at the airport, and the judge has granted an arrest warrant. I have officers ready to serve him with those charges and take him into custody. Since he's proved to be a flight risk, we'll request his passport and set his bail at $500,000."

Phil sat back in his office chair and took a deep breath, blowing it out slowly. He rolled his shoulders back and stretched his neck one way and then the next.

He walked out to the reception area. "Is Gabe back yet?"

Erin shook her head.

Phil paced up and down the narrow space between Erin's desk and the front door. The news buzzed in Phil's mind. Was it finally over?

"Is everything all right?" she asked.

"I sure hope so, or at least it's the beginning of all right. Bob's been taking money from the company."

Erin's mouth dropped open. "He's what? Is that why I've been rewriting contracts?"

"Yeah. Sorry I couldn't be clearer. Gabe helped me figure out what he was doing, why we were so short of money all the time."

Just then, Gabe pushed open the door of the lobby. She extended her hand to him.

"Well done, Gabe! So how can you both be so calm right now?"

Phil took a deep, soothing breath. "Between talking to Pastor Brad and Stefan Reid, I've found a new trust in God and His amazing provision. I've realized that it's not up to me to control everything."

He felt so thankful for Erin's understanding of just how intense things had been.

"Anyhow, Bob's being arrested at the airport about now. He was trying to flee to Jamaica. The charges are embezzlement and fraud."

"Fraud?" asked Erin.

"He was running two sets of invoices," Phil explained. "He showed me one set that balanced, but the creditors and suppliers saw the other set. Clients were overcharged and suppliers underpaid."

But thank goodness, this nightmare was coming to an end. Thanks to God, they would forge a way through, in no small part thanks to that new advertising campaign.

Phil turned and faced the newest hire. "Gabe, I can't thank God enough that you found our way to us."

"If there's anything else, let me know," Gabe replied. "I'm hanging out in the warehouse for the day. We've got to make sure to fulfill the quotas requested by our brand-new client."

"We have a brand-new client?" asked Phil.

"Yes. I was going to tell you about it when I had the chance this morning, but the day seems to have taken a minor detour."

Phil felt relieved that things were turning around so quickly, given all the balls he was being forced to juggle at the moment.

"Why don't you forward me the contract? I'll take a look and sign it," he said. "You can forward the design files directly to me as well. We'll also need to create an ad to fill Bob's job. Erin, can you put that together for me? We can't go long without an operations manager."

"Right away, Phil," said Erin. "But do you know Jared Jeriman very well? He's been working in the warehouse for a while. We could ask him to serve as temporary supervisor."

"You think he'd be good at the job?"

"Of the three techs on staff, he's the only one with a degree in computer engineering."

Phil smiled. "How do you remember these things, Erin?"

"That's why you pay me the big bucks."

His smile grew even wider.

"Gabe, head down and ask Jared if he'd be interested in taking on the warehouse operations temporarily."

"Done," Gabe replied.

As Gabe headed back to his office, Erin sat down and got to work on building the job recruitment ad. As for Phil, he walked over to a window and looked out at the dusky snowbanks melting on the tiny patch of lawn in front of the building.

God, You never cease to amaze me. You're taking care of the situation with Bob. You made a way for Gabe to be here to assist me. Thank You for Erin's administrative skills. I am overwhelmingly grateful for her incredible photographic memory that hones in on details. Thank You for making a way for new clients to become part of our business. Give me wisdom as I rebuild and retool this company. Lead me as I wrestle through the losses Samantha and I have gone through. Please help me forgive her completely. Help me battle the resentment I feel over being left out of her decision-making. Help me process the anger and hurt I feel.

Phil sat at his computer and began looking through the new contract Gabe had sent him. The product intrigued him. If he was right, it had the potential to revolutionize the takeout business and assist the environment at the same time.

He felt both sad and relieved about Bob's arrest. Maybe Samantha would feel free to return to the office part-time now. But as his dad used to say, "There's no use putting the cart before the horse." He needed to focus on the next steps: finish up in the office, drive to the wellness centre, and work hard on his marriage.

Focus, Phil, he told himself. *Focus!*

He hoped the work he'd done with Stefan and Pastor Brad was enough. His communication with his wife would either open the door to wholeness or prolong the wait before Samantha came home.

Thirty-Two

Rescheduled, then Rescheduled Again

The snowstorm had created interesting sculptures in the hedges surrounding the rehab centre. Although they were slowly melting, they would be unlikely to disappear before the next snowfall.

Samantha paced around her room. Today was the first time she and Phil would meet alone with the family counsellor. The long delay between her revelation about the abortion and being face to face with him again had her worried. Phil had been ignoring the subject during their nighttime conversations.

He hadn't seemed able to commit time to family counselling until the police investigation wrapped up. But then he had let her know that the situation had come to a head.

Samantha had taken the risk over the last few weeks of opening her heart to others and sharing her grief. To her surprise, once she'd gotten past herself she had found the bandwidth to focus on others. Cassidy, for example, was now a friend for life. She'd also eaten lunch with a woman named Angel. The woman's tattoos told a story, but Samantha hadn't heard it yet.

"Ready to head to the gym, Samantha?" asked the orderly.

"Yes. I need to dial down some of my nervous energy today. My husband's coming this afternoon."

The orderly led Samantha through the halls to the facility's gym. When they arrived, she immediately noticed Angel getting ready to use the bench press.

"Hi Sam," the tattooed woman said.

Samantha walked closer to help spot. "Hi Angel."

Over the course of the next hour, the two women moved from station to station. They'd almost finished the circuit when Angel's voice cut through Samantha's buzz.

"Sam, thanks for sharing your story the other day at grief group. I lost a baby at twenty-two weeks…"

Samantha reached over and touched Angel's arm.

"I felt so guilty," Angel said. "I didn't tell my partner about the abortion I had as a teen. I blamed myself for losing our baby, just like you did when you lost Micah."

"What day did your baby leave you?"

"October 16. Just over two years ago."

"Really?" Samantha shook her head in disbelief. "That's the same day we lost Micah."

"Wow! Maybe our kids are buddies up there."

"Maybe. Did you ever name your little one?"

Angel nodded. "Just this week, when we were working through the questionnaire Bonnie gave us."

"And?"

"Jolayne. We named her after my mom. Have you thought about naming the one… you know, the one you chose to…?"

Samantha's mind flashed to the room where she'd sat after the procedure was over. She'd shivered in the scant hospital gown, the ties trailing down her back.

She wrapped her arms around her middle and looked at Angel. "I haven't let myself go back there long enough to wonder."

"Maybe it's time."

Both women signed out of the gym and headed to their rooms.

Was it time?

Samantha took a quick shower before heading to her ADL session. She checked off her previous goals and then wrote a new one for the day. Nothing was more satisfying than seeing regular progress.

She straightened up her room and swiped her nightstand with the last remaining alcohol wipe. Did she have time to put laundry in the dryer before lunch and get it folded and put away before Phil arrived? He had planned to leave work early, since Mary Ann promised to pick Cami up from school and keep her overnight with Kristina. Those two girls were thick as thieves.

Heading back to the laundry room, Samantha put her clothes into the dryer and hung up the delicates on hangers to take back to her room. After leaving the hangers on the rack in her bathroom, she headed to the cafeteria. Today was looking like a great day.

———•••———

Phil wasn't having a great day. After dropping off Cami at school, he had realized halfway to work that he had forgotten his suitcase. After returning home to pick it up, he did one more walk through the house before leaving—and it was a good thing, because he noticed that Cami had forgotten her favourite stuffie on the bed. He picked it up and went over to Mary Ann's to drop it off. When she wasn't home, he stuck it inside the screen door.

He made it to work after skirting an accident and nearly hitting a cyclist who was in his blind spot. Why anyone would want to bike on the streets after the mother of all snowstorms, he'd never know.

"Erin, please tell me we've got coffee and something to snack on. I left my go cup sitting on my workbench in the garage."

Erin handed him a stale donut from yesterday's staff meeting and started a cup of coffee. "Hope this will carry you through."

"Thanks. I'm just grateful to have arrived in one piece."

"So much for getting here early so you could leave early."

Phil shrugged. "Oh well, the best laid plans. Gabe around?"

"He said he'd be back in the office by ten. Is that too late?"

"That's fine. Gives me time to sort out my priorities."

"I'm glad you're able to spend a little more time with Samantha. Will she come home soon?"

"They're going to evaluate her situation after two sessions to see how Samantha feels about becoming an outpatient."

"I'm rooting for you, Phil."

"Thanks, Erin, I appreciate it."

Phil's eagerness to get to Samantha overwhelmed him. He marvelled at the work God had been doing in his heart. This new burgeoning love for Samantha was based on God's love and forgiveness. It never ceased to amaze him.

It reminded him of a one-of-a-kind encounter he'd had with Pastor Brad recently. He'd sunk into the navy plaid armchair in the pastor's office one evening, feeling both physically and emotionally exhausted.

"You look different." Pastor Brad's gaze had felt like lasers into Phil's soul, cutting through his defences to reveal the darkness that dwelt there.

Phil had pushed himself out of the chair and paced. "I can't get past how long Samantha kept the abortion from me. I want to trust her again. I guess there's this fear that if I didn't know this about her, what else am I missing? I mean, it bothered her so much that she tried to take her own life."

He kept pacing and turning, pacing and turning, from the bookshelf to the doorway and back again.

"I hear anger more than fear. Why?"

"She didn't trust me! It took so long to win her trust in the first place, and she still withheld this important part of herself. How didn't I see it? I'd do anything for her. I've done everything possible to support her."

Pastor Brad stood up and faced Phil. "When you spoke your wedding vows, what words did you use? What promises did you make?

"The usual ones. We were too busy to write our own."

Pastor Brad moved to a filing cabinet and pulled out a folder. "Come. Read this over."

Phil took the folder, opened it, and read the notes written on the first page. These were the standard wedding vows everyone seemed to say. Where was he going with this?

"Yeah, these are the ones we used," Phil said.

"I'm going to leave you alone for a few minutes. Write down all the action words in these vows. Leave enough space beside them to describe how your marriage reflects these words. Then flip the vows over and answer the question on the back of the page."

Once left alone, Phil picked up a pen and jotted down the action words: love, honour, respect, cherish, care, partner, respect, forgive, care, and treasure. But his eyes kept coming back to two words: cherish and honour.

Guess I'll start with those, he thought. *How do I cherish Samantha?*

He had hired Glenda. And sometimes he gave her flowers just because he knew she liked them. He opened the door for her. He used to take Cami on Sundays so she could sleep. But how did he know that was the way she wanted to be cherished? Had he ever been vulnerable about losing his dad?

Honour? Hmm. Have I honoured her desire for deep conversation? Have I honoured her need to process things out loud?

He had certainly honoured her request to step away from Tailor-Made. But what about her desire for a smaller home, rather than the one that had pushed them financially?

Pastor Brad, I'm not sure I like where this is going.

He shifted in his seat, laid down the pen, and flipped the page over.

> Marriage is a covenant, not a contract. Just like a treaty, it is binding before the Creator as long as the sun shines; the grass grows, and the river flows. Is there anything that happened before your vows that would cause your spouse to doubt or distrust you?

Phil got up and paced in the small space. With each turn, the walls seemed to press him for answers. The vows on the desk interrogated him.

What about forgiveness? he asked himself. *Did you take an interest in and understand her feelings? When your passion overwhelmed you and you took instead of respecting her boundaries, what then? Did you forget what she saw as a child? What she experienced?*

———◦◦———

"Phil, it's eleven o'clock," Erin reminded him. "Didn't you say you needed to leave?"

He shook his head, freeing himself from the memory. "Right. Just let me copy you the final draft of the contract for this new client, then I'll get out of your hair."

Phil looked around his desk for his briefcase and slid his laptop into it. He grabbed his cell phone and headed out the door, where he met Gabe coming into the office.

Gabe smiled. "May everything you hope for come through in the next few days. I'll be praying."

"Thanks, Gabe."

As Phil drove the two hours to the rehab centre, he hummed to keep himself occupied. The song was something he had learned at a camp revival meeting a long time ago. He hadn't thought of it in years.

If you want to soar like an eagle,
  You've got to lay your burdens down.
  If you want to soar like an eagle,
  Put your hope and trust in the Lord,
  For He alone is able
  To deliver you from trouble.
  His strength is yours if you choose to wait on Him.

"God, I lay down my burden over the death of my baby," he prayed. "I lay down the guilt, the shame, and the grief I feel over this loss. I lay down any remaining anger and resentment I feel towards Samantha. I lay down my if-onlys and what-ifs. I choose to accept Your forgiveness for our decision to sin. I'm so grateful that one day Samantha and I will meet our children in heaven, where they experience Your love and will continue to be loved on by You for all eternity. Thank You for blessing us with our precious rainbow baby girl. I pray she will always know that she's just as cherished and treasured as our sons. We're grateful for our daughter. Watch over her and give her a wonderful time with Kristina. Keep the night terrors and nightmares away and may she have a good day at school. Keep her healthy. May she grow in wisdom and stature and in favour with God and man."

Tears rolled down his face as he prayed. He reached for a tissue to blow his nose and then grabbed another one to wipe his eyes so he could see more clearly. Gratitude overwhelmed him as he drove towards a fresh start.

At least, that's what he hoped for.

Thirty-Four

Are We There Yet?

Samantha folded her blue jeans and tucked the last pair of socks into her drawer. She looked up at the clock, willing it to be one o'clock already. Ten more minutes remained.

She picked up her journal and thumbed through this morning's writing exercise.

Communication Goals
1. Listen carefully before speaking.
2. Own your flaws.
3. Respond to criticism with empathy.
4. Be specific and don't assume the other person understands vague generalities.

Both she and Phil were guilty of ignoring the fourth goal. They had both kept their genuine struggles wrapped in generalities and assumed the other person knew exactly what was on each other's mind. When they'd each shared something significant and the other person hadn't agreed or understood, both had pulled back into their shells to avoid talking about the issue.

Today, they'd have support to improve in this area. In Janet, they would have an excellent coach. This gave Samantha confidence that their marriage would not only heal but grow stronger than ever. If she could respond to criticism with empathy instead of defensiveness, and avoid planning her arguments before hearing Phil out, that would go a long way.

Samantha closed her eyes. *God, help me to guard my lips today when I'm listening to the pain I caused Phil. Help me to own the flaws Phil may bring up in counselling. Help me also not to shrink back from the specifics of the hurt I experienced when Phil chose to "fix" my grief by giving me a housekeeper and help with Cami. Help us focus on how You brought us together. Regardless of where we were at in our relationship with You when we said our vows, we said those vows before You. Give us the grace to work on our relationship with the wisdom of the counsellors—and, when we go home, with Pastor Brad's encouragement.*

She took a deep breath, got up, and tapped on the door to her room. The orderly then led her to the entrance of the rehabilitation centre. It was a little too chilly outside, but the snow was melting off the roof. The sunlight reflected off of the remaining snowbanks, making it difficult to look towards the parking lot.

She peered through the windows of the front entrance, hoping to see Phil park the car.

"Waiting for me?"

Samantha whirled around when she heard Phil's teasing voice from behind her. "Phil, you're here early!"

"Not by much. Just finished signing in at the reception desk and bent down to pick up my carry-on when you walked into the lobby."

"How was your trip?"

"Well, I had a few adventures getting to work this morning, but the drive was uneventful. The highways were dry."

"That's good... but what do you mean, adventures?"

"I think I was a little distracted by the knowledge that I would be coming to see you. I had to go back for my suitcase."

Samantha smiled. That was almost identical to what had happened just before his trip to meet her grandmother. First he'd forgotten his cell phone charger, and then he'd gone back to get the engagement ring he'd left in his sock drawer.

This visit would take two whole days. It was just as significant to Phil as it was to her.

"I'm glad you made it here safe and sound, Phil."

"Me too."

Phil enveloped Samantha in a long hug. They stayed in the moment, leaning in, as Phil gently caressed Samantha's hair. Samantha's heart thudded with excitement as he cradled her. His expression of deep affection had won her trust so many years ago...

That is until that night when she had wanted more.

Samantha pulled away first and looked at Phil with a sweet smile playing on her lips. "I guess we're making progress, but we better head to our first activity."

She captured his hand in hers and tugged him towards his guest room so he could put away his carry-on. She wanted to linger there but knew their time together would be sweeter by working through more of the hard stuff.

"Where are we headed after this?" asked Phil. He clasped her around the waist and nuzzled her neck. "This seems like a great place to stay for a while."

"Never you mind, mister. Time to do some riding together, just to break the ice. You grabbed lunch on the way, right? Janet has an exercise for us. After supper, we'll have a process therapy session with Dr. Andrews. Then we get free time."

"Yes, I grabbed lunch." Phil tugged Samantha closer and whispered, "May I have a kiss?"

She gazed up at Phil's gorgeous hazel eyes flecked with gold. "Yes," she murmured.

The kiss embodied all their hopes for the future and signalled the return of passion and compassion in their marriage.

She pulled back a little to look into Phil's eyes.

Phil reluctantly moved away. "That was a wonderful hello, but we better go find Janet and get this rodeo started."

Samantha giggled all the way to the arena, feeling light-hearted in ways she hadn't felt for a very long time. Despite the crispness of the impending winter season, the warmth of new hope filled her like drinking hot chocolate at a hockey game.

She clung to Phil's arm as they walked, noting that the curtains of sadness draped over Phil's eyes had opened. Yes, her best friend had worked through his heartache and was on his way to forgiveness. Today would give them more tools to avoid the pitfalls they had fallen into during the dark times and enable them to move forward together rather than straining in opposite directions.

"You two look happy today," Janet said with a smile when they entered the arena. "I can fix that!"

Phil and Samantha looked at each other with a bit of trepidation.

"What kind of exercise do you have in mind?" Phil asked.

"This exercise is called Appendages, and it requires very specific communication. You get to link arms and work together to accomplish a task."

Phil felt suddenly enthusiastic. "Sounds fun!"

But Samanatha's definition of fun didn't necessarily align with his. "It sounds complicated..."

"Honey, we've got this. We've been through a lot. We've both worked on our issues. Now it's time to see if we can use what we've learned to move forward."

"You're right." She turned to Janet. "What do we have to do?"

"You'll link arms, and you can't use those arms for anything. Operating as one, Phil will control the left arm and you, Samantha, will control the right. Your task: halter either Duke or Star, then get a saddle on him or her. Give very specific instructions to each other about what you want each arm to do."

Certain this exercise would leave them sprawled in defeat, Samantha froze. She thought she'd gotten better at capturing negative thoughts, but this exercise felt unusually daunting.

"What's wrong, Sam?" Phil asked.

"I keep seeing my Grade Three self at play day."

"What happened?"

"Well, my partner was taller than me and had untied shoelaces. I kept stepping on them. She mashed her foot on top of mine and our forward momentum just kept going until we were both on the ground and couldn't figure out how to get up..."

"So you're thinking we're doomed before we even start?" As the words left Phil's mouth, he watched Samantha's facial features flatten. It was only their first hour together, and already he'd deflated her joy.

Kicking himself, he resolved to turn off the road of familiarity and take the road less travelled.

"Well, no, but..."

"Samantha, which horse are we going to halter? You've worked with both." Phil's tone was gentle but firm. Encouraged by the lifting of her eyes to his, he smiled in a way that he hoped would communicate his change of strategy.

Samantha spoke without hesitation. "Star."

"Let's get Star using the red halter. You grab it by the headpiece and I'll gather up the lead rope."

Together they walked over to Star.

"Hello, Star," Samantha said. "How is my girl doing today?"

"Looking mighty fine, if I say so myself." Phil laughed at his own joke.

"Keep a lid on it, Phil!" She jabbed him in the ribs. "Let's get this done."

"Got it, Sam I Am. Flirt later." Phil settled into his business mode, tamping down his urge to swoop her up in his arms. "Sam, slip the nose piece over Star's nose."

"Could you bend Star's right ear forward so I can slip the head piece over it? Now the left ear. Ouch, you stepped on my foot."

"Sorry, this is more awkward than I thought." Phil dropped the lead rope into the dirt of the arena. "Could you crouch down so you can pick up the snap part of the lead rope?"

"Could you gather up the extra so it doesn't brush against Star's legs? She hates it."

He nodded. "Okay. Could you pull back the lever and attach it to the right snaffle ring of her halter please?"

"With pleasure."

"Let's walk her over to that stall over there. If we tie her up to the post, it might be easier to saddle her."

Phil watched Samantha let go of the lead rope to scratch Star in her favourite spot, behind the left ear. Star swung her head around as if to say thanks and then backed up a step when she almost collided with Phil.

"Wow, Sam, you're so comfortable around her."

She'd never acted as if horses were important to her when they were at his mom's place. Phil thought back to the times he'd taken Samantha out to the tiny horse ranch his mother had loved.

Wait. Had he never taken her riding? Well, he'd avoided it ever since Buck was...

"Samantha, grab the lead rope with your right hand," he said. "Your horse is getting a little frisky."

"My horse, really? It's our horse today. Um, I don't know what to say. We've got to create a slip knot with our hands working together."

"We've got this, Samantha. Try thinking it through. If the instructions are unclear, I'll try it with you out loud first. Then you can take charge."

"First, drape the lead over the horizontal board. It should look like an upside U. Then hold the top of the U against the board."

He smiled. "Thanks for the word picture. Now pick up the free end of the lead rope and bend it up towards the top of the board. Go around the two lengths of the lead rope twice, underneath where you created the loop, and let the tag end rest on the bottom of the loop. Tug the long end of the lead rope, the one still attached to Star, to tighten the slip knot."

"Phil, can you pick up the loop and place it over the post?"

"And could you give the part of the lead rope attached to Star another tug to snug it up on the post?"

"Voilà! Okay! Let's go get Star's saddle. I see it on the sawhorse."

"I see it, too. Awaiting instruction, my lady."

"Didn't I just say, 'Let's go get Star's saddle'?"

"You did. However, there are a few saddles on sawhorses by the tack wall... and I don't know which one is Star's."

Samantha's lips pursed. "It's the one on the far left. The sawhorse underneath the tan cowboy hat."

"Let's move the saddle blanket and put it on Star. It's upside-down. Grab the right side with your thumb underneath and I'll do the same with my left. We'll flip it towards the wall."

"Like this?"

"Exactly. Now flip it and we'll lift it up on Star's back after we walk to her left side."

"That was rather clever, Phil. You're getting good at being specific."

"So are you!"

Together, they placed the saddle blanket on Star's back.

"You better tug it higher towards her neck," Samantha said. "She'll have twitched it too far down her back if we don't start it high enough."

"Good tip. You know her better than I do."

They walked back to the sawhorse.

"Phil, you can slide your hand underneath the pommel, or the saddle horn, and I'll grab underneath the seat. On the count of three, we'll lift the saddle off the sawhorse and brace it against our bodies, near our chest and linked arms. Careful not to trip on the stirrup."

Phil tugged his end of the saddle up a little higher, which caused Samantha to lose her grip.

The stirrup hit the ground in perfect position to trip them and Phil felt Samantha's fear fulfilled as the ground came up to meet his face.

Janet's peals of laughter sailed over their heads. It must have looked like something out of a slapstick comedy. How in the world were they going to extricate themselves now?

Thirty-Five

Extrication Troubles

Phil gingerly lifted his cheek off the saddle horn, wondering how he was going to explain that mark to his colleagues at work. Samantha tried to push herself off the back of the saddle but couldn't accomplish it one-handed.

"Watch it, Sam I Am. I don't need to make a dent on the other side of my face."

"Well, at least you didn't have the saddleback try to cleave you in half."

"Is anything broken?"

"I don't think so. Ready to figure out a way to get up and get this thing on Star?"

"That's the Sam I Am I know. Take the lead."

"Nope, been there, done that. It's your turn."

"On the count of three, let's push ourselves to our feet, but first we better get our feet closer to our chests. If you need to, lean towards me so I don't push you over again. One, two, three, push!"

The couple dusted one another off.

"Now what?" Samantha asked.

"Can you make sure we hook both stirrups and cinches over the saddle horn, Samantha?"

"Got it."

"Let's try this again by balancing the saddle against our bodies. You take the back and I'll get the front. Let's crouch down with our knees and reach under the saddle. On the count of three, we'll lift it to our chest, then stand up. One, two, three."

Samantha let out a squeal of victory as they embraced the saddle once again against their bodies. Phil felt a spiral of pride go through him as they moved towards Star in sync. They heaved the saddle upwards onto Star's back. Success!

"Samantha, would you swing down the left stirrup gently and unhook the front cinch from the saddle?"

She did as he asked.

"Great job! Now let's take a walk around Star." Phil slid his hand over Star's rump, gently guiding Samantha around Star. "Can you unhook the back cinch and let it fall to the ground?"

"Phil, I need some help. Can you loosen the knot a bit?"

He nodded. "Now let's take the right stirrup off of the horn now."

He was impressed as he watched Samantha lay the stirrup against Star's side.

"Okay, let's take a walk back to Star's left side and figure out how we're going to cinch things up in record time."

"Before we start, Phil, you should probably tug the saddle blanket up, so the saddle sits a little higher."

"Good idea. Now reach for the cinch strap and bring it towards my left hand."

"Could you pull the strap under and through the D ring of the cinch?" she asked.

"And can you grab the strap as I pull it through the saddle's D ring of the saddle and tighten?" When it was done, she tugged firmly on the leather strap. "Now, Star, don't you be huffing and puffing and blow your belly up. Phil, can you grab the pointy end of the strap with your left hand and move it up through both D rings again?"

He gritted his teeth. "Yes, there you go. Now grab it... I think it's short enough now to do the finishing tuck. But how do I find the right words to instruct you in that?"

After a few more fumbles, they had completed the job. Both inspected the saddle placement.

"Thank God," said Samantha. "Nothing's twisted, is it?"

"Nope. And just to be sure it's not too tight, would you mind trying to stick your finger between Star's chest and the cinch?"

"Check."

Then they moved to the back cinch.

"I think we should try one more hole higher," he remarked.

"You're right."

"Let's walk her around a little to see if the saddle's tight enough. You said she likes to puff up, right?"

Janet walked towards the couple as they led Star around the arena. "Well, how do you think you did?"

"I thought I did pretty well," Samantha replied. "Only once did I give unclear directions about where the saddle was. Phil had to ask for more information."

"How did you feel when Phil asked for that?"

"At first I felt exasperated that it hadn't been clear enough the first time. I'd thought he was looking in the same direction as I was."

"I was," Phil said. "Thanks for being more specific, even though my request bugged you."

Janet smiled. "Let's camp on this a little. I liked that phrase you used, 'looking in the same direction as I was.' That's key when you find yourselves miscommunicating, or talking past one another. As a couple, you're looking in the same direction, but extra info can clutter each other's view."

"Twice, Samantha deferred to me to take instructional leadership," Phil pointed out.

Samantha wondered if Janet would call that a good or bad idea in communication.

"Why do you think she did that?" Janet asked.

"I don't know. Maybe it was easier than trying to decide what to say."

Samantha felt startled. Suddenly, the flashback consumed her. She remembered herself trying to explain her point of view to her uncle, trying to get her thoughts out before he started taking apart her argument.

Janet peered at her. "Samantha?"

"If it's not clear to me, it's hard to explain myself," she said. "I shut down. It's easier to let someone else take the lead rather than sort out how I want to do a task and lead others."

"What does that mean to you, Phil? For instance, when you discuss a parenting issue with Samantha?"

"I guess I need to wait, ask questions, and be more patient for Samantha to get all her thoughts out."

Samantha offered, "I stop sharing my thoughts if I think Phil will cut me off. Or he'll pronounce some judgment because I'm taking too long. Or maybe because our ideas disagree."

"I guess I like to 'fix' the problem," Phil said. "Too much talking without a deadline for discussion makes me uncomfortable."

"Your business brain is showing, Phil." Samantha winked at him.

Janet held up the clipboard. It had a chart that divided the page into two columns, one for each of them. "I just thought I'd show how you did as a team." Under their names were tally marks. "Are you surprised by the result?"

Samantha stared at the results in surprise.

"I am," she said. "I thought I contributed more instructions than I actually did. I felt like it was more equal."

She felt uncertainty about her growth creeping in. Would she always defer to Phil? She didn't let him handle all the communication. She'd been having fun for the first time in a long while, working with Phil on a project.

"And I didn't know I was dominating the instructions again." He slipped his arm around Samantha.

Phil's uncertain tone relaxed Samantha.

"I didn't think you were," she said. "I was having fun. The second time through, we worked out the kinks from the first try. Although that fall to the ground may have created some new kinks to work out later tonight..."

Phil joined her in laughter.

"You both did a better job of listening to each other and being more specific," Janet said. "Phil, your level of ease around horses helped. But Samantha, you knew what the horse needed to feel secure. That's where your strength lies. You made sure Phil was aware of her likes and dislikes."

They took a moment to reflect on this.

"Can you think of other times where this pattern shows up in your marriage?" Janet continued. "If you're aware of this pattern, how does this change your future discussions?"

Samantha gave this some thought. "If you're wondering where this pattern came from, of me leaning into Phil's strengths and deferring my own thoughts... it started in college. Reading week was almost over and I was recovering from the abortion. Phil was on his way back to his internship in Silicon Valley. My friend's mom had just passed away from cancer. It felt like I was losing my mom all over again. Phil supported me in my grief. He left me groceries and clean laundry. And when he returned in July for our last year, he proposed to me in the Mendel Arts Conservatory. I said yes... and then my grandmother took over."

"Took over what?"

"You know, the wedding stuff."

Janet turned to Phil. "You had no input or influence at all?"

He shook his head. "I just focused on my last year of university and visiting Samantha on weekends. She seemed super stressed on the phone when we'd touch base midweek."

"I felt swamped with unit and lesson plans and trying to figure out how to wrestle a curriculum into submission," Samantha said. "Had to take on extra-curricular activities as well. Me, who had always done drama and band in high school, had to become a volleyball coach!"

"That must have been a little overwhelming."

"It was," she said. "All my life, academics came easy to me. With little effort, I excelled. Until my practicum. I felt so inept about how to organize my time and lessons. I couldn't think, couldn't put things together at all."

"Why do you think it was so hard?"

"The baby that should have been. His due date would have been September 21."

Phil reached out to Samantha and pulled her close. "I wish we could have been closer. When we saw each other on the weekends, how come you didn't share your struggles?"

"I didn't want to spoil our time together. It was my bright spot every month."

"Is that why you planned all those adventures for us?" Phil asked.

She nodded. "I wanted us to have memorable moments, not ones filled with frustrations and fears that I'd completely wasted my time becoming a teacher."

"Is that also why you limited our wedding planning time with your grandmother?"

"I just didn't want to spend any time arguing about this or that with anybody."

Phil reached out and took his wife's hand. "That explains why you switched to teaching elementary."

"Yes, no more high school students for me."

Janet interjected. "I take it you passed your practicum."

"I did," Samantha said. "But I still wasn't convinced about teaching ever again. The shame of it, though. No baby and no career? I'd be a failure."

Tears trickled down Samantha's face. She tried to hold them back, but it was no use. Phil wrapped his arms around her a little tighter as she sobbed.

"Let's try reframing," Janet said. "What if your abortion was the catalyst for positive changes in who you are as a person? You became a person unafraid to share your hurts and needs. Your practicum struggles were a way to focus on growth rather than perfection and performance. Let's reframe your story, Samantha. You can be a person who helps others find grace and hope for themselves."

"My abortion deception weakened our relationship," Samantha concluded. "Hiding sapped my creative energy and joy in finding new ways to engage my students. I built walls to prevent myself from being vulnerable. I deferred decision-making to Phil and Gran because I didn't want to make a huge mistake again..."

Samantha gasped. *I quit taking responsibility for making decisions? I agreed to teach a lower grade because I didn't want to think about pursuing a different career?*

"What's going on inside right now, Samantha?" Janet probed.

"I yielded my decision-making power to others around me."

"And your suicide attempt? Was that a way for you to take the power of control back?"

Phil released Samantha and she turned to face him. It felt like she'd pierced the final veil of darkness over her soul. She wanted Phil to see her heart again.

"Maybe? More like punish myself for what I did and stop hurting the most important people in my life. I thought God was punishing me when we lost Micah, but really I needed to punish myself."

Phil's soft strokes against her thumb soothed her.

—◦—

"Phil, why did you take on the role of decision maker?" Janet asked.

Samantha watched as the memories played across her husband's face.

"I think it started when my dad died." He closed his eyes. "My mom took on new roles at the horse farm, leaving me to figure things out on my own. My finances were tricky, so I sold my horse and pursued undergrad scholarships to pay my way through university. There were other kinds of bursaries available to commerce students, too." He sighed. "I was pretty confident about my decisions. Success followed... until my decision to hire Bob, that is. And my decision to surround Samantha with supports may have prolonged her pain, preventing her from coming face to face with the deeper issues in her life."

"I don't resent any of the things you did to help me," Samantha assured him. "But I didn't realize how checked out I had become."

Phil squeezed her hand. "I liked your idea to marry at Christmas. I wanted to do anything I could to make that happen."

"I should have reined in your idea to ride to the church in a carriage."

"And it might have been a better idea for you to wear a fur coat instead of that shimmery gossamer wrap..."

Janet chuckled. "That's the funny thing about life. There are no do-overs, just moving forward and changing what you do next." She looked over to the horse. "Notice what Star is doing right now?"

Phil and Samantha both turned to see Star's ears lowered and her back leg cocked.

"What's that posture mean, Phil?" Janet asked.

"The horse is relaxed."

"Is that significant, Samantha?" Janet asked.

Samantha felt peace course through her. "She's reflecting how we both feel."

I'm relaxed? she asked herself. *Yup, zero tension in my jaw, no tightness in my shoulders...*

"What now?" Samantha asked.

"That, my friend, is an excellent question," said Janet, leaning against the box stall. "Would you like to go home as an outpatient before Christmas?"

Phil pursed his lips. "What would that look like?"

"As a staff, we've already made a plan for this, and it rested on how well today's session went." She made eye contact with Samantha. "So what do you think about going home?"

Samantha moved closer to Phil, like a heat-seeking missile.

"I can't wait," she said, meeting Janet's gaze. "Would I be able to come back for regular visits? ADL check-ins via email?" Samantha paused. "I've got more edges I need to explore. Like working through the abandonment of my parents and the death of my grandmother. Maybe I could do more equine therapy with Cami. It could bring us closer in relationship and heal some of the hurts between us. I don't want Cami to go through the same things I went through."

Janet smiled. "Well, that's all I needed to hear. I'm proud of you."

A moment later, Janet turned and began walking back towards the main building. She clearly had some work to do to get ready for Samantha's release.

"Samantha?" Phil said, turning back to his wife.

"What's up?"

"Can I pray for us right now? I'm proud of you, too. I'm so grateful."

"Go ahead."

He closed his eyes. "Lord, thanks for this beautiful woman You gave me. You made her for me, and me for her. Thanks for allowing us to walk through these difficult circumstances, because they brought us back to You. Thank You for her sensitive heart. Thank You for her delight in creation and the arts. Lead her closer to You. Let her know who she is in You. Help her see herself as beloved by You. Silence the negative voices she hears. I'm so grateful You gave her a praying grandmother. Thank You for the way Pastor Brad reached out to us in our nightmare. Thank You for his investment of time and energy in discipling me so I could get a fresh understanding of what it really means to be a Jesus follower."

Thirty-Six

Ready for Transport

With her bags packed and ready for transport, Samantha headed to the barn. Time to say goodbye to Star.

She nodded to Janet on her way to Star's stall, picking up the soft brush on her way. Star nickered as she entered the stall.

"Hello to you, too, my beauty. I'm sure gonna miss you." She ran her hand over Star's warm winter coat. "Yeah, I know. 'Get brushing if you're gonna tease me like that.'"

Samantha pushed Star's head away from her shoulder and started brushing. She swished away her tears with one hand as she caressed Star's coat.

"Thank you, Star. You helped me reconnect with my feelings. I don't feel detached anymore. We had some good times. Don't forget me." Star's ears twitched in response. "Yeah, I know. You'll remember me. I'm the one who snivelled all over your coat every day."

She patted Star's rump as she moved to brush the other side.

"I'll see you after Christmas again. Cooperate for Janet. She's a good egg."

"Gee thanks, Samantha. Today's the day you head out?"

Samantha lifted her head at the sound of Janet's voice. "It is. I couldn't leave without saying goodbye."

"Does that include me, too?"

"Without you, I'd have never made it. I'm glad you're here. An alternative to talk therapy."

"Are you scheduled for outpatient visits?"

"I'll be back after Christmas for a weekend or two. I guess we'll see how things go after that. At least, that's what Dr. Andrews said."

"You've got this. You put in the work. It's been hard, but you've got tools now. Use them."

Janet headed out, with Duke trailing behind her.

Samantha wrapped her arms around Star and laid her head against the horse's neck. The soft warmth mingled with the musky scent of the barn. Samantha sighed. She'd miss this part of her daily routine.

With one last pat, she moved to the bench and took off the borrowed cowboy boots and headed back to the main building.

Life's curveballs were not one and done, though, and she was grateful for the opportunity to continue her healing. Last night, she'd shared her binder of routines with Phil. He'd absorbed the information at a snail's pace. She had even bristled about the changes Phil suggested—that is, until she found out they reflected the growth in Cami's eating habits.

"Ready to go?" asked Phil as he grabbed her suitcase and bag to put in the back of the vehicle.

"Yes. I'm looking forward to being back in my bed."

"Me too!"

Samantha turned beet red as she remembered the tender time of lovemaking they'd had the night before.

"Aww," he said. "Did I make you blush all over again?"

Samantha socked him in the shoulder.

"Babe, it was awesome to have you in my arms again. I'll never experience a tenth of that passion for anyone else." Phil tilted her chin and covered her lips with his own. "For better, for worse, for richer, for poorer, in sickness and in health, you are the only Sam I Am I want."

Samantha's fear melted all over again, and she relaxed and kissed him back with all her heart.

"Whoa there, girl. I've got to drive for the next hour and a half!"

"Guess I've still got it."

"No question."

Phil opened the car door for her. She nestled into her seat and belted herself in as Phil got in the driver's side. He turned on the engine, then turned and faced her.

"Honey, I'm so proud of all the hard work you've done in these last weeks. Please keep being honest with me once we get home. If I take over, remind me that it takes two to tango."

"I'm just so grateful you stayed, despite the way I treated you. Despite that I kept significant things from you."

Phil reached over and covered Samantha's hand with his own. "We're in this together because of one thing, God's magnificent grace. Want to pray before we drive away?"

"Yes."

"God, we thank You for this gift of life You've given both of us. Give us ears to hear each other's hearts. Give us hands to serve one another. We thank You for our sweet girl, Cami. Our rainbow baby. May all our struggles bring her good and not harm. Give us traveling mercies. Lead us and guide us."

Samantha hesitated, then spoke. "God, say hi to our boys and hug them for us. Give us courage as we enter back into the ebb and flow of daily life. Help us honour the new boundaries we've made in our relationship. Keep the worries of the business from overwhelming Phil right now as we wait to hear the trial's outcome with Bob. Thank You for giving us a new start. Amen."

Phil headed towards the highway. Samantha shrugged out of her coat and resettled her seatbelt. Nervous anticipation settled about her like a balloon coated with static electricity that crackled with excitement and worry. Home awaited her with all its familiar ruts of thinking, grooves of actions, and paths of communicating.

"A penny for your thoughts," Phil said. "Or should I say, a nickel?"

"On the one hand, I'm dreading going home. On the other, I can't make the car go fast enough."

"Hmmm, sounds familiar."

"In what way?"

"My thoughts are spinning like those of a hamster on crack. How do we continue on the path we've walked these past few months? Where will we trip up? Will we function better as a married couple? Will Cami be okay with only visiting Glenda once in a while instead of seeing her nearly every week? Will Bob go to prison? Will we get back the money he stole? Will the business stay afloat while we restore customer confidence?"

Samantha's laughter burst out like Old Faithful. "So glad I can join you on that hamster wheel! You nailed what's on my mind without hardly trying."

"So now that we've shared our angst, maybe we should talk about our hopes and dreams. What will our 'new' home be like? What do we hope it'll be like? What was it your counsellor said? Bringing your assumptions out into the open keeps them from turning on us in the dark?"

She nodded. "One of my hopes is getting baseball jerseys for the two teddy bears in the nursery, and putting Micah's and Matthew's names on them. I also want to burn their names into our leather gloves."

"I think we should name the first child we lost."

Samantha's swift intake of a breath alerted Phil that her emotions were high. He waited until a semi passed before reaching over for her hand.

He stroked her thumb gently. "Did I surprise you, Sam I Am? I even have a name to suggest."

Samantha reached for a tissue from the console and dabbed at the tears trying to salvage the makeup she'd put on. She gave up and grabbed several more tissues to blow her nose and keep the mascara rivulets from making her look like a zombie.

"You do?" Her voice sounded strangled in her own ears as she tried to force the words out. "Wh... what is it?"

"Morgan. It means 'dweller by the sea.' Our little one exists in God's presence, by the crystal sea. You have no need to fear that I'm holding your decision against you, like a gopher creating holes to trip us up as we relearn how to communicate and support each other better."

"You and your prairie pictures!" Samantha blew her nose again, sounding like a lost goose. "I love the name and its meaning. Thank you for giving me a new image to dwell on."

"I think I found it in Revelation 4."

Samantha scanned the passage on her phone and started reading it aloud to Phil.

"At once I was in the Spirit, and there before me was a throne in heaven with someone sitting on it. And the one who sat there had the appearance of jasper and ruby. A rainbow that shone like an emerald encircled the throne... Each of the four living creatures had six wings and was covered with eyes all around, even under its wings. Day and night they never stop saying: 'Holy, holy, holy is the Lord God Almighty, who was, and is, and is come.'"[3]

Phil spoke up. "It came to me as I pictured our son or daughter there. That's when my anger towards you melted. My shame disappeared. It was like standing on holy ground."

---

[3] Revelation 4:2–3, 8 (NIV).

Samantha pictured her little one with arms outstretched towards the Being on the throne, enraptured by the colours and activity going on in the throne room. It was another layer of grief exposed. Another stone removed from the backpack of burden and laid on the altar. Her shame and guilt slunk away as nail-pierced hands reached out to embrace rather than reject her.

"Samantha, look. Do you see what I see?"

She craned her neck to discover two sundogs on either side of the wintry sun. Awe crept over her. Who was she that the Creator would gift her with another sign of His love for her and His promise of hope rather than destruction?

"Thank you, Phil. I'm in awe of a God who is so powerful and tender. No wonder the angels, elders, and living creatures can't keep from crying out in amazement."

Samantha yawned so widely her jaw cracked.

"Why don't you see if you can catch a few minutes' sleep?" he said. "We'll be in Saskatoon in forty-five minutes. Then you'll power-grocery-shop while I get an oil change."

"Sounds good."

She leaned her seat back and scooted sideways to get more comfortable. She sighed and closed her eyes, the scenery holding no appeal. It was just dingy snow in the ditches and brown branches raised in protest against the bleak grey clouds. If nothing else, resting her eyes would feel good. She doubted she could sleep, but she'd try.

———◦———

Phil drove in silence, digesting the last few minutes of conversation. They'd perfected the dance of talking about daily life without ever dipping into the realm of hidden emotions surging beneath their benign words. Today's conversation had satisfied an ache he'd never named, just like the children he'd lost. Naming empowered them to recognize their loss together. It united them, linked them to vows made, and promised an ongoing future.

He took pleasure in hearing Samantha's breathing deepen as she fell asleep.

They'd just gotten to their turnoff when he nudged her awake. She yawned and stretched, shaking her head to scatter the last vestiges of sleep. She reached over and grabbed Phil's hand and didn't let go.

"Whatcha thinking about, honey?"

He enjoyed seeing Samantha's blue eyes focused on him, even if she was struggling not to yawn. Was she nervous about their next steps?

"I'm a little worried about how Cami will adjust to me being home."

"I think it's going to work out just fine. Remember what Janet said about creating daily rituals that support your relationship?"

"Yeah, I remember. Just worried that she'll resent me for trying to leave her for the rest of her life."

"Did you see any evidence of that resentment in the arena, or during our family chats?"

"No, but—"

"So is it time to take that thought captive, my dear wife?"

"You're right. I'm diving into the future and need to be present in the moment, not fixated on what happened in the past."

"We're almost at the grocery store. Do you have your list?"

"It's right here."

"I'll meet you in forty-five minutes. Don't forget the bags. They're in the backseat." Phil pulled up in front of the store and waited while Samantha removed the grocery bags. "See you in a little while, Sam I Am."

After getting an oil change, he returned to find Samantha pushing the cart towards him. Everything seemed to have gone well. Or had it?

He pushed the button to open the back hatch. "How'd it go, being back in the outside world?"

"No panic attacks or emotional breakdown over which bank card to use when facing the cashier."

"Ah. I didn't even realize that was one of your goals."

"It wasn't on the actual list. I added it while going through the frozen foods aisle."

"What was so bad about the frozen food aisle?"

"I couldn't decide which brand of fries to choose."

He shifted in his seat to look at Samantha. "Now you're just yanking my chain."

Relief undid the knotted muscles in his shoulders when he saw that she had, indeed, been joking.

"Just seeing if you're attuned to my needs there, mister," she said. "How many brands do we need? Yeesh!"

Samantha heaved the last bag of groceries out of the cart and placed it in the back of the SUV. She closed the hatch and then put the cart away.

Next, they headed off to collect Cami. When they pulled into the driveway, Phil noted the brand-new set of snowmen in Mary Ann's front yard. The vehicle lurched to a stop on the icy cement pad and Phil turned again to look at Samantha. Her breathing hitched and almost sounded a little choked.

"My driving's not that bad, is it, honey?"

She shook her head, unable to get a word out.

Phil grabbed her hand and drew it close to his chest. "Sweetheart, you've got all the tools to be an amazing mom. You've practiced them. We're together. You've got this. Tell me what's on your list to do when Cami comes in the door."

"Give her a hug. Hold her for as long as she'll let me. Put away the snack containers from her lunch bag." Her breathing began to normalize. "She hangs up her coat and opens her book bag to show me anything from school. If she has a book, she's supposed to put it in her safe space nook."

"Perfect. Let's go get our girl."

Phil skated across the front of the SUV to open the door for Samantha. Hand in hand, they went across the cul-de-sac and rang the doorbell.

Thirty-Seven

The Courtroom

Samantha stood beside the pillar of the courthouse, securely wrapped in Phil's arms. The new give-and-take had infused life back into their marriage. Today promised the end of a painful chapter and the beginning of a new one. One founded on the hope and future promised by the Creator for those who love Him.

The morning had felt long, but she was proud of how Phil had handled himself under cross examination. He'd done everything required of him, including presenting a plan for restitution.

She squeezed Phil's hand three times. Her insides melted under the slow kiss he placed just above her ear.

"Hey, you two lovebirds. Great job on the cross. You did everything we rehearsed."

Phil turned to his lawyer, Jeffrey Chamberlain.

"So it's just the summation left?" Phil asked.

"Yes, and then it's up to the jury. The judge will adjudicate the sentencing."

"Can I talk to Bob after court's adjourned, before the ruling and sentencing?"

"Will it be adversarial or confrontational?"

Phil sighed. "I just want him to know that I'll visit him if he wants me to come. I want him to add my name to his visitors list."

"The judge may not sentence him to jail. He might be placed under electronic surveillance."

"I'd still want to visit him."

"Duly noted. I can pass a note to the defence table to see if he's interested in having the discussion."

"Thank you." Phil looked to his wife, who wrapped her arms around his waist. "I just want to spend time with my family and my business. I look forward to not going to your office to prep every week."

Samantha tightened her grip on him. "I do too, mister! The fewer meetings in your life, the better."

Jeffrey pulled out his pager and glanced at it. "The judge will be back in fifteen minutes."

"Thanks. I really appreciate the effort you've put into this case."

"You're welcome, Phil. Now let's head back in."

Samantha tugged on Phil's arm. "I'm just going to duck into the washroom. Be there in a few."

Afterward she slid onto the bench behind the prosecutor's table and reached out to tap Phil on the shoulder. He turned around and reached to squeeze Samantha's hand. She squeezed back three times. He echoed her actions, a silent but constant reminder that their love was mutual.

"All rise for the Right Honourable Davis Carpenter."

The rumble of everyone getting to their feet reminded Samantha of a muted thunderstorm in the distance. Was it only four months ago when she'd sat over there in Bob's seat, wondering whether history would repeat itself and Cami would be left motherless? She'd faced the storm and overcome it, finding hope in the promises of a faithful Creator who walked her through deep waters.

What kind of storm awaited them now? Would the clouds clear?

Everyone sat and waited for the judge to call on each lawyer to present their summations. She listened to the defence and heard little that would mitigate the consequences that seemed to await Bob. Her joy diminished when she heard Bob ask for a period of five years to make his restitutions instead of two. The amount of money he'd taken was considerable. The sooner they got it back, the more financially secure they'd be.

"The defence rests, Your Honour."

The judge nodded to the prosecutor. "Mr. Chamberlain, you may proceed with your summation."

"Ladies and gentlemen of the jury, you've listened to the defence make a plea for a longer length of time for restitution. Was the same time available to Phil Camden when he had to repay his clients? Was he compensated for the time he spent trying to regain customer trust? How can a young startup recover from this? This wasn't just petty fraud. It amounted to well over one hundred thousand dollars. We request the full return of all funds taken from Tailor-Made Manufacturing, as well as additional compensation to cover Mr. Camden's legal fees and the damage caused to his reputation. The evidence is very clear and concise. Mr. Harrington's guilt is not in question, but the compensation is. The prosecution rests, Your Honour."

Phil whispered his thanks as his lawyer sat down.

He sat and listened as the judge gave the jury instructions and then dismissed them to deliberate. Bob rose and was taken back to his holding cell.

Jeffrey stood, and then Phil noticed the defence lawyer trying to get the Jeffrey's attention. Phil nudged him with his elbow.

Before leaving the courtroom, the defence lawyer passed them a note.

Phil smiled as he read it. It turned out that Bob had agreed to put him on the visitors list, after all.

He made his way out of the room to where Samantha was waiting.

"Ready to go pick up Cami from school?" he asked. "Maybe we can go out for burgers."

"Sounds like a plan. I'll text Mary Ann and let her know we'll handle the pickup today."

"Do you want to invite them out for lunch with us? And what do you think of asking Mary Ann to take Cami back to her place while we await the jury's verdict?"

"That might be a good idea."

As they got into the car, Samantha busied herself with texting.

A half-hour later, they pulled up to the pickup line at the elementary school. Cami jumped in after Samantha waved her over. She hopped out to close the door after making sure Cami buckled herself in.

"Mommy, Daddy, where are we going?"

"What do you think of going to that burger restaurant with the playground?" Samantha said.

"Yummy! Thanks, Mommy."

Phil grinned. "You thought this was Mom's idea? It was mine."

"Ooh... sorry, Daddy. Thank you!"

"Guess what, sugar plum?" Samantha asked. "Mary Ann and Kristina are meeting us there too. You're going on an adventure today. How does the Western Development Museum sound to you? The Festival of Trees is happening this week."

"You're not coming Mommy?" Cami's plaintive voice lingered in the air.

Samantha glanced at Phil, as if wondering how she should answer that.

Phil reached over and gave her hand a squeeze. "Go with Mary Ann if you want to, honey. You were with me every day this week when I needed you. Plus, we need some fresh ideas for Christmas decorations at the office. We're launching a contest for our clients to design 3D printed decorations around a theme. The winner gets a free advertising campaign courtesy of Gabe." Phil scanned Samantha's and Cami's faces. "I need some ideas."

Samantha looked at Cami in the back seat. "So are you and me going to help Daddy find some new Christmas tree decoration ideas?"

"Yes!" Cami looked from parent to parent, as though searching for any hidden worry or fear. Finding none, she carried on. "I hope there's a tree that has lots of purple sparkles and purple stars and snowflakes and purple everything on it."

Phil winked at Cami in the rearview mirror. "That's my girl. Ideas already!"

The telltale wrinkle between her brows had disappeared and she flashed her dimpled smile.

A few minutes later, Phil's shoulders eased as he pulled into the restaurant parking lot. The icy roads hadn't much improved since the snowstorm a month ago.

Samantha opened the door for Cami as she wriggled out of the booster seat. "Put your mitts on, honey. It's cold out today."

Cami reached back towards the floor of the back seat to locate her purple polka-dotted mittens. Samantha tugged her own hood up around her ears before reaching for Cami's hand.

To ward off the bitter Saskatchewan wind, Phil flipped up his coat collar and watched his precious girls thread their way through the parking lot, wishing he hadn't left his own gloves on the deacon's bench at home.

Although it would help when Bob paid back what he'd stolen, the money was beside the point. He and Gabe had worked hard to regain the confidence of their clients and suppliers over the past month. Gabe's facility with social media had paid the biggest dividend he could have dreamed. The videos he made attracted a lot of viewers, including a big venture capitalist who was now considering a seven percent investment deal in Tailor-Made. Assuming they accepted the deal, worth a hundred thousand dollars, their plan was to retool the warehouse and add new clients without cutting back on existing production. The additional capital would allow them to engage in more marketing than ever. They'd be in the black before they knew it.

"Mr. Slowpoke, are you frozen to the ground over there?" Samantha called from the door. "We're hungry and want to order!"

Cami had latched onto Kristina already. "Come on, Daddy, let's go!"

Phil skidded over the slick ice, doing his best Patrick Chan impression as he slid past the last car in the parking lot and came up behind Samantha.

He turned her around. "Fast enough for you now?"

"Yessiree, mister!" Then she whispered, "Meet you at home later to celebrate today's victory, in front of the fireplace under the afghan?"

He cupped her face with his hand and kissed her. The feel of her lips ignited deep longings in him for another weekend away where the two of them could rediscover one another.

"Ew! Gross, Daddy. I'm hungry!" Cami stamped her feet.

Phil nuzzled in close. "Oh, Sam I Am. I'm so glad we're together again. What would I do without my two favourite girls? Let's go feed our hungry girl!"

He grabbed one of Cami's hands as Samantha grabbed the other. Together they swung their rainbow baby through the doorway to the sound of giggles.

About the Author

Tamara Wanner's love affair with books began in Grade One. She pursued English as her major at the University of Saskatchewan and was torn between journalism and education. Her love of children won out.

Now retired, her career has touched the lives of students from kindergarten to Grade Twelve by inspiring others to write. She crafted plays to bring out her students' talents. Her church's Easter and Christmas programs also benefitted from her writing.

While farming with her husband, she joined a writers group called the Revisionists, which had several published authors including Sharon McFarlane, Larry Warwaruk, Tammy Wiens, Glenda MacFarlane, and Tony Peters. She loved the short stories of Alena Saxton and Margareta Fleuter. Their characters exemplified small-town connection.

She took a break while parenting their two chosen children. In 2019, a writers conference renewed her desire to share the transformational power of the gospel through story. Margaret Feinberg and Jonathan Merritt coached her through their Write Brilliant online course, and then she enrolled in the Flourish Writer's Academy. As a result, she believes there are to be more tales in her Legacy Reimaged Series. She resides in Moose Jaw, Saskatchewan with her husband Bill.

She once thought her legacy would end with her, but the Creator had a different idea. She won her husband's wedding band two years before they met. They waited nine years to be parents. She often wondered why her story didn't sound like the books she read, yet the legacy she received has been full of compassion and grace for those whose pages have been blotted with tears over miscarriage and infertility. Her writing walks alongside those who want to reimage their legacy by pointing them back to the One who created them.

You can learn more about it at www.legacyreimaged.com.

Tamara J. Wanner is also a singer-songwriter and can be found on any music streaming platform. She recently recorded "Soar Like an Eagle" and "Peace in the Battle." She hopes to get back to recording after the launch of *Rainbow Baby*.

Resources

Many authors and websites deserve credit for providing insights into the mental health of those who have experienced a miscarriage, stillbirth, or pregnancy termination.

"A Typical Day at Options," *Options Behavioral Health System*. Date of access: December 6, 2023 (https://www.optionsbehavioralhealthsystem.com/admissions/typical-day).

"Creating Rituals to Move through Grief," *GoodTherap*. June 27, 2011 (https://www.goodtherapy.org/blog/creating-rituals-to-move-through-grief).

David B. Feldman, "The Power of Rituals to Heal Grief," *Psychology Today*. September 28, 2019 (https://www.psychologytoday.com/ca/blog/super-survivors/201909/the-power-rituals-heal-grief).

Jennifer Paulson, "Safely Get in the Saddle with a Mountin Block," *Horse & Rider*. May 20, 2014 (https://horseandrider.com/training/safely-saddle-mounting-block-16336).

"How Art Therapy Will Help with Trauma," *Evolve*. Date of access: December 6, 2023 (https://evolvetreatment.com/blog/art-therapy-trauma).

Dr. Sarah Allen, "Tips for Coping After a Miscarriage," *Dr. Sarah Allen*. Date of access: December 6, 2023 (https://drsarahallen.com/miscarriage).

Kate Kripke, "13 Things You Should Know About Grief After Miscarriage or Baby Loss," *Postpartum Progress*. Date of access: December 6, 2023 (https://postpartumprogress.com/13-things-you-should-know-about-grief-after-miscarriage-or-baby-loss).

Dove Pressnall, "What I've Learned from Counseling Couples through Miscarriage," *Healthline*. June 12, 2017 (https://www.healthline.com/health/miscarriage-counseling-from-a-therapist).

Taylor M. Ham, *Equine Assisted Couples Therapy: An Exploratory Study* (Falls Church, VA: Virginia Polytechnic Institute and State University, 2013).

I have really enjoyed learning more about the Canadian justice system regarding embezzlement in the business place. I included the complexities and possibilities of 3D printing because they intrigue me.

"How to Make Money with a 3D Printer," *Printaworld*. September 22, 2021 (https://prtwd.com/guides/how-to-make-money-with-a-3d-printer).

"Guide to 3D Printing Materials: Types, Applications, and Properties," *Formlabs*. Date of access: December 6, 2023 (https://formlabs.com/blog/3d-printing-materials).

Annie Pilon, "25 Workplace Theft and Embezzlement Examples," *Small Business Trends*. August 4, 2023 (https://smallbiztrends.com/2023/08/embezzlement-examples.html).

"What Are Common Embezzlement Schemes?" *Bizmanualz.com*. Date of access: December 6, 2023 (https://www.bizmanualz.com/tighten-accounting-controls/what-are-common-embezzlement-schemes.html).

"Trial," *Government of Canada*. Date of access: December 6, 2023 (https://www.justice.gc.ca/eng/cj-jp/victims-victimes/court-tribunaux/trial-proces.html).

Noah and Lesley's story comes to life in Book 2 of the Legacy Reimaged Series: *Grafted In: An Adoption Story*.

To follow its journey to completion,
check out www.legacyreimaged.com and subscribe.